Defending His Own

BEVERLY BARTON

SILHOUETTE

Sensation

First published in Great Britain 1998
Large Print edition 2000
Silhouette Books Limited,
Eton House, 18-24 Paradise Road,
Richmond, Surrey, TW9 1SR

ISBN 0 373 04659 6

Set in Times Roman 15 on 16¼ pt.
34-1100-82765

Printed and bound in Great Britain
by Antony Rowe Ltd, Chippenham, Wiltshire

BEVERLY BARTON

has been in love with romance since her grandfather gave her an illustrated book of *Beauty and the Beast*. An avid reader since childhood, she began writing at the age of nine and wrote short stories, poetry, plays and novels throughout school and college. After marriage to her own 'hero' and the births of her daughter and son, she chose to be a full-time homemaker, a.k.a. wife, mother, friend and volunteer.

Six years ago she began substitute teaching and returned to writing as a hobby. In 1987 she joined the Romance Writers of America. Her hobby became an obsession as she devoted more and more time to improving her skills as a writer. Now her life-long dream of being published has come true.

To several very special ladies
whose friendships have meant so
much to me over the past few years.
Thank y'all for your support and
encouragement: Jean Tune,
JoAnn Courtney, Helen Everett
and Marsha Hunt.

Prologue

She must have taken the wrong turn off Cotton Lane. There was nothing out here but a bunch of cotton fields and an endless stretch of dirt road, apparently leading nowhere except in and out of the fields.

Deborah Vaughn slowed her dark blue Cadillac to a stop, shifted the gears into Park and picked up the piece of paper on which she'd written the directions. Despite the protection of her sunglasses, Deborah squinted against the sun's blinding glare. Holding up her hand to shield her eyes, she glanced down at the map and instructions she'd brought along to help her find the new development property her real estate firm had just purchased. Damn! She had turned off too soon.

Glancing around, she didn't see anywhere to make a turn, and she certainly had no intention of backing her car all the way to Cotton Lane. She'd just have to go a little farther and find some place to turn around.

Shifting the gears into Drive, she drove on. Within a few minutes she spotted what appeared to be the burned-out remains of an old shack. A wide, weed-infested path, marred with deep ruts, ran straight from the dirt road to where a shiny black Ford pickup had parked in knee-high grass behind the still-standing brick chimney.

Loud, pulse-pounding country music blared from the truck's radio.

Deborah assumed the truck belonged to the farmer who had planted the acres of cotton. She drove her Cadillac onto the path, intending to back up and head out the way she had come. The sun's glare blocked her vision, allowing her only partial vision of the open truck door. A man jumped out of the driver's side, and yelled a warning. She glanced toward the back of the truck where two men stood, one holding a gun to the other's head.

Sunshine reflected off the metal on the gun in the killer's hand. The gun fired. The wail of a steel guitar blasted from inside the truck. Deborah screamed. Blood splattered from the dead man's head. The killer turned abruptly and stared at the Cadillac, at the woman inside, then released his hold on the body. His victim slumped to the ground.

Deborah recognized the killer from his picture in the paper. She couldn't remember his name, but she knew he was somehow connected to that outlaw gang headed by Buck Stansell.

The man who'd leaped out of the truck pointed toward Deborah's car.

Dear God, she had to get away! Shifting the car into reverse, she backed out of the bumpy path and then headed the Cadillac toward Cotton Lane. She heard the truck's engine roar to life. Glancing back she saw the killer aim his gun out the window.

The Caddy sped down the dirt road, the black truck in hot pursuit. While the driver veered the truck off the side of the dirt road, partially into the open field, the killer aimed his gun toward Deborah. The truck closed in on the car, the truck's hood parallel to the Cadillac's left rear bumper. The killer fired; the bullet shattered the outside mirror. Deborah cried out, but didn't slow her escape, didn't take her eyes off the road ahead of her.

A cloud of dust flew up behind the Cadillac, providing a thin veil of protection between her and the men determined to overtake her. The truck picked up speed just as Deborah saw Cotton Lane ahead of her. Another bullet ripped through the driver's door.

They intended to kill her. She had no doubt in her mind. She'd seen the killer's face, the man who had murdered another in cold blood. She could identify him. And he knew it.

The minute she turned the Caddy onto Cotton Lane, she sped away from the truck. She had to escape. Had to find help. But who? Where? The police!

She didn't dare slow down enough to use her cellular phone. She had to make it to the police station before her pursuers caught her.

Where the hell was the police station in Leighton? *Think, dammit, Deborah! Think!*

She crossed Highway 72, paying little attention to whether or not traffic was coming from the other direction. The sleepy little town of Leighton, Alabama lay straight ahead. The truck breathed down her neck like a black dragon, the killer's gun spitting deadly lead fire.

A bullet sailed through the back glass, embedding itself in the dashboard. Deborah ran the Caddy straight through the town's one red light. The black truck slowed, but continued following her.

Deborah brought her car to a screeching halt at the side of the police station, a small metal building on the right side of the narrow street. Glancing behind her, she saw the black truck creep by. Lying down in the front seat, she eased open the door, crawled out and made a mad dash to safety.

A young officer jumped up from behind a metal desk when Deborah ran inside the station. ''What the hell's going on, lady? You look like the devil's chasing you.''

''He is.'' Deborah panted, wiping the perspiration from her face with the palm of her hand. She grabbed the approaching officer's shoulders. ''I just witnessed a murder.''

''You what?'' The young officer's face paled. ''Come on in and sit down.''

''I don't want to sit down,'' Deborah screamed. ''They're out there. Two of them. The killer and the man who was driving the truck. They followed me all the way into town. They shot at me. They were trying to kill me!''

''Good God!'' He shoved Deborah aside, drew his 9mm handgun and rushed outside.

The female officer who'd been listening to the conversation rushed over to Deborah and followed her when she headed for the door. Looking up and down the street, Deborah didn't see the truck. She leaned against the doorpost.

''Are you all right?'' the woman officer asked.

''I will be.''

The male officer let out a long, low whistle when he saw Deborah's Cadillac. ''Good thing they didn't get a lucky shot or you'd be dead, ma'am.''

''They're gone, aren't they?'' Deborah asked, realizing they wouldn't have hung around, making it easy for the police to arrest them.

''Yes, ma'am, looks that way.'' He walked toward her, shaking his head. "Just where did this murder take place?"

"Out past some cotton fields, somewhere off Cotton Lane."

"Don't suppose you recognized either man in the truck or the man you say they murdered?"

"I only recognized one of them," Deborah said. "The killer. He's one of Buck Stansell's gang. I remember seeing his picture in the paper when he went to trial a few months ago on drug-related charges."

"Lon Sparks?" the officer asked. "You saw Lon Sparks kill a man?"

"Yes, if that's his name…I saw him kill a man. Shot him in the head. Blood everywhere. All over the dead man. All over the killer." Deborah trembled, her hands shaking uncontrollably.

"Damn, ma'am, I sure wouldn't want to be in your shoes. Lon Sparks is a mean bastard, if you'll pardon me saying so." The officer returned his gun to his holster.

"Shut up, Jerry Don, can't you see she's already scared out of her wits." Putting an arm around Deborah's shoulder, the female officer led her back inside the station. "We'd better get hold of the chief and then call the sheriff. If the killing took place out past Cotton Lane, then it's a county matter."

"Everything will be all right," Jerry Don said. "You're safe here with us, Miss…er… Miss…?"

"Deborah Vaughn."

"Come on over and sit down, Miss Vaughn, and tell me exactly what happened," The female officer said.

"May I use your phone first?" Deborah picked up the telephone on the officer's desk. "I'm expected at home for dinner and my mother will worry if I'm late."

Her hands trembled as she dialed the number. "Mother, I'm afraid I'll be running a little late. You and Allen go ahead and have dinner without me. No. No, everything's all right. I just ran into a little car trouble out here in Leighton. Nothing I can't handle."

Nothing she couldn't handle. That's right, Deborah. You're tough, aren't you? You can handle anything that's thrown your way. You don't need anyone to take care of you. You've been taking care of everyone else for so long, you wouldn't know how it felt to admit you needed someone.

Well, it looked like the time had come. If the police wanted her to live long enough to testify against a cold-blooded killer, someone was going to have to protect her from Buck Stansell's outlaws.

Chapter 1

He had sworn he'd never come back to Sheffield, Alabama. But never say never. Ashe McLaughlin had discovered that anyone so absolutely certain often wound up eating his own words. And in his case, the taste was mighty bitter.

He had been gone eleven years, and little had changed. Except him. He had changed. He was older. Smarter. Harder.

He chuckled to himself. Harder? Hell, folks in northwest Alabama had considered him a real bad boy, one of those McLaughlins from Leighton, his daddy nothing but a white trash outlaw. But Ashe hadn't been as tough as everyone thought. He had hated the legacy of poverty and ignorance his family had given him. He'd wanted more. He'd fought long and hard to better himself. But Wallace

Vaughn had destroyed Ashe's dreams of being accepted in Colbert County.

Eleven years ago he'd been told to leave town or else—or else he would have done jail time.

Now, here he was returning to a town that hadn't wanted his kind. He couldn't help wondering if anyone other than his grandmother would welcome him home. He supposed Carol Allen Vaughn would be glad to see him. After all, she'd been the one who'd asked him to take this job. He was probably a fool for agreeing to act as Deborah's bodyguard.

Deborah Vaughn. No amount of time or distance had been able to erase her from Ashe's memory.

He parked his rental car in the circular drive in front of the old Allen home, a brick Greek Revival cottage on Montgomery Avenue. His grandmother had once been the housekeeper here for the Vaughn family.

Walking up to the front door, he hesitated before ringing the bell. He'd never been allowed to enter the house through the front door but had always gone around to the back and entered through the kitchen. He remembered sitting at the kitchen table doing his homework, sharing milk and cookies with Deborah, and sometimes her older cousin Whitney. That had been a lifetime ago.

He rang the doorbell. What the hell was he doing here? Why had he allowed Carol Vaughn's dare to goad him into returning to a town he hated? Deb-

orah needs you, she'd said. Are you afraid to see
her again? she had taunted him.

He was not afraid to see Deborah Vaughn again.
After ten years as a Green Beret, Ashe McLaughlin
was afraid of nothing, least of all the girl who had
betrayed him.

A plump, middle-aged woman opened the door
and greeted him with a smile. "Yes, sir?"

"I'm Ashe McLaughlin. Mrs. Vaughn is expect-
ing me."

"Yes, please come inside. I'll tell Miss Carol
you're here."

Ashe stepped into the gracious entrance hall
large enough to accommodate a grand piano as well
as a large mahogany and gilt table with an enormous bouquet of fresh flowers in the center. A
sweeping staircase wound upward on the left side
of the room.

"If you'll wait here, please." The housekeeper
scurried down the hall toward the back of the
house.

He'd been summoned home. Like a knight in the
Queen's service. Ashe grinned. Better a knight than
a stable boy, he supposed. Why hadn't he just said
no? *I'm sorry, Mrs. Vaughn, but whatever trouble
Deborah has gotten herself into, you'll have to find
someone else to rescue her.*

God knows he had tried to refuse, but once he'd
heard that Deborah's life was in real danger, he had

wavered in his resistance. And Carol Vaughn had taken advantage of the weakness she sensed in him.

"Ashe, so good of you to come, dear boy." The voice still held that note of authority, that hint of superiority, that tone of Southern gentility.

He turned to face her, the woman he had always thought of as the personification of a real lady. He barely recognized the woman who stood before him. Thin, almost gaunt, her beautiful face etched with faint age lines, her complexion sickly pale. Her short blond hair was streaked with gray. She had once been full-figured, voluptuous and lovely beyond words.

She couldn't be much more than fifty, but she looked older.

Caught off-guard by her appearance, by the drastic change the years had wrought, Ashe stared at Carol Vaughn. Quickly recovering his composure, he took several tentative steps forward and held out his hand.

She clasped his big, strong hand in her small, fragile one and squeezed. "Thank you for coming. You can't imagine how desperately we need your help."

Ashe assisted Carol down the hallway and into the living room. The four-columned entry permitted an unobstructed view of the room from the foyer. The hardwood floors glistened like polished metal in the sunlight. A blend of antiques and expensive reproductions bespoke of wealth and good taste.

"The sofa, please, Ashe." She patted his hand. "Sit beside me and we'll discuss what must be done."

He guided her to the sofa, seated her and perched his big body on the edge, not feeling comfortable in her presence. "Does Deborah know you sent for me?"

"I haven't told her," Carol said. "She's a stubborn one, that girl of mine. She's always had a mind of her own. But she's been a dutiful daughter."

"What if she doesn't agree to my being here?" He had known Deborah when she was seventeen, a plump, pretty girl who'd had a major crush on him. What would she look like now? And how did she feel about him after all these years?

"Mazie, please bring us some coffee," Carol instructed the housekeeper who stood at the end of the hallway. "And a few of those little cakes from the bakery. The cinnamon ones."

"Refreshments aren't necessary, Mrs. Vaughn. Really." Ashe felt ill at ease being entertained, as if his visit were a social call. "I'm here on business. Remember?"

"Mazie, go ahead and bring the coffee and the cakes, too." Carol turned her attention to Ashe. "Times change, but good manners don't. Of course my mother would be appalled that I had welcomed a gentleman, unrelated to me and not a minister, into my home when I am quite alone.''

"Coffee will be fine, Mrs. Vaughn.''

"You used to call me Miss Carol. I much prefer that to the other. Your calling me Mrs. Vaughn makes us sound like strangers. And despite your long absence from Sheffield, we are hardly strangers, are we, Ashe?''

"No, ma'am, we're not strangers.''

"Mazie has prepared you a room upstairs. I want you with Deborah at all times.'' Carol blushed ever so lightly. "Or at least close by.''

"Has she received any more threats since we spoke two days ago?''

"Mercy, yes. Every day, there's a new letter and another phone call, but Charlie Blaylock says there's nothing more he can do. And I asked him why the sheriff was incapable of protecting innocent citizens.''

"Has a trial date been set for Lon Sparks?'' Ashe asked.

"Not yet. It should be soon. But not soon enough for me. I can't bear the thought of Deborah being in danger.''

"She just happened to be in the wrong place at the wrong time.'' Ashe knew what that was like. And he knew as well as anyone in these parts just how dangerous Buck Stansell and his band of out-

laws could be. For three generations, the Stansell
bunch, along with several other families, had cornered the market on illegal activities. Everything
from prostitution to bootlegging, when the county
had been dry. And nowadays weapons and drugs
dominated their money-making activities.

"She insists on testifying." Carol glanced up
when she saw Mazie bringing the coffee. "Just put
it there on the table, please."

Mazie placed the silver service on the mahogany
tea table to the left of the sofa, asked if there would
be anything else and retreated to the kitchen when
told all was in order.

"Do you prefer your coffee black?" Carol
asked.

"Yes, ma'am. Thank you." When his hostess
poured the coffee and handed it to him, Ashe accepted the Haviland cup.

"I will expect you to stay in Sheffield until the
trial is over and Deborah is no longer in danger."

"I've already assured you that I'll stay as long
as is necessary to ensure Deborah's safety."

"And I will send the sum we agreed upon to
your agency in Atlanta on a weekly basis."

"You and I have come to an agreement on
terms," Ashe said. "But unless Deborah cooper-
ates—"

"She will cooperate."

Ashe widened his eyes, surprised by the vigor of

Carol Vaughn's statement. Apparently her fragile physical condition had not extinguished the fire in her personality.

The front door flew open and a tall, gangly boy of perhaps twelve raced into the living room, tossing a stack of schoolbooks down on a bowfront walnut commode.

"I made a hundred on my math test. See. Take a look." He dashed across the room, handed Carol his paper and sat down on the floor at her feet. "And guess what else, Mother? My team beat the hel...heck out of Jimmy Morton's team in PE today."

Carol caressed the boy's blond hair, petting him with deep affection. "I'm so proud of you, Allen."

The boy turned his attention to Ashe, who stared at the child, amazed at his striking resemblance to Deborah. Ashe's grandmother had mentioned Allen from time to time in her letters and phone calls. He'd always thought it odd that Wallace and Carol Vaughn had had another child so late in life. When Wallace Vaughn had run Ashe out of town eleven years ago, the Vaughns had had one child—seventeen-year-old Deborah.

"Who's he?" Allen asked.

"Allen, this is Mr. McLaughlin. He's an old friend. He and Deborah went to school together."

"Were you Deborah's boyfriend?" Allen scooted around on the floor until he situated himself just right, so he could prop his back against the Queen Anne coffee table.

"Allen, you musn't be rude." Carol shook her index finger at the boy, but she smiled as she scolded him.

"I wasn't being rude. I was just hoping Mr. McLaughlin was here to ask Deborah for a date. She never goes out unless it's with Neil, and she told me that he isn't her boyfriend."

"I must apologize for Allen, but you see, he is very concerned that Deborah doesn't have a boyfriend," Carol explained. "Especially since he's going steady himself. For what now, Allen, ten days?"

"Ah, quit kidding me." Allen unlaced his shoes, then reached up on top of the tea table to retrieve a tiny cinnamon cake. He popped it into his mouth.

Ashe watched the boy, noting again how much he looked like Deborah as a young girl. Except where she had been short and plump with small hands and feet, Allen was tall, slender and possessed large feet and big hands. But his hair was the same color, his eyes an almost identical blue.

"Hey, what do we know about Mr. McLaughlin? We can't let Deborah date just anybody." Allen returned Ashe's penetrating stare. "If he gets serious about Deborah, is he the kind of man who'd make her a good husband?"

The front door opened and closed again. A neatly

attired young woman in a navy suit and white blouse walked into the entrance hall.

"Now, Allen, you're being rude again," Carol said. "Besides, your sister's love life really isn't any of our business, even if we did find her the perfect man."

"Now what?" Deborah called out from the hallway, not even looking their way. "Mother, you and Allen haven't found another prospect you want me to consider, have you? Just who have you two picked out as potential husband material this time?"

Carrying an oxblood leather briefcase, Deborah came to an abrupt halt when she looked into the living room and saw Ashe sitting beside her mother on the sofa. She gasped aloud, visibly shaken.

"Come in, dear. Allen and I were just entertaining Ashe McLaughlin. You remember Ashe, don't you, Deborah?"

"Was he your old boyfriend?" Allen asked. "Mother won't tell me."

Ashe stood and took a long, hard look at Deborah Vaughn…the girl who had proclaimed her undying love for him one night down by the river, eleven years ago. The girl who, when he gently rejected her, had run crying to her rich and powerful daddy.

The district attorney and Wallace Vaughn had

given Ashe two choices. Leave town and never come back, or face statutory rape charges.

"Hello, Deborah."

"What are you doing here?"

She had changed, perhaps even more than her pale, weak mother. No longer plump but still as lovely as she'd been as a teenager, Deborah possessed a poise and elegance that had eluded the younger, rather awkward girl. She wore her long, dark blond hair tucked into a loose bun at the nape of her neck. A pair of small golden earrings matched the double gold chain around her neck.

"Your mother sent for me." Ashe noted the astonished look on her face.

Deborah, still standing in the entrance hall, gazed at her mother. "What does he mean, you sent for him?"

"Now, dear, please come in and let's talk about this matter before you upset yourself."

"Allen, please go out in the kitchen with Mazie while I speak with Mother and Mr. McLaughlin."

"Ah, why do I have to leave? I'm a member of this family, aren't I? I shouldn't be excluded from important conversations." When his sister remained silent, Allen looked pleadingly at his mother, who shook her head.

"Do what Deborah says." Carol motioned toward the hallway. "This is grown-up talk and although you're quite a young man, you're still not old enough to—''

"Yeah, yeah. I know." Allen jumped up and ran out of the room, his eyes downcast and his lips puckered into a defiant pout.

"What's going on?" Deborah marched into the living room, slamming her briefcase down atop Allen's books on the antique commode. She glared at Ashe. "What are *you* doing here?"

"As Ashe said, I sent for him." Tilting her chin upward, Carol straightened her thin shoulders.

"You what?"

"Calm yourself," Carol said.

"I am calm." Deborah spoke slowly, her teeth clenched tightly.

"Ashe works for a private security firm out of Atlanta." Carol readjusted her hips on the sofa, placing her hand down on the cushion beside her. "I've hired him to act as your bodyguard until the trial is over and you're no longer in any danger."

"I can't believe what I'm hearing." Deborah scowled at Ashe. "You've brought this man back into our lives. Good God, Mother, do you have any idea what you've done?"

"Don't speak to me in that tone of voice, Deborah Luellen Vaughn! I've done what I think is best for everyone concerned."

"And you?" Deborah looked directly at Ashe. "Why would you come back to Sheffield after all these years? How on earth did my mother persuade you to return?'' Deborah's rosy cheeks turned pale, her lips quivered. ''What—what did she tell you?''

''I told him that your life had been threatened. I explained the basic facts.'' Carol turned to Ashe. ''This is what he does for a living, and I'm paying him his usual fee, isn't that right, Ashe?''

''This is strictly a business arrangement for me,'' Ashe replied. ''My services are for hire to anyone with enough money to afford me.''

Where was the sweet girl he'd once known? The laughing, smiling girl who'd been his friend long before she'd become his lover one hot summer night down by the river. He had never regretted anything as much as he had regretted taking Deborah's virginity. He'd been filled with rage and half drunk. Deborah had been with him that night, trying to comfort him, and he had taken advantage of her loving nature. But she'd paid him back.

''I don't want you here. Keep a week's salary for your trouble.'' Deborah nodded toward the door. ''Now, please leave.''

''No!'' Reaching out, Carol grabbed Ashe by the arm. ''Please, don't leave. Go in the kitchen and have some cookies with Allen.''

''Mother! Think what you're saying.''

''Please, Ashe. Go out into the kitchen for a few minutes while I speak with Deborah.''

Ashe patted Carol on the hand, then pulled away

from her. "I won't leave, Miss Carol. It would take an act of congress to get me out of Sheffield."

He smiled at Deborah when he walked past her, halting briefly to inspect her from head to toe, then proceeding down the hallway and through the door leading to the kitchen.

Heat and cold zigzagged through Deborah like red-hot and freezing blue shafts of pain. Ashe McLaughlin. Here in Sheffield. Here in her home. And he'd seen Allen!

"He can't stay."

"Come over here, dear." Carol patted the sofa seat. "You've needed him for such a long time, Deborah, but now more than ever. You know I disagreed with your father's assessment of Ashe, but I loved your father and never would have gone against his wishes. But once Wallace died, I begged you to let me contact Ashe. He's kept in touch with Mattie all these years. We could have asked him to come home at any time."

"He kept in touch with his grandmother, not with us. He left this town and didn't look back. He never once called me or wrote me or..." Deborah crossed the room, slumped down on the sofa beside her mother and folded her hands in her lap. "I need to phone the office and let them know I won't be back in this afternoon. I had planned to just drop Allen off, but I saw the car in the drive and wondered who... I don't want Ashe McLaughlin here."

"But I do." Carol's blue eyes met her daughter's blue eyes, stubborn, determined and equally strong. "We both know that I'm only in remission. The cancer could worsen at any time and I'll have to go in for more surgery. I could die without ever seeing you happy."

"You honestly think Ashe McLaughlin can make me happy? Get real, Mother." Deborah lowered her voice to a snarling whisper. "The man seduced me when I was seventeen, dropped me like a hot potato and left town two months later, never bothering to find out whether or not he'd gotten me pregnant."

"I think you should know that—"

"If you're convinced I need a bodyguard then have the private security agency send someone else. Tell them we want someone older or younger or... Hell! Tell them anything, but get rid of Ashe."

"I believe he still cares about you." Carol smiled, deepening the faint lines in her face.

"Mother!"

"It's been eleven years, Deborah, and you haven't had one serious relationship in all that time. Doesn't that tell you anything about your own feelings?"

"Yes. It tells me that I'm a smart girl. I learn from my mistakes."

"It tells me that you've never gotten over Ashe

McLaughlin, that somewhere deep down, in your heart of hearts, you're still in love with him.''

Deborah couldn't bear it. Her mother's words pierced the protective wall she had built around her heart. She didn't love Ashe McLaughlin. She hated him. But she knew only too well how fine a line there was between love and hate.

''I've hardly had time to date, let alone find the man of my dreams. Have you forgotten that I was in my senior year of college when Daddy died and I had to complete my courses for my degree and step in at Vaughn & Posey?'' Deborah paused, waiting for her mother to comment. Carol said nothing.

''Then I had to earn my Realtors' license and work damn hard to fill Daddy's shoes at the firm,'' Deborah said. ''Over the last few years while other firms have floundered, I've kept Vaughn & Posey in the black, making substantial gains each year. Over the last five years, we've been involved in two different subdivision developments.''

Carol held up her hand, signaling acquiescence. ''I know what a busy young woman you've been. But other people lead busy lives and still find time for romance.''

''I don't need any romance in my life. Have you also forgotten how my foolishly romantic illusions about love nearly destroyed my life eleven years ago?''

"Of course I haven't forgotten. But there's more at stake than my desire to see you and Ashe settle things between you. Your life is in danger—real danger. Charlie Blaylock can only do so much. You need twenty-four-hour-a-day protection, and Ashe is highly qualified to do the job I've hired him to do."

"What makes him so highly qualified?"

"He was a Green Beret for ten years and joined, what I am told, is the best private security agency in the South. If you won't agree to his staying here for any other reason, do it for me. For my peace of mind."

"Mother, really. You're asking a great deal of me, aren't you? And you're putting Allen at risk. What if Ashe were to suspect the truth? Do we dare take that kind of chance? How do you think Allen would react if he found out that everything we've told him is a lie?"

Tears gathered in the corners of Deborah's eyes. She blinked them away. No tears. Not now. She cried only when she was alone, where no one could see her. Where no one would know that the strong, dependable, always reliable Deborah Luellen Vaughn succumbed to the weakness of tears. Since her father died, she had learned to be strong—for her mother, for Allen, for those depending upon Vaughn & Posey for their livelihoods.

"Even if Ashe learns the truth, he would never tell Allen."

"How can you be so sure?"

"Intuition."

Deborah groaned. Sometimes her mother could be incredibly naive for a fifty-five-year-old woman. "I don't want Ashe McLaughlin to become a part of our lives."

"He's always been a part of our lives." Carol glanced up at the oil painting of Allen at the age of three, hung over the fireplace beside the portrait of a three-year-old Deborah. "All I ask is that you allow him to stay on as your bodyguard until after Lon Sparks's trial. If you feel nothing for Ashe except hatred, then his being here should do nothing more than annoy you. Surely you can put up with a little annoyance to make your dying mother happy."

"You aren't dying!"

"Please, dear, just talk to Ashe."

Sighing deeply, Deborah closed her eyes and shook her head. How could she say no to her mother? How could she explain what the very sight of Ashe McLaughlin had done to her? Wasn't she already going through enough, having to deal with testifying against a murderer, having to endure constant threats on her life, without having to put up with Ashe McLaughlin, too?

"Oh, all right, Mother. I'll talk to Ashe. But I'm not promising anything."

"Fine. That's all I ask." Gripping the arm of the sofa for support, Carol stood. "I'll go in the kitchen and see how Ashe and Allen are getting along, then I'll send Ashe out to you."

Standing, Deborah paced the floor. Waiting. Waiting to face the man who haunted her dreams to this very day. The only man she had ever loved. The only man she had ever hated. Stopping in front of the fireplace, she glanced up at Allen's portrait. He looked so much like her. Their strong resemblance had made it easy to pass him off as her brother. But where others might not see any of Ashe in Allen's features, she could. His coloring was hers, but his nose was long and straight like Ashe's, not short and rounded like hers. His jaw tapered into a square chin unlike her gently rounded face.

Now that Allen was ten, it was apparent from his size that he would eventually become a large man, perhaps as big as Ashe, who stood six foot three.

But would Ashe see any resemblance? Would he look at Allen and wonder? Over the years had he, even once, asked himself whether he might have fathered a child the night he had taken her virginity?

"Deborah?"

She spun around to face Ashe, who stood in the

hallway. Had he noticed her staring at Allen's portrait?

"Please come in and sit down."

He walked into the living room, but remained standing. "I came back to Sheffield as a favor to your mother." *And because she dared me to face the past.* "She sounded desperate when she called. My grandmother told me about Miss Carol's bout with cancer. I—"

"Thank you for caring about my mother."

"She was always good to Mama Mattie and to me. Despite what happened between the two of us, I never blamed your mother."

What was he talking about? What reason did he have to blame anyone for anything? He'd been the one who had left Sheffield, left an innocent seventeen-year-old girl pregnant.

"Mother has gotten it into her head that I need protection, and I don't disagree with her on that point. I'd be a fool to say I'm not afraid of Buck Stansell and his gang. I know what they're capable of doing. I saw, firsthand, how they deal with people who go against them."

"Then allowing me to stay as your bodyguard is the sensible thing to do."

How was it, he wondered, that years ago he'd thought Whitney Vaughn was the most beautiful, desirable creature on earth, when all along her little cousin Deborah had been blossoming into perfection? Although Whitney had been the woman he'd wanted, Deborah was the woman he'd never been able to forget.

"I would prefer your agency send another representative. That would be possible, wouldn't it? Surely, you're no more eager than I am for the two of us to be thrown together this way."

"Yes, it's possible for the Dundee Agency to send another agent, but your mother wants me. And I intend to abide by her wishes."

Deborah glared at him, then regretted it when he met her gaze head-on. She didn't like the way he was looking at her. As if…as if he found her attractive.

"You could speak to Mother, persuade her to agree to another agent."

"Yes, I could speak to your mother, but I don't think anything I say will dissuade her from having me act as your personal bodyguard." Ashe took a tentative step toward Deborah. She backed away from him. "Why is it that I get the feeling Miss Carol would like to see something romantic happen between you and me?"

Deborah turned from him, cursing the blush she felt creeping into her cheeks. When he placed his hands on her shoulders, she jerked away from him, rushing toward the French doors that opened up onto a side patio. She grasped the brass handle.

"I'm not interested in forming any kind of relationship with you other than employer and employee,'' Ashe said. ''I agreed to act as your bodyguard because a fine, dear lady asked me to, as a personal favor to her. That's the only reason I'm here. You don't have to worry that I'll harass you with any unwanted attention.''

Deborah opened the French doors, walked outside and gazed up at the clear blue sky. Autumn sky. Autumn breeze. A hint of autumn colors surrounded her, especially in her mother's chrysanthemums and marigolds that lined the patio privacy wall.

Why should Ashe's words hurt her so deeply? It wasn't as if she still loved him. She had accepted the fact, long ago, that she had meant nothing to him, that Whitney had been the woman he'd wanted. Why would she think anything had changed?

Ashe followed her out onto the side patio. ''It wasn't easy for me to come back. I never wanted to see this place again as long as I lived. But I'm back and I intend to stay to protect you.''

''As a favor to my mother?''

''Partly, yes.''

She wouldn't face him; she couldn't. ''Why else would you come back to Sheffield?''

''Your mother asked me if I was afraid to face the past. She dared me to come home.''

''And were you afraid to face the past?''

"I'm here, aren't I? What does that tell you?"

"It tells me that you have a soft spot in your heart for my mother because she was kind to your grandmother and you and your cousin, Annie Laurie. And it tells me that you're the type of man who can't resist a dare."

"If I'm willing to come back to Sheffield, to act as your personal bodyguard because it's what Miss Carol wants, then it would seem to me that you should care enough about her to agree to her wishes. All things considered." He moved over to where Deborah stood near the miniature waterfall built into the privacy wall.

Turning her head slightly, she glanced at him. He had changed and yet he remained the same. Still devastatingly handsome, a bit cocky and occasionally rude. The twenty-one-year-old boy who'd made love to her had not completely vanished. He was there in those gold-flecked, green eyes, in that wide, sensuous mouth, in those big, hard hands. She jerked her gaze away from his hands. Hands that had caressed her intimately. Hands that had taught her the meaning of being a sexual woman.

How could she allow him to stay in her home? How could she endure watching him with Allen, knowing they were father and son?

Was there some way she could respect her mother's wishes and still keep the truth from Ashe?

"Let's understand something up front," Deborah

said, facing him, steeling herself not to show any emotion. "I don't want you here. I had hoped I'd never see you again as long as I lived. If I agree to your acting as my bodyguard until the end of the the trial, to please Mother, you must promise me, here and now, that once I am no longer in any danger, you'll leave Sheffield and never return."

"Do you honestly think I'd want to stay?"

"Promise me."

"I don't have to promise you anything. I don't owe you anything." He glared at her, into those bright, still innocent-looking blue eyes and wanted to grab her and shake her until her teeth rattled. Who the hell did she think she was, giving him orders, demanding promises from him?

"You're still as stubborn, as bullhcaded, as aggravating as you ever were," she said.

"Guilty as charged." He wanted to shout at her, to tell her she seemed to be the same little girl who wanted her own way. But this time she couldn't go running to Daddy. This time Wallace Vaughn couldn't force him to leave town. Nobody could. Most certainly not Deborah.

"We seem to be at an impasse."

"No, we're not. Once I settle in, pay a few visits on family and get the lay of the land, so to speak, you're stuck with me for the duration." When she opened her mouth to protest, he shook his head. "I won't promise you anything, but I can tell you this,

I don't intend to stay in Alabama one day longer than necessary. And while I'm here, you don't have anything to fear from me. My purpose is to protect you, not harm you.''

They stared at each other, face-to-face, two determined people, neither giving an inch. Finally Deborah nodded, then looked away.

''Dinner is at six-thirty, if you care to join us,'' she said.

''Fine. I'll be back from Mama Mattie's before then.'' Ashe hesitated momentarily, overwhelmed with a need to ask Deborah why. Why had she gone running to her daddy eleven years ago? Had his rejection made her hate him that much?

''I'll have Mazie prepare you a room, if Mother hasn't already seen to it.''

''Thanks.'' There was no reason to wait, no reason to keep looking at her, to continue wondering exactly what it was about this woman that had made her so unforgettable. He tried to smile, but the effort failed, so he turned and walked back inside the house.

Deborah balled her hands into fists. Taking and releasing a deep breath, she said a silent prayer, asking God to keep them all safe and to protect Allen from the truth. A truth she had kept hidden in her heart since the day he was born, since the day she agreed to allow her son to be raised as her brother.

Chapter 2

As Ashe drove his rental car up Montgomery Avenue, into the downtown area of Sheffield, he noticed the new businesses, mostly restaurants—Louisiana, Milestones and New Orleans Transfer. Come what may, Southerners were going to eat well. Mama Mattie's homespun philosophy had always been that if folks spent their money on good food, they wouldn't need to spend it on a doctor.

Mama Mattie. How he loved that old woman. She was probably the only person he'd ever truly loved. The only person who had ever really loved him. He could barely remember a time during his growing up years when he hadn't lived with her. He had faint memories of living in a trailer out in Leighton. Before he'd started school. Before his daddy had caught his mama in bed with another man and shot them both.

The courts had sentenced JoJo McLaughlin to life in prison, and that's where he'd died, seven years later.

Mama Mattie had tried to protect Ashe from the ugly truth, from the snide remarks of unthinking adults and the vicious taunts of his schoolmates. But his grandmother had been powerless to protect him from the reality of class distinction, from the social snobbery and inbred attitudes of elite families, like the Vaughns, for whom she worked.

If he'd had a lick of sense, he would have stayed in his place and been content to work at the service station during the day and at the country club as a busboy on weekend nights. But no, Ashe McLaughlin, that bad boy who'd come from white trash outlaws, had wanted to better himself. It didn't matter to anyone that he graduated salutatorian of his high school class or that he attended the University of North Alabama on an academic scholarship. He still wasn't good enough to associate with the *right people*.

He had thought Whitney Vaughn cared about him, that their passionate affair would end in marriage. He'd been a fool. But he'd been an even bigger fool to trust sweet little Deborah, who professed to be his friend, who claimed she would love him until the day she died.

Crossing the railroad tracks, Ashe turned off

Shop Pike and drove directly to Mama Mattie's neat frame house.

When he stepped out of the car, he saw her standing in the doorway, tall, broad-shouldered, her white hair permed into a halo of curls around her lean face.

He had sent her money over the years. Wrote her occasionally. Called her on her birthday and holidays. Picked up special gifts for her from around the world. She had asked him to come home a few times during the first couple of years after he joined the army, but she'd finally quit asking.

She wrote him faithfully, once a month, always thanking him for his kindness, assuring him she and Annie Laurie were well. Sometimes she'd mention that Miss Carol had dropped by for a visit, and told him what a precious little boy Allen Vaughn was. But she never mentioned Deborah. It was as if she knew he couldn't bear for her name to be mentioned.

Mattie Trotter opened the storm door, walked out onto the front porch and held open her arms. Ashe's slow, easy gait picked up speed as he drew closer to his grandmother. Taking the steps two at a time, he threw his arms around Mama Mattie, lifting her off her feet.

"Put me down, you silly boy! You'll throw out your back picking me up." All the while she scolded, she smiled, that warm, loving smile Ashe well remembered from his childhood.

Placing her on her feet, he slipped his arm around her waist, hugging her to his side. She lacked only a few inches being as tall as he was. "It's so good to see you again, Mama Mattie."

"Come on inside." She opened the storm door. "I've made those tea cakes you always loved, and only a few minutes ago, I put on a fresh pot of that expensive coffee you sent me from Atlanta."

Ashe glanced around the living room. Small, not more than twelve by fourteen. A tan sofa, arms and cushions well-worn, sat against the picture window, a matching chair to the left. The new plaid recliner Ashe had sent her for Christmas held a fat, gray cat, who stared up at Ashe with complete disinterest.

"That's Annie Laurie's Mr. Higgins. She's spoiled him rotten," Mattie said. "But to be honest, I'm pretty fond of him myself. Sit down, Ashe, sit down."

He sat beside her on the sofa. She clasped his hands. "There were times when I wondered if I'd ever see you again. I'm an old woman and only God knows how much longer I'm going to be in this world."

"Don't talk like that. You'll live to be a hundred."

Releasing his hands, she looked directly into his eyes. "Have you seen Deborah?"

"Yeah, Mama Mattie, I've seen Deborah Vaughn."

"She turned out to be a beautiful woman, didn't she?"

"She was always beautiful, just not...not finished."

"Miss Carol looks bad, doesn't she?" Mattie shook her head sadly. "That bout she had with cancer a while back took its toll on her. She's in remission now, but we all live in fear she'll have a relapse."

"She aged more than I'd expected," Ashe said, recalling how incredibly lovely Carol Vaughn had once been. "But nothing else has changed about her. She's still a very kind lady."

"So is Deborah."

"Don't!" Ashe stood abruptly, turning his back on his grandmother, not wanting to hear her defend the woman who had been responsible for having him run out of town eleven years ago.

Mattie sighed. "I still say you judged her wrong. She was just a child. Seventeen. You rejected all that sweet, young love she felt for you. If she went to her daddy the way you think she did, then you shouldn't hold it against her. My God, boy, you took her innocence and then told her you didn't want her."

"It wasn't like that and you damn well know it."
Ashe needed to hit something, smash anything into
a zillion pieces. He hated remembering what he'd
done and what his stupidity had cost him.

"Don't you swear at me, boy." Mattie narrowed
her eyes, giving her grandson a killing look.

"I'm sorry, Mama Mattie, but I didn't come by
to see you so we could have that old argument
about Deborah Vaughn." Ashe headed toward the
kitchen. "Where are those tea cakes?"

Mattie followed him, busying herself with pouring coffee into brown ceramic mugs while Ashe
devoured three tea cakes in quick succession. He
pulled out a metal and vinyl chair and sat down at
the table.

"They taste just the same. As good as I remember."

He would never forget walking into the
Vaughns' kitchen after school every day, laying his
books on the table and raiding Mama Mattie's tea
cake tray. More often than not, he and Annie Laurie
rode home with Miss Carol when she picked up
Deborah and Whitney from school.

Whitney had ignored him as much as possible,
often complaining to her aunt that she thought it
disgraceful they had to be seen with *those children*.
He supposed her haughty attitude had given him
more reason to want to bring her down to his level,
and eventually he'd done just that. He hadn't been

Whitney's first, but he hadn't cared. She'd been hot and eager and he'd thought she really loved him.

All the while he'd been drooling over Whitney, he hadn't missed the way Deborah stared at him, those big blue eyes of hers filled with undisguised adoration.

"Thinking about those afternoons in the Vaughn kitchen?" Mattie asked.

"What is it with you and Miss Carol? Both of you seem determined to resurrect some sort of romance between Deborah and me." Ashe lifted the coffee mug to his lips, sipped the delicious brew and held his mug in his hand. "Deborah and I were never sweethearts. We weren't in love. I liked her and she had a big teenage crush on me. That's all there ever was to it. So tell me what's going on?"

"Neither one of you has ever gotten married."

"Are you saying you'd like to see me married to Deborah?" Ashe's laughter combined a snicker, a chuckle and a groan. "It's never going to happen. Not in a million years. Wherever did you get such a crazy idea?"

"You came back home when Miss Carol called and told you that Deborah was in trouble, that her life was in danger," Mattie said. "In eleven years nothing I've said or done could persuade you to return. And don't try to tell me that you came back because of Miss Carol. You could have sent another man from that private security place where you work. You didn't have to come yourself and we both know it.''

"Miss Carol asked for me, personally. I knew how sick she'd been. You've told me again and again that you were afraid she might die.''

''So knowing Buck Stansell is probably out to stop Deborah from testifying didn't have anything to do with your coming home? You don't care what happens to her?''

''I didn't say I don't care. I wouldn't want anything to happen to her.'' When Miss Carol had first telephoned him and explained the situation, his blood had run cold at the thought of anyone harming Deborah. Despite what she'd done to him, he couldn't help remembering the sweet, generous, loving girl he'd known since she was a small child. He had thought she didn't matter to him, that he didn't even hate her anymore. But he'd been wrong. He cared. He cared too damned much. Now that he'd seen Deborah again, he was worried that he couldn't act as her bodyguard and keep their relationship on a purely business level. And that could be dangerous for both of them. If he was smart, he'd call Sam Dundee and tell him to put another agent on the first available flight out of Atlanta.

But where Deborah Vaughn was concerned, he'd never been smart. Not when he had ignored her to pay court to her older cousin. Not when he'd accepted her comfort and love when Whitney had rejected him. And not when he'd been certain she would never betray him to anyone, least of all her father.

Mattie poured herself a second cup of coffee, broke a tea cake in two and popped half into her mouth. Chewing slowly, she watched Ashe. When he turned around and caught her staring at him, he smiled.

"All right. I admit it. Part of the reason I agreed to Miss Carol's request was because I don't want to see anything happen to Deborah. There. I said it. Are you satisfied?"

Mattie grinned, showing her perfect, white dentures. "You ought to go have a talk with Lee Roy and Johnny Joe. They're working for Buck Stansell, you know."

"Yeah, I figured as much, since their daddy and mine were both part of that gang years ago, along with Buck's daddy."

"Well, I don't trust Johnny Joe, but I always saw something in Lee Roy that made me think he was a mite better than that bunch of trash he came from."

"Hey, watch what you're saying, Mama Mattie. You're talking about my family." Ashe grinned.

"Your daddy's family, not mine, and not yours. I think Johnny Joe took after his daddy and his Uncle JoJo, where Lee Roy reminds me a bit of your daddy's sister. She wasn't such a bad girl. She and your mama always got along.''

"You think Lee Roy and Johnny Joe know something about the threats against Deborah?'' Ashe asked.

"Can't nobody prove nothing, but folks know that Buck Stansell was behind that killing Deborah witnessed. Whoever's been sending her those notes and making those phone calls, you can bet your bottom dollar that Buck's behind it all.''

"What do you know about this Lon Sparks? I don't remember him.''

"No reason you should. He showed up around these parts a few years back. I hear he come up from Corinth with a couple of other guys that Buck recruited when he expanded his drug dealings.''

"How do you know so much, old woman?'' Ashe laid his hand over his grandmother's where it rested beside her coffee cup.

"Everybody hears things. I hear things. At the beauty shop. At the grocery store. At church.''

"After I've settled in and made my presence known, I'll take a ride out to Leighton and see how my cousins are doing.''

"You be careful, Ashe. Buck Stansell isn't the kind of man to roll over and play dead just because Deborah's got herself a bodyguard.''

"Don't you worry. I'm not stupid enough to underestimate Buck. I remember him and his old man. I've come up against their type all over the world.''

"While you're taking care of Deborah and Miss Carol and that precious little Allen, make sure you take care of yourself, too.'' Mattie squeezed her grandson's big hand.

The back door swung open and a tall, thin young woman in a sedate gray pantsuit walked in and stopped dead still when she saw Ashe.''

"Oh, my goodness, it's really you!'' Annie Laurie threw herself into Ashe's arms. "Mama Mattie said you'd come home, but I wasn't so sure. You've been away forever and ever.''

Mr. Higgins sneaked into the kitchen, staring up at Annie Laurie, purring lightly.

Ashe held his cousin at arm's length, remembering the first time he'd seen her. She'd been a skinny eight-year-old whose parents had been killed in an automobile accident. Mama Mattie, Annie Laurie's mother's aunt, had been the child's closest relative and hadn't hesitated to open her home and heart to the girl, just as she had done for Ashe. "Here, let me have a good look at you. My, my. You sure have grown. And into a right pretty young lady.''

Blushing, Annie Laurie shoved her slipping glasses back up her nose. "You haven't seen me since I was thirteen.''

Hearing a car exit the driveway, Ashe glanced out the window in time to see a black Mercedes backing up, a familiar looking redheaded guy driving.

"Your boyfriend bring you home from work?" Ashe asked.

Annie Laurie's pink cheeks flamed bright red. She cast her gaze down toward the floor, then bent over, picked up Mr. Higgins and held him in her arms.

"Stop teasing the girl," Mattie said.

"He's not your boyfriend?" Ashe lifted her chin.

"He's my boss."

"Your boss?"

"That was Neil Posey," Mattie said. "You remember him. He's Archie Posey's son. He's partners with Deborah in their daddies' real estate firm."

"You work for Vaughn & Posey Real Estate?" Ashe asked. "I guess Mama Mattie told me and I'd just forgotten."

"I'm Neil's...that is Mr. Posey's secretary. And he's not my boyfriend. He's Deborah's...I mean, he likes her."

"What?" Ashe laughed aloud. Neil Posey was Deborah's boyfriend? That short, stocky egghead with carrot red hair and trillions of freckles.

"I've tried to tell Annie Laurie that Deborah isn't interested in Neil just because he follows her around like a lovesick puppy dog." Mattie shook her head, motioning for Ashe to let the subject drop. "Are you staying for supper? I've got some chicken all thawed out. It won't take me long to fry it up."

"Sorry, Mama Mattie, I'm expected for dinner at the Vaughns', but I'm looking forward to some of your fried chicken while I'm home."

"You be sure and tell Deborah and Miss Carol I asked about them," Mattie said. "And, here, take Allen some of my tea cakes. He loves them as much as you used to when you were his age."

Ashe caught an odd look in his grandmother's eyes. It was as if she knew something she wanted him to know, but for some reason didn't see fit to tell him. He shook off the notion, picked up his coffee mug and relaxed, enjoying being home. Back in his grandmother's house. Back with the only real family he'd ever known.

Deborah checked her appearance in the cheval mirror, tightened the backs of her pearl earrings and lifted the edge of her neckline so that her pearl necklace lay precisely right. Ashe McLaughlin's presence at their dinner table tonight had absolutely nothing to do with her concern about her appearance, she told herself, and knew it was a lie. Her undue concern *was* due to Ashe, and so was her nervousness.

Didn't she have enough problems without Ashe reappearing in her life after eleven years? How could her mother have thought that bringing that man back into their lives could actually help her? She'd almost rather face Buck Stansell alone than have to endure weeks with Ashe McLaughlin at her side twenty-four hours a day.

Of course, her mother had been right in hiring a personal bodyguard for her. She had to admit that she'd considered the possibility herself. But not Ashe!

Ever since she had inadvertently driven up on the scene of Corey Looney's execution, she had been plagued by nightmares. Both awake and asleep. Time and again she saw the gun, the blood, the man's body slump to the ground. Even in the quiet of her dark bedroom, alone at night, she could hear the sound of the gun firing.

Shivers racked Deborah's body. Chill bumps broke out on her arms. The letters and telephone calls had begun the day the sheriff arrested Lon Sparks. At first she had tried to dismiss them, but when they persisted, even the local authorities became concerned.

Colbert County's sheriff and an old family acquaintance, Charlie Blaylock, had assigned a deputy to her before and during the preliminary hearing, but couldn't spare a man for twenty-four-hour-a-day protection on an indefinite basis. Charlie had spoken to the state people, the FBI and the DEA, hoping one or more of the agencies' interest in Buck Stansell's dealings might bring in assistance and protection for Deborah.

But there was no proof Buck Stansell was involved, even though everyone knew Lon Sparks worked for Stansell. The federal boys wanted to step in, but murder in Colbert County was a local crime. They'd keep close tabs on the situation, but couldn't become officially involved.

Charlie had been the one to suggest hiring a private bodyguard. Deborah had agreed to consider the suggestion, never dreaming her mother would take matters into her own hands and hire Ashe McLaughlin.

Closing the door behind her, Deborah stepped out into the upstairs hallway, took a deep breath and ventured down the stairs. When she entered the foyer, she heard voices coming from the library, a room that had once been her father's private domain. Her mother had kept the masculine flavor of the room, but had turned it into a casual family retreat where she or Deborah often helped Allen with his homework. The old library was more a family room now.

She stood in the open doorway, watching and listening, totally unnoticed at first. Her mother sat in a tan-and-rust floral print chair, her current needlepoint project in her hand. She smiled, her gaze focused on Allen and Ashe, who were both sitting on the Tabriz rug, video-game controls in their hands as they fought out a battle on the television screen before them.

"You're good at this," Allen said. "Are you sure you don't have a kid of your own you play with all the time?"

Deborah sucked in a deep breath, the sting of her son's words piercing her heart. She couldn't bear the way Allen looked at Ashe, so in awe of the big, friendly man he must never know was his father.

"I don't have any kids of my own." Ashe hadn't thought much about having a family. His life didn't include a place for a wife and children, although at one time, a family had been high on his list of priorities—eleven years ago when he'd thought he would marry Whitney Vaughn and carve a place for himself in local society. Hell, he'd been a fool in more ways than one.

"You should be thinking about a family, Ashe," Carol Vaughn said, laying aside her needlework. "You're how old now, thirty-two? Surely you've sowed all the wild oats a man would need to sow."

Ashe turned his head, smiled at Carol, then frowned when he caught sight of Deborah standing in the doorway. "I haven't really given marriage a thought since I left Sheffield. When a man puts his trust in the wrong woman, more than once, the way I did, it makes him a little gun-shy."

Deborah met his fierce gaze directly, not wavering the slightest when he glared at her with those striking hazel eyes...gold-flecked green eyes made even more dramatic since they were set in a hard, lean, darkly tanned face.

Ashe realized that he could not win the game of staring her down. Deborah Vaughn had changed. She was no longer the shy, quiet girl who always seemed afraid to look him in the eye. Now she seemed determined to prove to him how tough she was, how totally immune she was to him.

With that cold, determined stare she told him that he no longer had any power over her, that the love-sick girl she'd once been no longer existed. Her aversion to him came as no great surprise, but what did unsettle him was her accusatory attitude, as if she found him at fault.

All right, he had taken her innocence when he'd had no right to touch her, but he'd told her he was sorry and begged her to forgive him. He had rejected her girlish declaration of love as gently as he'd known how. If he'd been a real cad, he could have taken advantage of her time and again. But he'd cared about Deborah, and his stupidity in taking her just that one time had made him heartsick.

But he had not ruined her life. It had been the other way around. She had almost ruined his a couple of months later by running to her daddy. Why had she done it? Had she hated him that much? Did she still hate him?

Carol glanced at her daughter. ''Deborah, come

join us. Mazie tells me dinner will be ready promptly at six-thirty.''

''She's always punctual. Dinner's at six-thirty every night,'' Deborah said.

''She's prepared Allen's favorite. Meat loaf with creamed potatoes and green peas,'' Carol said.

''Hey, pal, that's my favorite, too.'' Ashe elbowed Allen playfully in the ribs.

Allen leaned into Ashe, toppling the big man over onto the rug. Within seconds the two were wrestling around on the floor.

Deborah looked from father and son to her mother. Nervously she cleared her throat. When no one paid any heed to her, she cleared her throat again.

''Come sit down.'' Carol gestured toward the tufted leather sofa. ''Let the boys be boys. They'll tire soon enough.''

When Deborah continued staring at Allen and Ashe rolling around on the floor, both of them laughing, Carol stood and walked over to her daughter.

''Allen needs a man in his life.'' Carol slipped her arm around Deborah's waist, leading her into the room. ''He'll soon be a teenager. He's going to need a father more than ever then.''

''Hush, Mother! They'll hear you.''

Carol glanced over at the two rowdy males who

stopped abruptly when their roughhousing accidently knocked over a potted plant.

"Uh-oh, Allen, we'll be in trouble with the ladies now." Rising to his knees, Ashe swept up the spilled dirt with his hands and dumped it back into the brass pot.

"Don't worry about it," Carol said. "I'll ask Mazie to run the vacuum over what's left on the rug."

Deborah glanced down at her gold and diamond wristwatch. "It's almost six-thirty. I'll check on dinner and tell Mazie about the accident with the plant."

The moment Deborah exited the room, Allen shook his head, stood up and brushed off his hands. "What's the matter with Deborah? She's acting awful strange."

"She's nervous about the upcoming trial, but you know that, Allen." Carol smiled, first at Allen and then at Ashe. "Our lives have been topsy-turvy for weeks now."

"No, I'm not talking about that." Allen nodded toward Ashe. "She's been acting all goofy ever since Ashe showed up here today." He turned to Ashe. "Nobody ever answered my question about whether you and Deborah used to be an item."

"Allen—" Carol said.

"Deborah and I were good friends at one time." Ashe certainly couldn't say anything negative about his sister to the boy. "I'm four years older, so I dated older girls."

"Deborah had a crush on Ashe for years," Carol said.

When Ashe glanced at Carol, she stared back at him, her look asking something of him that Ashe couldn't comprehend.

"She liked you, but you didn't like her back?" Allen asked. "Boy, were you dumb. Deborah's pretty and about the nicest person in the world."

"Yeah, Allen, I was pretty dumb all right. I'm a lot smarter now."

"Well, if Deborah gives you a second chance this time, you won't mess things up, will you?" Allen looked at him with eyes identical to Deborah's, the purest, richest blue imaginable.

"I'm not here to romance your sister," Ashe said. "I'm here to protect her, to make sure—"

Carol cleared her throat; Ashe realized he was saying too much, that they wanted the boy protected from the complete, ugly truth.

"Ashe is here to act as Deborah's bodyguard. You know, the way famous people have bodyguards to protect them from their overzealous fans. Well, Ashe is going to make sure the reporters and people curious about the trial don't interfere with her life in any way."

"The kids at school say Buck Stansell will try to kill Deborah if she tells in court what she saw that man do,'' Allen said, looking directly to Ashe for an explanation. "Is that true?''

"No one is going to hurt Deborah while I'm around.'' Ashe placed his hand on the boy's shoulder. "And I'll be here until after the trial, maybe a little longer.''

Carol Vaughn sighed. Ashe glanced at the doorway. Deborah had returned and was looking straight at him, her eyes filled with pain and fear and something indiscernible. Longing? Ashe wondered. Or perhaps the remembrance and regret of longing?

Deborah willed herself to be strong, to show no sign of weakness in front of Allen and her mother or in Ashe's presence. She'd heard Ashe say that no one would hurt her while he was around. For one split second her heart had caught in her throat. He had sounded so determined, so protective, as if he truly cared what happened to her.

"Dinner is ready.'' Damn, her voice shouldn't sound so unsteady. She had to take control. "Is everything all right?''

"Fine,'' Carol and Ashe said in unison.

Rushing across the room, Allen threw his arms around Deborah. "I'll help Ashe protect you. You'll have two men in your life now, and we'll make sure nobody bothers you.''

Deborah hugged her son to her, threading her fingers through his thick blond hair. "I feel very safe, knowing that I have you two guys looking out for me.''

Carol Vaughn steered Allen and Ashe into the hall. ''You two wash up and meet us in the dining room.'' She slipped her arm around Deborah's waist. ''Come, dear.''

Carol managed to keep the conversation directed on Allen during the meal, telling Ashe about the boy's exploits since early childhood. Deborah wished her mother didn't have her heart set on re-uniting them all. There was no way it would ever happen. She and Ashe didn't even like each other. She certainly had good reason not to like Ashe, and it seemed he thought he had reason to dislike her.

''I told Mazie to save the apple pie for tomorrow night's dinner,'' Carol said. ''Ashe brought us some of Mattie's delicious homemade tea cakes.''

''I love Mama Mattie's tea cakes,'' Allen said.

Jerking his head around, Ashe stared at Allen. Had he heard correctly? Had Allen Vaughn referred to Ashe's grandmother as Mama Mattie?

''Mattie insisted Allen call her Mama Mattie.'' Carol laid her linen napkin on the table. ''She said that she liked to think of Allen as a grandchild.''

Deborah strangled on her iced tea. Lifting her napkin to her mouth, she coughed several times. Her faced turned red. She glared at her mother.

''Let's have Mazie serve the tea cakes in the library with coffee for us and milk for Allen.'' Easing her chair away from the table, Carol stood.

Allen followed Carol out of the dining room, obviously eager for a taste of Mattie Trotter's tea cakes. Deborah hesitated, waiting for Ashe. He halted at her side as he walked across the room.

"You look lovely tonight," he said. What the hell had prompted that statement? He'd thought it, and made the remark before thinking.

"Thank you."

She wore blue silk, the color of her eyes. And pearls. A lady's jewel. Understated and elegant.

"We've tried to protect Allen from the complete truth," she said. "He's so young. And he and I are very close. He was only four when Daddy died, and he tries to be our little man."

"He knows more than you think." Ashe understood her need to protect the boy; on short acquaintance he felt an affinity with Deborah's brother and a desire to safeguard him. "Anything made public, he's bound to hear sooner or later. You're better off being up front with him."

"Just what do you know about ten-year-old boys?"

"I know they're not babies, that a boy as smart as Allen can't be fooled."

"It's not your place to make decisions where—"

The telephone rang. Deborah froze. Ashe wished he could erase the fear he saw in her eyes, the somber expression on her face. "Have you had your number changed? Unlisted?"

"Yes." She swallowed hard.

"It's for you, Miss Deborah." Mazie stood in the doorway holding the portable phone. "It's Mr. Posey."

Letting out a sigh, Deborah swayed a fraction. Ashe grabbed her by the elbow.

"Are you all right?" he asked.

Deborah took the phone from Mazie, placed her hand over the mouthpiece and looked at Ashe. "Go ahead and join Mother and Allen in the library."

"Neil Posey?" Ashe asked. "Has he changed any or do his buddies still call him Bozo?"

Deborah widened her eyes, glaring at Ashe as if what he'd said had been sacrilege. *Go away. Now.* She mouthed the words. Grinning, Ashe threw up his hands in a what-did-I-say gesture, then walked out of the room.

"Neil?"

"I thought perhaps you'd like to take a drive," he said. "It's such a lovely autumn night. We could stop by somewhere for coffee later."

"Oh, that's such a sweet thought, but I'm afraid... Well, tonight just isn't good for me. We...that is, Mother has company tonight."

"I see. I'm disappointed of course, but we'll just make it another night."

"Yes, of course."

"See you tomorrow," Neil said. "Yes. Tomorrow." Deborah laid the phone down on the hall table.

Before she took three steps, the telephone rang again. She eyed it with suspicion. Don't do this to yourself. Answer the damned thing. It's not going to bite you.

"Hello. Vaughn residence."

"Deborah?" the man asked.

"Yes."

"Telling the sheriff what you saw was your first mistake. Testifying in court will be your last mistake."

"Who is this?" Sheriff Blaylock had put a tap on their telephones, the one in her bedroom and the one in the library. Damn, why hadn't she remembered not to answer the portable phone?

"This is someone concerned for your safety."

"How did you get our number?" She gripped the phone with white-knuckled ferocity.

"Change it as many times as you want and we'll still keep calling."

"Leave me alone!" Deborah's voice rose.

Ashe appeared before her, grabbed the phone out of her hand and shoved her aside. She stared at him in disbelief.

"Ms. Vaughn won't be taking any more phone calls." He ended the conversation, laid the phone on the hall table, then grabbed Deborah by the arm.

"From now on, you're not to answer the phone. Mazie or I will screen all the incoming calls."

The touch of his big hand on her arm burned like fire. He was hard, his palm warm. She looked up at him, saw the genuine concern in his eyes and wanted nothing more than to crumple into his arms. It would be so easy to give in to the fear and uncertainty that had plagued her since she had witnessed Corey Looney's death. Ashe was big and strong, his shoulders wide enough to carry any burden. Even hers. She wanted to cry out to him "Take care of me," but she couldn't. She had to be strong. For herself. For her mother and Allen.

"Please, don't mention the phone call to Mother. It will only worry her needlessly."

"Needlessly?" Ashe grabbed Deborah by the shoulders. "You're so cool and in control. You're not the girl I used to know. She would have been crying by now. What changed you so much?"

You did. The words vibrated on the tip of her tongue. They would be so easy to say, so difficult to explain. "I grew up. I took on the responsibilities Daddy left behind when he died so suddenly."

Ashe ran his hands up and down her arms. She shivered. For one instant he saw the vulnerable, gentle girl he'd once liked, the Deborah who had adored him. "You won't answer the telephone, at home or at work."

"All right."

"And I won't mention this call to Miss Carol."

"Thank you."

He could barely resist the urge to kiss her. She stood there facing him, her defiant little chin tilted, her blue eyes bright, her cheeks delicately flushed. God, but she was beautiful. But then she always had been. Even when he'd fancied himself in love with Whitney, he hadn't been immune to Deborah's shy, plump beauty.

"If you ever need to let down your defenses for a few minutes, to stop being strong all the time for your mother and brother, I'll be around." He released her, but continued looking directly at her.

She nodded her head, turned and walked away from him.

He didn't want to care about her. Dammit! All these years he'd never been able to forget her. Or the fact that she had betrayed him to her father. Or that she had been a virgin and he had taken advantage of her. And he could never forget when she'd told him she loved him that night, he had seen a depth of emotion on her face he'd never seen again.

He waited in the entrance hall for a few minutes, wondering how the hell he was going to do his job protecting Deborah from the bad guys, when what she desperately needed was protection from him.

Chapter 3

"Mother had Mazie put your bag in here," Deborah said. "One of the guest rooms. It's right across the hall from mine."

"I'm sure it'll be fine." Ashe followed her into the room. Over the years he had stayed in some fancy places. It wasn't as if the finer things in life impressed him the way they once had. But even now, after all these years, he couldn't suppress the satisfaction of knowing he'd be sleeping in a guest room at the Vaughns' house.

Deborah flipped on the overhead light, revealing a room done tastefully in shades of tan and green. The antique oak bedroom suite, masculine in its heavy lines and massive size, would have overwhelmed a smaller room.

"Mother's room is to the right." Deborah returned to the hall. Ashe stood in the doorway.

"And that's Allen's room." She pointed to the open door from which a blast of loud music came, then quieted. "He forgets and plays it too loud sometimes, but he's trying to be more considerate, for Mother's sake."

"I suppose it's been difficult for her trying to raise a young boy, alone, especially at her age." Ashe caught a glimpse of Allen darting around in his room, apparently straightening things.

"Mother is an incredible lady, but she hasn't been alone in raising Allen. I've been with her, taking as much responsibility for him as I possibly could."

"I'm sure you have. I just meant she's raised him without a father, without a man around to help her."

Deborah noticed Ashe watching their son. No! She had to stop thinking that way. Allen Vaughn was her brother.

"He's picking up because he plans to invite you in. He has a lot of questions to ask you about being a bodyguard."

"He's quite a boy, isn't he?" Ashe looked at Deborah. "He reminds me of you. Same coloring. Same quick mind."

"Yes, Allen and I are very much alike." But there are things about him that remind me of you, she wanted to say. Even before Ashe had come back into their lives, she had found similarities between Allen and the man who had fathered him. Now that they'd be together all the time, would those similarities become even more apparent?

"He's big for his age, isn't he?" Ashe asked. He'd thought it strange that Allen was so tall for a ten-year-old. Deborah couldn't be more than five-four, about the same height as Miss Carol; and Wallace Vaughn had been short and stocky.

"Yes." She smiled, thinking about how Ashe had looked as a boy of ten. He had been a part of her life for as long she could remember. He'd come to live with Mattie Trotter when he was only six, right after his mother's death. Deborah had grown up accustomed to seeing Ashe in the kitchen and out in the garden, during the summers and after school, until he'd grown old enough for part-time jobs.

"What are you thinking about?" Ashe couldn't quite discern that faraway look in her eyes. Whatever thoughts had captured her, they must have been pleasant.

"I was thinking about when we were kids. You and little Annie Laurie, Whitney and I." She could have lied, but why should she? They could not change the past, neither the good nor the bad. What had happened, had happened.

"How is Whitney?"

Deborah hadn't thought Ashe's interest in her cousin would create such a sharp pain inside her heart. *Don't do this to yourself! It doesn't matter any more. Whitney is not your rival. You don't love Ashe McLaughlin.*

"She's as well as anyone could be married to George Jamison III."

"What does that mean, exactly?"

"It means that George is quite content to live off Whitney's money, and the two of them have never had children because Whitney is too busy trying to raise the little boy she married."

"I'd say Whitney got what she deserved, wouldn't you?" He could remember a time when he had longed to make Whitney Vaughn his wife. He'd been a fool. She had wanted Ashe for one thing and one thing only. She had enjoyed the sense of danger and excitement she found having an affair with a bad boy her friends considered beneath them.

"She could have married you, couldn't she? You never would have deserted *her.* And you wouldn't have lived off her inheritance." Deborah turned toward her room.

Ashe gripped her by the elbow, pulling her toward him. Jerking her head around, she glared at him. "Your cousin didn't want to marry me. Remember?" he said. "She thought I wasn't good enough for her. But you didn't think that, did you, Deborah?"

He said her name all soft and sexy and filled with

need. The way he'd said it that night. She tried to break away, to force herself into action, to terminate the feelings rising within her. No, she had never thought she was too good for Ashe. She had adored him for as long as she could remember and held her secret love in her heart until the night he'd turned to her for comfort.

He had taken the comfort she'd offered—and more. He'd taken all she had to give. And left her with nothing.

No, that wasn't true. He had left her with Allen.

"Did you change your mind, later? After—" Ashe began.

"No, I… The difference in our social positions isn't what kept us apart and we both know it."

"What about now?" he asked.

"What do you mean?" She looked at him, questioning his statement, daring him to ask her what she thought of the man who had come back into her life after deserting her eleven years ago.

"I'm the hired help around here." His lips were so close that his breath mingled with hers. "Would Miss Deborah ever fool around with the hired help?"

"You're being offensive." She tried to pull away from him; he held fast. Her heartbeat drummed in her ears.

They stared at each other. Defiant. Determined. Neither backing down.

"Hey, Ashe, come in my room and let me introduce you to Huckleberry," Allen called out from down the hallway.

Allen's interruption immediately broke the tense spell. Deborah breathed a sigh of relief; Ashe loosened his hold on her arms.

"Allen, does Mother know you've brought Huckleberry inside?" Deborah asked as she eased her body away from Ashe.

A large tan Labrador retriever stood beside Allen, the dog's tongue hanging out, his tail wagging as the boy stroked his back.

Ashe grinned. "Where does Huckleberry usually stay?"

"Outside," Deborah said. "But occasionally Mother allows Allen to bring him inside."

"Come on." Allen waved at Ashe. "I want to show you my room. Deborah helped me redo the whole thing last year. It's a real guy's room now and not a baby's room anymore."

"Is your mother having a difficult time letting Allen grow up?" Ashe asked.

"Yes, I suppose she is. But he is the baby, after all."

"Come on, Ashe." Allen motioned with his hand.

"Coming?" Ashe asked Deborah.

"Yes, in a minute. You go ahead."

Ashe gave Huckleberry a pat on the head when

he entered Allen's domain. He'd speak to Deborah and Miss Carol about allowing the dog to remain inside. A dog as big as Huckleberry could act as a deterrent to anyone foolish enough to break into the house.

Allen's room was indeed a *real guy's room.* Posters lined one wall. Dark wooden shutters hung at the windows. A sturdy antique bed, covered in blue-and-green plaid, and a huge matching dresser seemed to be the only antique items in the room. A color television, a CD player, a VCR and a tape recorder filled a wall unit beside a desk that held a computer, monitor and printer.

"This is some room, pal. I'd say your sister made sure you had everything a guy could want."

"Yeah, she let me get rid of everything baby-ish." Allen grabbed Ashe by the hand. "Come take a look at these. This is one of my hobbies."

Allen led Ashe over to a shiny metal trunk sitting at the foot of his bed. Lying atop the trunk were two brown albums.

"What have you got here?"

"My baseball card collection."

Deborah stood in the hallway, listening, waiting. How was she going to protect Allen from Ashe McLaughlin when she was finding it difficult to protect herself from him? The moment he'd pulled her close, the moment he'd said her name in that husky, sexy voice of his, she'd practically melted.

No other man had ever made her feel the way Ashe did.

Damn him! Damn him for having the same dizzying effect on her he'd always had. Eleven years hadn't changed the way she wanted him. If she thought she would be immune to Ashe's charms, then she'd been a total fool. If she wasn't careful, she'd wind up falling in love with him all over again.

She couldn't let that happen. And she couldn't allow Ashe to find out that Allen was his son.

Deborah walked down the hall, stopping in the doorway to Allen's bedroom. Ashe and Allen sat on the bed, Huckleberry curled up beside them, his head resting on a pillow. A lump formed in Deborah's throat.

Please, dear Lord. Don't let anyone else notice what I see so plainly—the similarities in boy and man.

''How long were you a Green Beret?'' Allen asked.

''Ten years.''

''Wow, I'll bet that's one exciting job, huh? Did you ever kill anybody?''

Deborah almost cried out, not wanting Ashe to discuss his life in the special forces with their ten-year-old son. She bit her lip and remained silent, waiting for Ashe's reply.

''Yes, Allen, I've killed. But it isn't something

I like to talk about. It was my job to get rid of the
bad guys, but killing is never easy.''

"That's what you're here in Sheffield to do, isn't
it?'' Allen asked. "You're here to protect Deborah
against the bad guys, and if you have to, you'll kill
them, won't you?''

"I hope it doesn't come to that,'' Ashe said.
"But, yes, I'll do whatever it takes to keep Deborah
safe.''

"How long have you been a bodyguard?''

"I started working for Sam Dundee last year,
right after I left the army.''

"Why'd you leave the Green Berets?''

Deborah cleared her throat, stepped inside Allen's room and gave him a censuring stare. "I think
you've asked Ashe enough questions for one night.
Save a few for later.''

"Ah, Deborah, can't he stay just a little while
longer?'' Allen whined in a typical childlike man-
ner. "I was going to ask him about the two of you
when you were kids.'' Allen turned his attention to
Ashe. "Did you ever kiss Deborah when you two
were teenagers?''

"Allen!'' Deborah scolded, her voice harsher
than she had intended.

"Yes, I kissed Deborah.'' Ashe watched her
closely, noting that she wouldn't look at him, that
she had balled her hands into fists and held them
rigidly at her hips.

"I knew it! I knew it!" Allen bounced up and down on the bed. "You two were a thing, weren't you?"

"No, Allen." Deborah trembled inside, and prayed the shivers racing through her body didn't materialize externally. "Stop jumping up and down on the bed."

"You sure are being a grouch." Settling back down on the side of the bed, Allen glanced back and forth from Deborah to Ashe. "What's the big secret about you two being an item when you were teenagers? Is it a big deal that Ashe was your boyfriend?"

"We've told you that Ashe wasn't my boyfriend," Deborah said. No, he'd never been her boyfriend, just her lover for one night. One night that had changed her life forever. "We were friends."

"Then why did he kiss you?" Allen asked.

Deborah looked to Ashe, her gaze pleading with him, then she glanced away quickly. "Sometimes an occasion arises when a friend might kiss another friend," Deborah said.

The look on Allen's face plainly said he didn't believe a word of it.

"Deborah and I were friends all our lives," Ashe explained. "Then not long before I left Sheffield, we thought we could be more than friends. That's when I kissed her. But it didn't work out. So you see, Allen, your sister was never actually my girl-friend.''

"Do you have a girlfriend now?"

"Allen!" Rolling her eyes heavenward, Deborah shook her head in defeat. "Enough questions for one night."

Ashe laughed. "I remember being the same way when I was his age. I used to drive Mama Mattie nuts asking her so many questions. I guess it's the age. The whole world is a mystery when you're ten."

"I guess it's a guy thing, huh, Ashe?"

Allen looked at Ashe McLaughlin with such ad-oration in his eyes that Deborah almost cried. There had been a time when she, too, had adored Ashe. It was so easy to fall under his spell, to succumb to his charm. Maybe her son had inherited her weakness.

"Curiosity isn't a guy thing," Ashe said. "I re-member a time when your sister's curiosity got the minister in big trouble."

"What?" Allen grinned, stole a quick glance at Deborah and burst into laughter. "Deborah did something she wasn't supposed to do? I can't be-lieve it. She always does the right thing."

"Well, she made the mistake of walking in on Reverend Bently and the new choir director, a very attractive lady," Ashe said.

"I asked Mother, right in the middle of her study

club meeting, why Reverend Bently would kiss Miss Denise.'' Deborah smiled, remembering the utter horror on her mother's face and the loud rumble of ladies' voices rising in outrage as they sat in Carol Vaughn's garden, dropping their finger sandwiches and spilling their tea.

"How'd you know, Ashe? Were you there? Did you see it happen?"

"Allen, that's enough questions," Deborah said. "You've got school tomorrow and I have work. Besides, Ashe hasn't even settled in yet. Save the rest of your million and one questions for another day."

"Ah…ahh… All right."

"Deborah told me all about it when I stopped by to pick up Mama Mattie that evening after I got off from work. Your sister was only twelve then, and at that age she used to tell me everything."

Not everything, Deborah thought. Not then, not later, and certainly not now. She never told him how much she loved him. Not until that night by the river. But he'd known she had a crush on him, just as he was aware, now, that she was afraid of him, afraid of how he made her feel.

"Deborah's right, pal. It's getting late." Ashe ruffled the boy's thick blond hair, hair the exact shade Deborah's had been as a child. "I'll be around for several weeks. You'll have a chance to ask me a lot more questions."

Deborah waited in the hallway until Ashe walked past her and toward his own room. He hesitated in the doorway.

"You were always special to me," he said. "I trusted you in a way I didn't trust another soul."

She stood in the hall, staring at his back as he entered his room and closed the door. She shivered. What had he meant by that last statement? Was he accusing her of something? He had trusted her. Well, she had trusted him, too. And he had betrayed her. He had taken her innocence, gotten her pregnant and left town.

Whatever had gone wrong between them hadn't been her fault. It had been his. He hadn't loved her. He'd used her. And afterward, when she'd poured out her heart to him, he'd said he was sorry, that he never should have touched her.

Ashe McLaughlin had regretted making love to her. She could never forget the pain that knowledge had caused her. Even if she could forgive him, she could never forget what he'd said to her eleven years ago… *But I don't love you, Deborah. Not that way. What we did tonight shouldn't have happened. I'm sorry. It was all my fault. Forgive me, honey. Please forgive me.*

Tears gathered in the corners of her eyes. She walked the few steps to her open bedroom door, crossed the threshold, closed the door quietly and, once alone, wiped away her tears.

* * *

"All of Ms. Vaughn's calls are to be screened. That means the caller must identify him or herself and must be someone Ms. Vaughn knows. Otherwise the call will be directed to me. Is that understood?"

Ashe McLaughlin issued orders to the office staff of Vaughn & Posey, the men obviously intimidated, the women enthralled. Standing six-foot-three, broad-shouldered and commanding in his gray sport coat, navy slacks and white shirt, Ashe was the type of man to whom no one dared utter a word of protest.

Listening to Ashe give orders, Deborah waited in her office doorway, Neil Posey at her side. When the staff, one by one, turned their heads in her direction, she nodded her agreement with Ashe. He'd made it perfectly clear to her before they arrived at work that he would be in charge of her life, every small detail, until she was no longer in danger.

Ashe turned to Annie Laurie, who had worked as Neil's secretary for the past five years, and was doing double duty as Deborah's secretary while hers was out on maternity leave. "Carefully check all of Deborah's mail. Anything suspicious, bring to me. And I'll open all packages, no matter how innocent looking they are. Understand?"

"Of course, Ashe." Despite her mousy brown hair and out-of-style glasses, plain little Annie Laurie had grown into a lovely young woman.

Deborah tried not to stare at Ashe, but she found herself again inspecting him from head to toe as she had done at breakfast this morning. No wonder all the females in the office were practically drooling. Although his clothes were tailored to fit his big body, on Ashe they acquired an unpretentious casualness. He wore no tie and left the first two buttons of his shirt undone, revealing a tuft of dark chest hair.

"Who does he think he is coming in here issuing orders right and left?" Neil Posey whispered, his tone an angry hiss. "When you introduced him as your bodyguard, I assumed you would be giving him orders, not the other way around."

"Ashe can't do the job Mother hired him to do unless I cooperate." Deborah patted Neil on the shoulder. "Ashe is here to protect me. He's a trained professional."

"He hasn't changed. He's as damn sure of himself as he ever was." Neil took Deborah's hand in his. "I don't like the idea of that man living in your house, sleeping across the hall from you."

"He could hardly protect me if he stayed at a motel."

"Why Ashe McLaughlin? Good grief, Deb, you were in love with the guy when we were in high school." Neil's eyes widened. He stared directly at Deborah. "You don't still...the man doesn't mean anything to you now, does he?"

"Lower your voice." She had told Neil time and again that she couldn't offer him more than friendship. She'd never led him on or made him any promises. Perhaps it was wrong of her to go out with him from time to time, but he was such a comfortable, nonthreatening date.

"I'm sorry," Neil said. "It's just I'd hate to see him break your heart. You mooned around over him for years and all he could see was Whitney."

"Yes, Neil, I know. Can we please change the subject?"

Deborah caught a glimpse of Ashe going from desk to desk, speaking personally to each Vaughn & Posey employee. Ashe looked up from where he was bent over Patricia Walden's desk and smiled at Deborah. He'd seen her staring at him, watching while Patricia fluttered her long, black eyelashes at him. Deborah forced a weak smile to her lips.

"Look at him flirting with Patricia, and her a married woman!" Neil sucked in his freckled cheeks, making his long, narrow face appear even more equine than usual.

"Neil, close the door, please. We need to discuss the Cotton Lane Estates. I'm afraid we've allowed my situation to interfere in our moving ahead on this project."

Neil closed the door, followed Deborah across the room, waited until she sat, then seated himself. "We have the surveyor's report. No surprises there.

I've had Annie Laurie run a check on the deed. Everything is in order. Mr. and Mrs. McCullough have agreed to our last offer. I'd say, despite your problems, things are moving ahead quite smoothly.''

"We should have had this deal wrapped up a week ago. Have Mr. and Mrs. McCullough come in today and let's get everything signed, sealed and delivered. We've still got several months of good weather, so if we can give Hutchinson the go-ahead, he can move his crews in there and cut the roads we'll need before we divide the land into one-acre lots.''

"I'll give the McCulloughs a call. Since he's retired, they shouldn't have any problem driving down from Decatur this afternoon.''

"Fine. And thanks for handling things while my life has been turned upside down lately.''

Neil smiled, that widemouthed grin that showed all his teeth. "You know I'd do anything for you, Deb. Anything.''

The door opened and Ashe McLaughlin walked in, making no apologies for interrupting. "Make time at lunch to go with me to see Sheriff Blaylock. I want to arrange for one of his men to keep an eye on you tomorrow while I do a little investigating on my own.''

"I don't think that's necessary,'' Neil said.

"Whenever you need to do your *investigating,* I'll be more than happy to stay with Deborah.

"Neil—" Deborah wanted to caution her friend, but she didn't get the chance.

"Look, Posey, I appreciate the fact you're Deborah's friend, but you're a realtor. I'm a professional bodyguard. If I can't be at Deborah's side, I want another professional to be there. One of the sheriff's deputies."

"I can assure you that I'd die to protect Deborah."

"That may be so, but once they kill you, what would keep them from killing her?" Ashe ignored Deborah's pleading look that said not to crush Neil Posey's ego. But Ashe didn't give a damn about Posey's ego. He simply wanted to make sure the man understood he wasn't equipped to play hero. "Do you own a gun? Do you carry it with you? Have you ever killed a man?"

"No, I don't own a gun and I most certainly have never killed another human being." Neil shuddered, obviously offended at the thought.

"It's all well and good to be willing to die to protect Deborah, but it's just as important to be willing to kill, or at least maim an assailant, in order to protect her."

"I'll arrange to go with you to see Charlie Blaylock," Deborah said, her tone sharp. She wanted Ashe to know how displeased she was with him.

There had been no need to humiliate Neil. "Thank you for your offer, Neil. I'd feel completely safe with you, but..." She nodded in Ashe's direction. "Mother is paying Mr. McLaughlin a small fortune, so I plan to get our money's worth out of him."

"Yes, well...I understand." With shoulders slumped, Neil slinked out of Deborah's office like a kicked dog.

She marched across the room, slammed shut the door and turned on Ashe. "How dare you make Neil feel less than the man he is! What gave you the right to humiliate him that way?"

"My intention wasn't to humiliate Neil. Hell, I have no reason to dislike the man, to want to hurt him. My intention was to show him that he's useless as a bodyguard."

"Did you have to do it in front of me?" She looked down at her feet. "Neil has a crush on me."

Ashe laughed. "That must be the reason Annie Laurie can't get to first base with him."

Deborah snapped her head up, her eyes making direct contact with Ashe's. She smiled. "I've done everything but offer to pay for their wedding to get Neil interested in Annie Laurie. He can't seem to see past me to take notice of what a wonderful girl Annie Laurie is and how much she adores him."

Ashe stared at Deborah, his expression softening as he remembered another stupid man who had been so blinded by his passion for one woman that he'd allowed a treasure far more rare to slip through his fingers. Unrequited love was a bitch.

"I'm sorry if you think I was too rough on Neil. Annie Laurie had told me he liked you, but I had no idea he fancied himself in love with you. I'll tread more lightly on his ego from now on."

"Thank you, Ashe. I'd appreciated it."

A soft knock sounded at the door, breaking the intensity of Deborah's and Ashe's locked stares.

"Yes?"

Annie Laurie cracked open the door, peeked inside and held out a bundle of mail. "I've checked through these. The one I put on top looks odd to me. Whoever sent it used one of Deborah's business cards as a mailing label."

"Hand me that letter and place the others on the desk," Ashe said.

Annie Laurie obeyed Ashe's command. Deborah glanced from Annie Laurie's worried face to the letter in Ashe's hand. She waited while he turned the envelope over, inspecting it from every angle. He held it up to the light.

"Does this look pretty much like the other letters you've received?" he asked.

"The others were typed," Deborah said. "This is the first time they've used my business card."

Ashe walked over to Deborah's desk, picked up her letter opener and sliced the envelope along the spine. Lifting out a one-page letter, he laid the opener down, spread apart the white piece of stationery and read aloud the message, which had been typed.

"Don't show up in court. If you do, you'll be sorry."

Deborah glanced at Annie Laurie who seemed to be waiting for something. "Is there something else?" she asked.

Tilting her head to one side and casting her gaze downward, Annie Laurie smiled. "Megan stopped by to see you. She's got Katie with her."

"Oh." Deborah returned Annie Laurie's smile. "I suppose everyone's passing Katie around as if she were a doll. Tell Megan I'll be out in just a minute."

Annie Laurie slipped out of the office, silently closing the door behind her.

"What was that all about? Who are Megan and Katie?"

"Megan is my secretary. She's on maternity leave. Katie is her two-week-old baby girl."

Ashe shook his head. "You've just received another threatening letter and you're concerned with coochie-cooing over your secretary's new baby?"

"I've received a letter very similar to the one you hold in your hand every day since Lon Sparks was arrested," Deborah said. "And I get at least one threatening phone call a day. But it isn't every day that Katie goes for her two-week checkup and Megan brings her by to see us.''

Ashe grinned. God bless her, Deborah hadn't really changed. Not nearly as much as he thought she had. And certainly nowhere near as much as she tried to make everyone think. Underneath all that tough, career woman exterior lay the heart of the sweet, caring girl she'd been years ago. He supposed he should have realized that Deborah was perfectly capable of handling both roles, that sophistication and success didn't exclude the more nurturing qualities that made Deborah such a loving person.

''You go visit with mother and baby,'' Ashe said. ''I'll phone Sheriff Blaylock and let him know we'll be stopping by around noon. We'll let him add this letter to his collection.''

''It won't do any good.'' Deborah opened the door. ''There are never any fingerprints, nothing unique about the stationery. They're all mailed from Sheffield. And the typewriter isn't much of a clue. Hundreds of people in this area have access to the same brand.''

''Whoever's doing this is experienced. He's no amateur.''

''Buck Stansell may be a redneck outlaw, but he's a professional redneck outlaw.''

''Yeah, his family's been in the business for several generations.'' Ashe glanced around Deborah's office. ''Kind of like the Vaughns have been in real estate for three generations.''

''Don't assume that I'm taking the threats lightly,'' she said, her hand on the doorpost. ''I'm shaking in my boots. But I have a business to run, people who count on Vaughn & Posey for their livelihoods. And I have a mother who's in bad health and a ch…a brother who's only a child.''

''Who has access to your business cards?''

''What?''

''Could just anybody get one of these cards?'' Ashe waved the envelope in the air.

''Oh, yes, anybody could get one.'' Deborah walked into the outer office. ''Megan, we're so glad you stopped by. Who's got Katie? Come on, Helen, give her to me.''

Ashe stood in the doorway, watching Deborah hold her secretary's baby. She looked so natural, as if cuddling a baby in her arms was something she did all the time. Why wasn't she married, with children of her own? A woman like Deborah shouldn't be single, still living at home with her mother and little brother. She should be hustling a pack of kids off to school and baseball games and cheerleader practice. She should be holding her own child in her arms.

Ashe didn't mean to eavesdrop, but when Megan pulled Deborah aside into the corner near her office, he remained standing just behind the partially closed door.

"I want to thank you again for the bonus you gave me," Megan said. "Bennie is so proud, he would never have accepted the money if you hadn't convinced him it was a bonus and that Mr. Posey had given the same amount to his secretary. Annie Laurie even went along with our little fib."

"It was a bonus," Deborah said. "A baby bonus. I think every baby should have a fully equipped nursery."

"We could never have afforded everything without that bonus. And after that, you didn't have to bring another gift to the hospital." Megan looked down at the pink-and-white ruffled dress her daughter wore. "It looks beautiful on her, don't you think?"

Ashe closed the door. Still the do-gooder. Still the tenderhearted pushover. No, Deborah hadn't changed. She was older, more beautiful, more experienced and certainly more sophisticated. But she was still the girl he'd considered his friend, the girl with whom he would have trusted his soul.

Was it possible that she had no idea what her father had done to him? Had he misjudged her all these years? Maybe she hadn't run to Wallace Vaughn and cried rape. But even if she hadn't falsely accused him, she'd still told her father that the two of them had made love. Surely she would have known how her father would react.

Even after Ashe had left town, Wallace Vaughn had slandered him. It had become public knowledge that Deborah's father had run Ashe Mc-Laughlin out of Sheffield.

All the old feelings came rushing back, bombarding him with their intensity. All the love, the hate, the fear and the uncertainty. Maybe Carol Vaughn had been right. He hadn't returned to Sheffield before now because he was afraid to face the past, to find out the truth, to confront Deborah and Whitney.

But he was back now, and there was no time like the present to meet the ghosts of his past head-on.

Chapter 4

Charlie Blaylock had been a friend of her father and Deborah suspected he'd always had a soft spot in his heart for her mother. He asked about Carol every time he ran into Deborah, and his concern certainly seemed a bit more than neighborly.

Deborah tried to relax as she sat in Charlie's office listening to him explain the details of the Lon Sparks case to Ashe, and exactly what he could and could not do to protect Deborah against Buck Stansell and his bunch of outlaws.

"When Carol asked my advice about hiring a private bodyguard for Deborah, I was all for it." Charlie gazed out the window that overlooked the parking area. He moved with a slow, easy stride, all six feet five inches, three hundred pounds of him. "We don't have a smidgen of proof that Buck and his boys are involved in the threats Deborah's been receiving. If we had any proof, we could make a move to stop them. But even if we caught the guy who's making the phone calls, Buck would just have somebody else take up where he left off.''

"I'm planning on paying a visit to Lee Roy and Johnny Joe.'' Ashe stood, walked across the room, and stopped at Charlie's side. "I want you to have one of your men stay with Deborah while I drop in on my cousins.''

Charlie lifted his eyebrows. "When were you planning on visiting the Brennan brothers?''

"Tomorrow. Bright and early.''

"I've tried to tell Ashe that I've survived for a couple of weeks now without his constant protection.'' Deborah squirmed around in the uncomfortable straight-back chair in which she sat. "I'll be perfectly all right at the office for a couple of hours.''

"I'll have somebody stop by the house around seven in the morning and stay with Deborah until you finish your business and get back to Sheffield.'' Charlie laid his big hand on Ashe's shoulder, gripping him firmly. "I was surprised when Carol told me she was hiring you. Last I'd heard, you were still in the army. The Green Berets, wasn't it?''

"I left over a year ago.'' Ashe looked down at Charlie's hand resting on his shoulder, all friendly like.

Ashe figured Charlie Blaylock knew exactly

what his old friend, Wallace Vaughn, had done to him eleven years ago. Although Charlie had been sheriff even then, Wallace had brought the district attorney with him when he'd had his little talk with Ashe. And Sheffield's chief of police had been waiting right outside the door, waiting to arrest Ashe if he hadn't agreed to leave town and never return. But Charlie would have known what Wallace had been up to, perhaps had even given him a little advice on how to get rid of that white trash boy who had dared to violate Wallace's precious daughter.

Charlie gave Ashe's shoulder another tight squeeze, then released him. "Carol wants you here. She's convinced herself that nobody else can protect Deborah. I'll do everything I can to cooperate with you."

"I'll keep that in mind."

Removing the most recent threatening letter from his coat pocket, Ashe dropped it on Charlie's desk. "You might want to have this examined, but I'd say it's clean."

"Another one?" Charlie asked. "This has become a daily occurrence, hasn't it?"

"I expect you'll notify the big boys, keep them informed on every detail. Let them know that I've arrived, if you haven't already called them." Walking across the room, Ashe held out his hand to Deborah. "Let's go get a bite of lunch."

Deborah started to take his hand, then hesitated when Charlie spoke.

"What makes you think anybody else is involved in this case?" Charlie picked up the envelope from his desk, glancing at it casually as he turned it over.

"Buck Stansell has the drug market cornered in this county. And if Corey Looney's death was drug related, the DEA is already unofficially involved." Ashe dropped the hand he'd been holding out to Deborah.

She glanced back and forth from Charlie's flushed face to Ashe's cynical smile. The big boys? The DEA? No one had told her that Corey Looney had been executed because of a drug deal.

"What are y'all—" Deborah began.

"I don't know what you're talking about." Charlie laid the envelope on his desk, rested his hand on the back of his plush leather chair and looked Ashe straight in the eye.

"My boss is a former agent," Ashe said. "All Sam Dundee had to do was make a phone call. I know everything you know, Blaylock. Everything."

"Stop it, both of you!" Deborah jumped up, slammed her hands down on her hips and took a deep breath. "I have no idea what y'all are talking about, but I'm tired of you acting as if I'm not in the room. I'm the person whose life is in danger. *I'm* the one who should know *every-thing!*"

Ashe grabbed her by the elbow, forcing her into action as he practically dragged her out of Charlie's office. "I'll tell you whatever you need to know at lunch."

"Whatever I need to know!" She dug in her heels in the hallway.

Ashe gave her a hard tug. She fell against him and he slipped his arm around her. "It's a beautiful fall day. Let's pick up something and take it down to Spring Park for a picnic."

Deborah jerked away from him. She couldn't bear being this close to him. Despite their past history, she could not deny the way Ashe made her feel—the way no other man had ever made her feel.

"What was all that between you and Charlie?" Deborah stood her ground, refusing to budge an inch, her blue eyes riveted to Ashe's unemotional face. "For a minute there I thought he wanted to take a punch at you."

Ashe glanced around the corridor, listening to the sound of voices from the adjoining offices. "This isn't the time or the place."

"Just tell me this, is the DEA involved in this case?"

"Unofficially." Ashe grabbed her by the arm again. "Come on. We'll get lunch, go to the park and talk."

"All right." She followed his lead, outside and into the parking lot.

She didn't resist his manhandling, macho jerk that he was. Ashe's brutally masculine qualities had fascinated her as a teenager. Now they irritated and annoyed her. Yet she had to admit, if she was totally honest with herself, that she couldn't imagine any other bodyguard with whom she'd feel more secure.

There was a strength in Ashe that went beyond the normal male quality. It had been there, of course, years ago, but she recognized it now for what it was. Primitive strength that came from the core of his masculinity, the ancient need to beat his chest and cry out a warning to all other males.

Deborah shivered. Everything male in Ashe called to all that was female within her. If he claimed her, as he once had done, would she be able to reject him? A need to be possessed, protected and cherished coursed through her veins like liquid fire, heating her thoughts, warming her femininity.

When he opened the passenger door of his rental car and assisted her inside, she glanced up at him. Her heartbeat roared in her ears. Ashe hesitated just a fraction of a second. He looked at her lips. She resisted the urge to lick them.

"Where's a good place to get take-out close

by?'' He shut the door, walked around the hood of the car and got in on the driver's side.

''Stephano's on Sixth Street has good food.'' She clutched her leather bag to her stomach. ''It's on the left side of the street, so you may want to turn off on Fifth and make the block.''

When she returned home this evening, she'd tell her mother that this wasn't going to work, having Ashe as her bodyguard. Even if he kept her safe from Buck Stansell, another few weeks of being near Ashe would drive her insane.

Ashe picked up a couple of meatball subs, colas and slices of sinfully rich cheesecake. Gazing down into the bag, Deborah shook her head.

''This is too much food. I can't eat all of this. I have to watch my...'' She left the sentence unfinished. She'd been about to tell Ashe McLaughlin that she had to watch her weight. Of course she had no need to tell him; he could well remember what a plump teenager she'd been.

''Splurging one day won't spoil that knockout figure of yours.'' Ashe kept his gaze focused on the road as he turned the car downward, off Sixth Street, and into the park area beneath the hill.

He thought she had a knockout figure? Was that the reason he couldn't seem to take his eyes off her all morning? Why he watched every move she made at the office? The thought of Ashe approving of her figure sent pinpricks of excitement rushing through her. Idiot! She chastised herself. You shouldn't care what he thinks. You shouldn't care what any man thinks, least of all Ashe. He didn't want you when you were a plump teenager, and you don't want him now. So there.

Liar! Good or bad. Right or wrong. You still want Ashe McLaughlin. You've never wanted anyone else.

"Is there a woman in your life back in Atlanta?" She heard herself ask, then damned herself for being such a fool. How could she have asked him such a question?

Ashe parked the car in the shade, opened his door and turned to take their lunch bag from Deborah. "No one special," Ashe said. "Women come and go, but there's been no one special in my life since I left Sheffield eleven years ago."

Whitney, Deborah thought. Her cousin had been the only special woman in Ashe's life. Jealousy and pity combined to create a rather disturbing emotion within Deborah. Both feelings constituted an admission that she still cared about Ashe.

And she didn't want to care. God in heaven, she didn't dare care. He had taken her innocence, broken her heart and left her pregnant. What woman in her right mind would give a man like that a second chance?

But then, Ashe hadn't said or done anything to indicate he wanted a second chance.

"This place hasn't changed much, has it?" Ashe looked around Spring Park, a small area of trees, playground equipment and picnic tables surrounding a small lake fed by an ancient underground spring.

"It's a bit lonely this time of day and this late in the season. Most of the activity takes place over there—" Deborah pointed to the south of the park "—at the golf course."

Ashe chose a secluded table on the west side of the park, near a cove of hedge apple trees, their bare branches dotted with mistletoe. The spring's flow meandered around behind them on a leisurely journey toward Spring Creek. Laying down the paper sack, Ashe removed the white napkins and spread out their lunch. He handed Deborah a cup and straw. She avoided touching his hand when she accepted the offering.

"Are you afraid of me?" he asked, swinging his long legs under the picnic table.

Deborah sat across from him, gripping the plastic container of food as she placed the cola on the concrete table. "Why should I be afraid of you? You're here to protect me, aren't you?"

"I wasn't asking if you were afraid that I might physically harm you. We both know that's ridiculous. I'm asking why your hands tremble whenever you think I might touch you. And why you have a difficult time looking directly at me. Your eyes give you away, honey.''

She undid the plastic covering her meatball sandwich. ''I feel awkward around you, Ashe. I guess I'm just not as sophisticated as the women you're accustomed to these days. Maybe what happened between us in the past didn't affect your life the way it did mine.''

No, Ashe didn't suppose what had happened between them had affected his life the way it had hers. She had gone on as if nothing had happened, secure in her family's love and support and Wallace Vaughn's money. Maybe she'd suffered a broken heart for a while until she'd found another boyfriend. But he had paid a high price for their night of passion. He had lost his dream. His big plans of becoming one of the area's movers and shakers had turned sour.

''You don't look like you've fared too badly.'' Ashe surveyed her from the top of her golden blond hair, all neatly secured in a fashionable bun at the nape of her neck, to the length of shapely legs partially hidden beneath the picnic table. ''You're successful, beautiful and rich.''

Did he actually have no idea what he'd done to her? Of course he didn't know about the child they had created together, but how could he have forgotten his adamant rejection, his cruel words of regret, his deliberate avoidance of her in the days and weeks following their lovemaking?

''Whenever we're together, I can't seem to stop thinking about... I suppose it's true what they say about a woman never forgetting her first lover.''

Her words hit him like a hard blow to the stomach. He sucked in air. Why did she sound so innocent, so vulnerable? After all this time, why did the memories of that night haunt him? Why did the thought of a young girl's passionate cries still echo in his mind? ''And a guy never forgets what its like to take a virgin, to be her first. I never meant for it to happen. One minute you were comforting me and the next minute—''

''You don't have to tell me again that you wished it hadn't happened, that you regretted making love to me the minute it was over. You made that perfectly clear eleven years ago! Do you think I don't know that you were pretending I was Whitney all the while you were...''

Deborah lifted her legs, swung them around and off the concrete bench and jumped up, turning her back to Ashe. The quivering inside her stomach escalated so quickly it turned to nausea.

Dammit! Is that what she actually thought? That he had pretended she was Whitney? Yes, he'd thought he was in love with Whitney, but the minute she announced her engagement to George Jamison III, there at the country club where he worked, he'd begun to doubt his love. And when she had laughed in his face and told him he'd been a fool to think she'd ever marry a loser like him, all the love inside him had died. Murdered by her cruelty.

Ashe got up and walked over to Deborah. He wanted to touch her, to put his arms around her and draw her close. She stood there, her shoulders trembling, her neck arched, her head tilted upward. Was she crying? He couldn't bear it if she was crying.

"Deborah?"

She couldn't speak; unshed tears clogged her throat. Shaking her head, she waved her hands at her sides, telling him to leave her alone.

"I did not pretend you were Whitney." He reached out to touch her, but didn't. He dropped his hand to his side. "I might've had a few drinks to dull the pain that night, but I knew who you were and I knew what I was doing."

"You were—" she gasped for air "—using me."

How could he deny the truth? He had used her. Used her to forget another woman's heartless rejection. Used her to salve his bruised male ego. Used her because she'd been there at his side, offering her comfort, her love, her adoration.

"Yeah, you're right. I used you. And that's what I regretted. I regretted taking advantage of you, of stealing your innocence. But I didn't regret the loving.''

The unshed tears nearly choked her. The pain of remembrance clutched her heart. He didn't regret the loving? Was that what he'd just said?

He grabbed her shoulders in a gentle but firm hold. She tensed, every nerve in her body coming to full alert. She couldn't bear for him to touch her, yet couldn't bring herself to pull away.

''I told you I was sorry for what happened, that I regretted what I'd done.'' Ashe couldn't see Deborah's face; she kept her back to him. But in his mind's eye he could see plainly her face eleven years ago. There in the moonlight by the river, her face aglow with the discovery of sexual pleasure and girlish love, she had crumpled before his very eyes when he'd begged her to forgive him, told her that what happened had been a mistake. She had cried, but when he'd tried to comfort her, she had lashed out at him like a wildcat. He'd found himself wanting her all over again, and hating himself for his feelings.

''I've never felt so worthless in my life as I did that night.'' Deborah balled her hands into fists. She wanted to hit Ashe, to vent all the old bitterness and frustration. She wanted to scream at him, to tell him that he'd left her pregnant and she hated him for not caring, for never being concerned about her welfare or the child he had given her.

He turned her around slowly, the stiffness in her body unyielding. She faced him, her chin lifted high, her eyes bright and glazed with a fine sheen of moisture.

"When I took you, I knew it was you. Do you understand? I wanted you. Not Whitney. Not any other woman."

"But you said…you said—"

"I said it shouldn't have happened. It shouldn't have. I didn't love you, not like I should have. I couldn't offer you marriage. What I did was wrong."

She quivered from head to toe, clinching her jaws tightly, trying desperately not to cry. She glared at him, her blue eyes accusing him.

Dear God, he had hurt her more than he'd ever known. After all these years, she hadn't let go of the pain. Was that why she'd gone to her father? Is that why she'd accused him of raping her? Or had she accused him? Was it possible that the rape charges had been Wallace's idea? The thought had crossed his mind more than once in the past eleven years.

"Neither of us can change the past," he said. "We can't go back and make things right. But I want you to know how it really was with me. With us."

"It doesn't matter. Not any more." She tried to pull away from him; he held her tight.

"Yes, it does matter. It matters to me and it matters to you."

"I wish Mother had never brought you back." Deborah closed her eyes against the sight of Ashe McLaughlin, his big hands clasping her possessively.

"She's doomed us both to hell, hasn't she?" Ashe jerked Deborah into his arms, crushing her against him. "I would have made love to you a second time that night and a third and fourth. I wanted you that much. Do you understand? I never wanted anything as much as I wanted you that night. Not Whitney. Not my college degree. Not being successful enough to thumb my nose at Sheffield's elite."

Her breathing quickencd. Her heart raced wildly. She wanted to run. She wanted to throw her arms around Ashe. She wanted to plead with him to stop saying such outrageous things. She wanted him to go on telling her how much he'd wanted her, to tell her over and over again.

"Why…why didn't you tell me? That night? All you kept saying was that you were sorry." Deborah leaned into him, unable to resist the magnetic pull of his big body.

"You wanted me to tell you I loved you. I couldn't lie to you, Deborah. I'd just learned that night that I didn't know a damned thing about love."

"Ashe?"

He covered her lips with his own. She clung to him, returning his kiss with all the pent-up passion within her. The taste of her was like a heady wine, quickly going to his head. It had been that way eleven years ago. The very touch of Deborah Vaughn intoxicated him.

He thrust his tongue into her mouth, gripped the back of her head with one hand and slipped the other downward to caress her hip. He grew hard, his need pulsing against her. She wriggled in his arms, trying to get closer. Their tongues mated in a wet, daring dance. A prelude to further intimacy.

When they broke the kiss to breathe, Ashe dropped his hand to her neck, circling the back with his palm. His moist lips sought and found every sweet, delicious inch of her face.

Deborah flung her head back, exposing her neck as she clung to him, heat rising within her, setting her aflame. Ashe delved his tongue into the V of her blouse, nuzzling her tender flesh with his nose. Reaching between them, he undid the first button, then the second, his lips following the path of his fingers.

A loud blast rent the still autumn air. Ashe knocked Deborah to the ground, covering her body with his as he drew his 9mm out of his shoulder holster.

"Keep down, honey. Don't move."

"Ashe? What happened? Did—did someone shoot at us?" She slipped her arms around his waist.

Lifting his head, Ashe glanced around and saw nothing but an old red truck rounding the curve of the road, a trail of exhaust smoke billowing from beneath the bed. He let out a sigh of relief, but didn't move from his position above Deborah. He waited. Listening. Looking in every direction, lifting himself on one elbow to check behind them.

"Ashe, please—"

"It's all right." After returning his gun to its holster, he lowered himself over her, partially supporting his weight with his elbows braced on the ground. "I'm pretty sure the noise was just a truck backfiring."

"Oh." She sighed, then looked up into Ashe's softening hazel eyes. Eyes that only a moment before had been clear and trained on their surroundings. Now he was gazing down at her with the same undisguised passion she'd seen in them when he had unbuttoned her blouse.

Her diamond hard nipples grazed his chest. His arousal pressed against her. She needed Ashe. Needed his mouth on her body. Needed him buried deep inside her. Needed to hear him say that he wanted her more than he'd ever wanted anything or anyone.

"It's safe for us to get up now, isn't it?" She

heard her own breathless voice and knew Ashe would realize how needy she was.

"I don't think it's safe for us anywhere, honey. We're in danger from each other here on the ground or standing up."

When he lowered his mouth, brushing her lips with his, she turned her head to the side. But she still held him around the waist, her fingers biting into his broad back.

"Eleven years ago, you weren't much more than a girl. What you felt was puppy love. And I was a confused young man who didn't have the foggiest idea what love was all about. But I was older and more experienced. I take the blame for everything." Ashe kissed her cheek, then drew a damp line across to her ear. "We're both all grown up now. Whatever happens between us, happens between equals. No regrets on either side. No apologies. I want you. And you want me."

She shook her head, needing to deny the truth. If she admitted she wanted him, she would be lost. If they came together again, for him it would be sex, but for her it would be love. Just like last time. She couldn't have an affair with Ashe and just let him walk out of her life after the trial. She couldn't give herself to him and risk having her heart broken all over again.

"Please, let me get up, Ashe. I'm not ready for this." She shoved against his chest. He remained on top of her, unmoving, his eyes seeking the truth of her words.

Nodding his head, he lifted himself up and off her, then held out his hand. She accepted his offer of assistance, taking his hand and allowing him to pull her to her feet. She brushed the blades of grass and crushed leaves from her dress, redid the open buttons and straightened the loose strands of her hair.

"I need to get back to work," she said, not looking directly at him. "Let's take this food back to the office with us. We'll be safer there. We won't be alone."

Without a word, Ashe gathered up their sandwiches, returning them to the paper bag. She was right. They'd both be a lot safer if they weren't alone. He intended to do everything in his power to protect Deborah, to make sure no harm came to her. But could he protect her from what they felt for each other? From the power of a desire too powerful to resist?

Later that day Ashe stood in the doorway of Allen's room watching Deborah help the boy with his homework. She played the part of his mother convincingly. He wondered how long she had substituted for Miss Carol. Ever since illness had sapped Miss Carol's strength and she lived in constant fear the cancer would return?

No one seeing Deborah and Allen together could deny the bond between sister and brother. Her whole life seemed to revolve around the boy, and he so obviously adored her.

While Allen struggled with the grammar assignment, he eased his right hand down to stroke Huckleberry's thick, healthy coat.

"Remember, Allen, it's rise, rose, risen," Deborah said. "Do this one again."

Nibbling on the tip of his pencil eraser, Allen studied the sentence before him. "Hmm-hmm."

Ashe remembered how Deborah had struggled with algebra. When he had tutored her, downstairs at the kitchen table, she'd sat there nibbling on her eraser, a perplexed look on her face identical to Allen's. Ashe had been the one who'd had trouble with grammar, and Deborah had helped him write more than one term paper.

Gripping his pencil in his left hand, Allen scribbled the sentence across the sheet of notebook paper, then looked up at Deborah. "Is that right?"

Checking his work, she smiled. "Yes, it's right. Now go on to the next one." She glanced up and saw Ashe. Her smile vanished. Standing, she moved her chair from Allen's right side to his left, shielding him from Ashe's view.

Why had she moved? he wondered. It was as if she were protecting Allen. But from what? Surely not from him.

Ashe walked into the room. Huckleberry lifted his head from the floor, gave Ashe a quick glance, recognized him as no threat and laid his head back down, his body pressed against Allen's foot.

"Hey, Ashe." Allen looked up from his homework paper. "I'm almost finished here, then we can play a video game on the computer."

"Maybe Ashe doesn't want to play," Deborah said, standing up, placing her body between Ashe and her brother. "We've had a long day. Maybe he wants to read or watch TV alone for a while."

"I'm alone all the time in my apartment in Atlanta," Ashe said. "I like being part of a family. Allen and I are pals. I think we enjoy doing a lot of the same things."

"Oh. I see." Did he spend all his time in his Atlanta apartment alone? She doubted it. A man like Ashe wouldn't be long without a woman. She pictured the entrance to his apartment. The thought of a revolving door flashed through her mind.

"Your sister used to have a problem with algebra," Ashe said, walking around Deborah to sit down in the chair she had vacated. "English grammar seems to be your downfall just like it was mine. I guess guys have a difficult time choosing the right words, huh?" Ashe glanced up at Deborah, who glared down at him.

"I don't have to sweat making good grades in anything except this." Allen punched his paper with the tip of his pencil. "I've got three more sentences to go, then watch out, Indiana Jones!"

Allen leaned over his desk, reading from his book. He jotted down the sentence, choosing the correct verb tense. Ashe watched the way his un-tutored handwriting spread across the page, like so much hen scratch. The boy's penmanship was no better than his own. Another shortcoming a lot of guys had in common.

Ashe noticed a crossword puzzle book lying on the edge of the desk. He loved working the really tough ones, the ones that often stumped him and stimulated his mind. He'd been a dud at English grammar, but he was a whiz at figuring out puzzles, even word puzzles.

Ashe picked up the book. "Have you got an extra pencil?"

Allen opened his desk drawer, retrieved a freshly sharpened number two and handed it to Ashe. "You like crossword puzzles, too?"

"Love 'em." Taking the pencil and sticking it behind his ear, Ashe opened the book, found the most complicated puzzle and studied it.

He felt Deborah watching him. What the hell was the matter with her? "Are you planning on hanging around and cheering us on while we play Indiana Jones and the Last Crusade?"

"No. I just want to make sure Allen finishes his homework."

"I'll make sure he does. Go wash out your lingerie or something. Read a good book. Call your boyfriend." Ashe's expression didn't alter as he named off a list of alternatives to standing guard over her brother.

"I told you Deborah doesn't have a boyfriend. She won't give any guy the time of day." Allen never looked up from his paper.

Ashe glanced down at the puzzle. "What's another word for old maid?"

Allen smothered his laughter behind his hand, sneaking a peek at Deborah out of the corner of his eye.

"Try the word *smart,*" Deborah said. "As in any smart woman dies an old maid, without having to put up with a man trying to run her life."

"Spinster." Ashe acted as if he hadn't heard Deborah's outburst. Jerking the pencil from behind his ear, he printed the letters into the appropriate boxes.

"Hey, you're left-handed just like me," Allen said, his face bursting into a smile.

Deborah's heart sank. No. She mustn't panic. A lot of people were left-handed. There was no reason for Ashe to make the connection.

"We seem to have a lot in common." Ashe couldn't explain the rush of emotion that hit him. Like a surge of adrenaline warning him against something he couldn't see or hear, touch, taste or feel. Something he should know, but didn't. And that sense of the unknown centered around Allen Vaughn. Ashe found himself drawn to the boy, in a way similar yet different from the way he'd been drawn to Deborah when they'd been growing up together.

"Ashe, I... We need to talk," Deborah said.

He glanced up at her. Her face was pale. "Can't it wait until later? Allen and I are looking forward to our game."

"This won't take long." She nodded toward the hallway.

He laid down the puzzle book and pencil, stood up and patted Allen on the back. "You finish your homework while I see what Deborah wants that's so important it can't wait."

"Hurry," Allen said. "I'm almost through."

Deborah led Ashe out into the hallway, closing Allen's bedroom door behind him. "Please don't let Allen become too fond of you. He's at an age where he wants a man around, and he seems to idolize you. He thinks you're something special."

"So what's the problem?" Ashe asked. "I like Allen. I enjoy spending time with him. Do you think I'm a bad influence on him?"

"No, that isn't it."

"Then what is it?"

"If you two become close—too close—it'll

break his heart when you leave Sheffield. He's just a little boy. I don't want to see him hurt.''

Ashe pinched her chin between his thumb and forefinger, tilting her downcast eyes upward, making her look directly at him. ''Who are you afraid will get too close to me? Who are you afraid will be brokenhearted when I leave? Who, Deborah? You or Allen?''

She hardened her stare, defying him, standing her ground against the overwhelming emotions fighting inside her. ''You won't ever break my heart again, Ashe McLaughlin. I know you aren't here to stay, that you're in Sheffield on an assignment, just doing your job. But Allen is already forming a strong attachment to you. Don't encourage him to see you as a…a…big brother.''

''A father figure, you mean, don't you? Allen needs a father. Why hasn't Carol ever remarried and given him a father? Or why haven't you married and given him a brother-in-law?''

''I don't think my personal affairs or my mother's are any of your business.''

''You're right.'' He released her chin.

''Please don't spend so much time with Allen. Don't let him start depending on you. You aren't going to be around for very long.''

''What should I do to entertain myself at night?'' he asked. ''Should I play bridge with your mother and her friends? Should I watch the Discovery channel on TV downstairs in the library? Should I invite a lady friend over for drinks and some hanky-panky in the pool house? Or should I come to your bedroom and watch you undress and see your hair turn to gold in the moonlight? Would you entertain me to keep me away from Allen?''

Her hand itched to slap his face. She knotted her palm into a fist, released it, knotted it again, then repeated the process several times.

''If you hurt my…my brother, I'll—''

He jerked her into his arms, loving the way she fought him, aroused by the passion of her anger, the heat of her indignation. ''I'm not going to hurt Allen. You have my word.''

Ceasing her struggles, she searched his face for the truth. ''And I don't want to hurt you, Deborah. Not ever again. No matter what we've done to each other in the past, we don't have to repeat our mistakes.''

''You're right,'' she said breathlessly. ''Do your job. Act as my bodyguard until the trial is over and the threats stop. There's no need for you to become a temporary member of the family. None of us need a temporary man in our lives.''

Was that what he was? Ashe wondered. A temporary man. Never a permanent part of anything. Just there to do a job. It hadn't mattered before, that he didn't have a wife or children. That his life held so little love, so little commitment. Why had being back in Sheffield changed all that? Being around families again, his family and Deborah's, brought to mind all his former hopes and dreams. Dreams of living in one of the big old houses in Sheffield, of becoming a successful businessman, of showing this town how far he'd come—from the depths of white trash, from the McLaughlins of Leighton. And the biggest part of his dream had been the society wife and the children she'd give him. Children who would never know the shame he'd felt, would never face the prejudice he'd fought, would never be looked at as if they were nothing.

"I'll do my job. I'll be careful not to let Allen become too attached to me. And I won't come into your bedroom and make slow, sweet love to you. Not unless you ask."

He didn't give her a chance to say a word. Turning, he marched down the hall, opened Allen's door and walked in, never once looking back at Deborah.

"Hell will freeze over, Ashe McLaughlin, before I ever ask you to make love to me again!" she muttered under her breath.

Chapter 5

A passel of hounds lay in the dirt yard surrounding the double-wide trailer. A brand-new cherry red Camaro, parked beside an old Ford truck, glistened in the morning sun. A long-legged, large-breasted brunette with a cigarette dangling from her lips flung open the front door and ushered three stair-step-size children onto the porch. Her voice rang out loud and clear.

"Get your rear ends in the car. I ain't got all morning to get you heathens to school."

The children scurried toward the Camaro. The wom-an turned around, surveyed Ashe from head to toe and grinned an I'd-like-to-see-what-you've-got-in-your-pants-honey kind of grin.

Ashe leaned against the hood of the rented car he had parked several feet off the gravel drive leading to Lee Roy Brennan's home. He eyed the smiling woman.

"Well, hello." She gave the youngest child a shove inside the car, never taking her eyes off Ashe. "You here to see Lee Roy?"

"Yeah. Is he around?"

"Could be." She ran her hand down her hip, over the tight-fitting jeans that outlined her shapely curves. "Who wants to know?"

"How about you go tell Lee Roy that Ashe McLaughlin wants to see him?"

"Well, Mr. Ashe McLaughlin, you sure do look like you're everything I ever heard you were." She stared directly at his crotch, then moved her gaze up to his face. "Lee Roy says you been in the army. One of them Green Berets. A real tough guy."

Ashe glanced at the three children in the Camaro. People like this didn't care what they said or did in front of their kids. He had vague memories of his old man cursing a blue streak, slapping his mother around and passing out drunk. Yeah, Ashe knew all about the low-class people he'd come from and had spent a lifetime trying to escape.

"Go tell Lee Roy his cousin wants to see him," Ashe said.

The woman's smile wavered, her eyes darting nervously from Ashe to the trailer. "Yeah, sure. He heard you was back in these parts."

Ashe didn't move from his propped position against the hood of his car while Lee Roy's wife went inside the trailer. Three pairs of big brown eyes peered out the back window of the Camaro. Ashe waved at the children. Three wide, toothy smiles appeared on their faces.

"Hey, cousin. What's up?" Lee Roy Brennan stepped out onto the wooden porch connected to his trailer, his naked beer belly hanging over the top of his unsnapped jeans.

"Just paying a social call on my relatives." Ashe lowered his sunglasses down on his nose, peering over the top so that his cousin could see his eyes. Ashe had been told that he possessed a look that could kill. Maybe not kill, he thought, but intimidate the hell out of a person.

"You run them kids on to school, Mindy." Lee Roy swatted his wife's round behind.

She rubbed herself against the side of his body, patting him on his butt before she sauntered off the porch and strutted over to the car. She gave Ashe a backward glance. Although he caught her suggestive look in his peripheral vision, he kept his gaze trained on Lee Roy.

"Come on in and have a cup of coffee. Johnny Joe just got up. He's still in his drawers, but he'll be glad to see you."

Standing straight and tall, Ashe accepted his

cousin's invitation. Lee Roy slapped Ashe on the back when they walked inside the trailer.

"Didn't think I'd ever see you around these parts again. Not after the way old man Vaughn run you out of the state."

Ashe removed his sunglasses, dropped them into the inside pocket of his jacket and glanced over at the kitchen table where Johnny Joe, all five feet eight inches of him, sat in a wooden chair. Swirls of black hair covered his stocky body, making him look a little like an oversize chimpanzee.

"Heard you was back. What the hell ever made you agree to hire on as a bodyguard for that Vaughn gal?" Johnny Joe picked up a mug with the phrase Proud to be a Redneck printed on it. "I figured you wouldn't have no use for that bunch."

Lee Roy wiped corn flake crumbs out of a chair, then turned to lift a mug off a wooden rack. "Have a seat. You still like your coffee black?"

"Yeah." Ashe eyed the sturdy wooden chair, a few crumbs still sticking to the side. Sitting down, he placed his hands atop the table, spreading his arms wide enough apart so that his cousins could get a glimpse of his shoulder holster.

Lee Roy handed Ashe a mug filled with hot, black coffee, then sat down beside his brother. "You're working for some fancy security firm in Atlanta now, huh? Got your belly full of army life?"

"Something like that," Ashe said. "And private security work pays better, too."

The brothers laughed simultaneously. Ashe didn't crack a smile.

"You bleeding old lady Vaughn dry?" Johnny Joe asked. "After what her old man almost did to you, I figure you got a right to take 'em for all you can get."

Ashe glared at Johnny Joe, the hirsute little weasel. He hadn't taken after the McLaughlin side of the family in either size, coloring or temperament. No, he was more Brennan. Little, dark, smart-mouthed and stupid.

"Shut up, fool." Lee Roy swatted his younger brother on his head. "Ashe wouldn't have come back to take care of Deborah Vaughn just for the money."

"You doing her again, Ashe?" Johnny Joe snickered.

Lee Roy slapped him up side his head again, a bit harder.

"What the hell was that for?" Johnny Joe whined.

"Don't pay no attention to him." Lee Roy looked Ashe square in the eye. "It's good to see you again. We had some fun together, back when we was kids. You and me and Evie Lovelady."

"Yeah, we had some good times." Ashe had liked Lee Roy better than any of his McLaughlin relatives and the two of them had sowed some pretty wild oats together. Fighting over Evie Lovelady's favors. Getting drunk on Hunter McGee's moonshine in the backseat of Lee Roy's old Chevy. Getting into fights with Buck Stansell when he cheated at cards.

Another life, a lifetime ago.

"This ain't just a social call to get reacquainted with relatives," Lee Roy said. "Spit it out, whatever it is you come here to say."

"I understand you two are working for Buck Stansell. Is that right?"

Johnny Joe opened his mouth to respond, but shut it quickly when his older brother gave him a warning stare.

"Buck took over the business when his old man died a few years back." Lee Roy picked up his coffee mug, took a swig, then wiped his mouth with the back of his big hand. "Our old man and yours both worked for Buck's daddy."

"I know who my daddy worked for and what he did for a living," Ashe said, laying his palms flat on the table. "I've chosen to work on the other side of the law. And right now, my main concern is Deborah Vaughn's safety."

"I see." Lee Roy studied the black liquid in his mug.

"She ain't in no danger as long as she keeps that pretty little mouth of hers shut," Johnny Joe said.

"Dammit, man, you talk too much." Lee Roy turned to Ashe. "You ought to stay out of things that ain't none of your business. What happens to Deborah Vaughn shouldn't be your concern."

Ashe leaned over the table, glanced back and forth from one brother to the other, finally settling his hard stare on Lee Roy. "Deborah Vaughn is very much my concern, and what happens to her is my personal business."

"Are you saying that there's still something between the two of you? Hell, man, I'd have figured—"

"I will take it personally if anything happens to her. If one hair on her head is harmed, I'll be looking for the guy who did it. Do I make myself clear?"

"Why are you telling us?" Lee Roy asked.

"I'm asking you to relay the message." Ashe shoved back the chair and stood, towering over his seated cousins. "Tell Buck Stansell that Deborah Vaughn is my woman. She's under my protection. This isn't just another job to me."

"You sure you want to tangle with ol' Buck?" Johnny Joe grinned, showing his crooked teeth, three in a row missing on the bottom.

"I've trapped and gutted meaner bastards than Buck Stansell, and you can tell him that. Buck and his friends don't want to tangle with me. If I have to come after them, I will."

"You sure do talk big," Johnny Joe said. "But then you always did. Just 'cause you been in the Green Berets—"

"Shut up!" Lee Roy said.

"I know that the local, state and federal authorities would all like to see Buck behind bars." Ashe walked toward the door. "So would I. But you tell him that my only interest in him and his business is my woman's safety. If he leaves her alone, I'll leave him alone. Pass that advice along."

"Yeah, I'll do that," Lee Roy said. "Can't say whether or not Buck will take the advice, but it's possible that whoever's out to get Deborah Vaughn might listen. Her being your woman just might make a difference. To certain people."

Ashe smiled then, nodded his head and walked out the door. He'd bet money that before he was halfway back to Sheffield, Lee Roy and Johnny Joe would be on their way to see Buck Stansell.

Ashe parked his rental car in the lot adjacent to Vaughn & Posey Real Estate. Walking up the sidewalk, he almost laughed aloud when he saw the sheriff's deputy pacing back and forth just inside the office entrance. The fresh-faced kid looked like a posted sentry marching back and forth.

When Ashe opened the door, the deputy spun around, taking a defensive pose, then relaxed when he recognized Ashe.

"No problems here, Mr. McLaughlin. Not even a phone call or a letter."

"Good. Tell Sheriff Blaylock that I said you did a fine job. Thanks—" Ashe glanced at the boy's name tag "—Deputy Regan."

The young man grinned from ear to ear. "Ms. Vaughn's taking care of some personal business right now, but she agreed to keep her door open so she wouldn't be out of my sight."

Ashe slapped the deputy on the back. "I'll take over now. I appreciate your diligence in keeping Ms. Vaughn safe for me."

Ashe noticed Deborah in her office, standing to the side of another woman, whose back was to him. Deborah glanced at him, her face solemn.

The young deputy backed out of the office like a servant removing himself from the presence of his king. Ashe nodded a farewell to the boy, then focused all his attention on Deborah and the other woman.

He heard a rather loud hiss, then someone cleared their throat. Looking around, he saw Annie Laurie motioning for him to come to her.

"What's up?"

"Shh...shh." She flapped her hands in the air and shook her head. "Whitney Jamison—" Annie Laurie pointed to Deborah's office "—is in there right now. She came prancing in here with her nose in the air, looking all over the place for you."

Ashe sat down on the edge of Annie Laurie's desk, leaned over and whispered, "What makes you think she was looking for me?"

"She said so, that's how I know." Annie Laurie kept her voice low. "She took one look at the deputy and asked what he was doing here. Deborah told her he was on temporary guard duty. Then Whitney asked what was the problem, had you already deserted her? Then that bitch laughed. I wish Deborah had slapped her face."

"Aren't you overreacting just a little?"

"No, I don't think I am. Do you suppose for one minute that Whitney will let Deborah forget that you once asked Whitney to marry you and she dumped you, that she made you look like a fool?"

"Maybe I'd better go on in there and make sure there's not a catfight." Ashe grinned.

"Wipe that stupid grin off your face," Annie Laurie said. "Deborah Vaughn is not the type of lady to get into a catfight over any man, not even you, cousin dear."

Ashe laughed, but took note of Annie Laurie's words. She was right. Deborah wasn't the catfight type by any stretch of the imagination. But if she was, and she did choose to go one-on-one with Whitney, he'd place all his money on Deborah.

Ashe walked into Deborah's office, stopping directly behind Whitney, who was obviously unaware of his presence.

"It's going to be a delightful evening. Simply everyone will be there. You must come. If you don't, I'll never forgive you. After all, George's fortieth birthday celebration should be something for him to remember."

"Of course I'll be there," Deborah said. "I wouldn't miss it."

Deborah looked over her cousin's shoulder, making direct eye contact with Ashe, who couldn't seem to erase the lopsided grin off his face. The very sound of Whitney's voice grated on his nerves. Why had he never noticed how whiny she sounded?

"You mean we'll be there, don't you?" Ashe stepped to one side, placing himself beside Deborah's desk.

Whitney spun around, a cascade of long black curls bouncing on her shoulders, settling against her pink silk blouse. "Ashe!"

She stared at him, her eyes hungry, her mouth opening and then closing as she bit down on her bottom lip. Whitney Vaughn Jamison was still beautiful, erotically beautiful with her dark hair and eyes and slender, delicate body.

Over the years there had been a few times when he'd wondered how he'd feel if he ever saw her again. Now he knew. He didn't feel a damned thing. Except maybe grateful she'd rejected him. Despite her beauty, there was a noticeable hardness in her face, a lack of depth in those big, brown eyes. He'd been too young and foolish to have seen past the surface eleven years ago.

"Whitney, you haven't changed a bit." It was only a small lie, a partial lie. She'd grown older, harder, hungrier.

"Well, darling, you've certainly changed. You've gotten bigger and broader and even better looking." Rushing over to him, she slipped her arms around his neck and kissed him boldly on the mouth.

She all but melted into him. Ashe did not return her kiss. He eased her arms from around his neck, held her hands in his for a brief moment, then released her and took a step over toward Deborah.

"What's this big event you've invited Deborah and me to attend? Something special for ol' George's birthday?" Ashe took another step in Deborah's direction.

"His fortieth birthday." Whitney pursed her lips into a frown. "And he's being a beast about getting older. I think it really bothers him that I'm so much younger."

"Not that much younger," Ashe said. "If I recall, you're thirty-four."

Whitney gasped, then smiled and purred as she gave Ashe another hungry look. "Of course you'd remember. You probably remember a lot of things about me, don't you, Ashe?"

"Not really, Whitney. To be honest, I haven't given you more than a passing thought over the years."

Ashe slipped his arm around Deborah's waist. Glaring at him, she opened her mouth to protest. He tightened his hold on her. She wriggled, trying to free herself.

"Deborah, on the other hand, I never forgot." He pulled her close to his side, smiled at her and barely kept himself from laughing out loud when he saw the stricken look on her face.

"Well, don't tell me you were cheating on me with my little cousin behind my back." Whitney pasted a phony smile on her heavily made-up face.

"Sort of like the way you cheated on me with George?" Ashe asked.

"That was years ago. Surely you don't still hold that against me?" Whitney fidgeted with the shoulder strap on her beige leather purse.

"Whitney, I appreciate your stopping by to invite me—" Deborah gasped when Ashe squeezed her around the waist "—us to George's birthday party." She glared at Ashe. "We'll be there."

"I'll be looking forward to seeing you again, Ashe. The party's at the country club." Whitney's genuine smile returned with a vengeance.

When she didn't receive the reaction from Ashe she'd hoped to evoke, she waved at him with her index finger. "Until next Saturday night."

The moment Whitney exited the office, Deborah jerked out of Ashe's embrace, stormed across the room and slammed the door.

"Just what was that all about?" Deborah anchored her hands on her hips.

"I think your cousin was coming on to me. What do you think?"

"Of course, she was coming on to you. My God, I expected her to drag you down on my desk and jump on top of you at any minute."

Ashe chuckled, then coughed and covered his mouth when he noticed Deborah's face reddening and her eyes widening.

"I was not referring to the way Whitney threw herself at you," Deborah said. "I was talking about your dragging me into your arms, accepting her invitation on *our* behalf and telling her that I was the one you never forgot."

"Oh, that."

"Yes, that!"

"You had already accepted her invitation when I walked in, hadn't you? All I did was let Whitney know that you didn't go anywhere without me these days."

"I could have, and would have, explained to her that as my bodyguard, you'd have to accompany me." Deborah dropped her hands to her sides. "That doesn't explain your manhandling me in front of Whitney or your reason for saying what you did.''

''I put my arm around you because I wanted Whitney to think that there's more than a business arrangement between the two of us.''

''But there isn't.''

''Of course there is. Do you honestly think I came back to Sheffield, to a town I swore had seen the last of me, to lay my life on the line for a woman who pretends she hates me, simply as a favor to a woman who was once kind to me and my grandmother?''

''Yes. That's what you told me.''

''Doing a favor for Miss Carol was only part of my reason for accepting this job.'' Ashe realized that he'd been lying to himself as well as Deborah about his reasons for accepting Carol Vaughn's dare. ''I wasn't lying when I told Whitney that you were the one I never forgot.''

Deborah's vision blurred. Her ears rang with the pounding of her heart. ''Don't—'' she threw up her hands in front of her as if to ward him off ''—please, don't. Whitney was the one. You loved her. Don't you dare lie to me!''

''You and I need to have a long talk and get a few things straight, but I doubt this is the time or the place.'' Ashe heard the phones in the outer office ringing and the buzz of voices. ''Whitney doesn't mean a damn thing to me. You, on the other hand, do. I'm here to protect you. And you'll be a lot safer if everyone thinks you're—''

A loud knock on the outer office door interrupted Ashe midsentence. Opening the door, Annie Laurie walked in with a package in her hands.

''This just came for Deborah. There's no return address.'' Annie Laurie held the square box out in front of her. ''Something inside there is ticking!''

Deborah stood deadly still staring at the box. Ashe took the package out of Annie Laurie's hands. Listening, he heard the steady *tick, tick, tick* coming from inside the cardboard container.

''Don't panic, and don't scare the others in the office,'' Ashe said. ''Go back to your desk and call the Sheffield police. Talk to Chief Burton. Tell him to send whatever kind of bomb squad he has over here, pronto.''

''You think it's a bomb?'' Annie Laurie gulped, then started backing out of the office. ''What do we do?''

''You and Deborah get everyone outside. Tell them you'll explain once you're out. Walk them across the street. And make sure everyone stays there.''

''What about you?'' Deborah asked.

''I'm going to set this box down on your desk and follow you all outside.''

Deborah shoved a stricken Annie Laurie out of the office, then rounded all her employees together and ushered them outside, while Annie Laurie phoned the police. Deborah started into Neil's office, but Annie Laurie reminded her that Neil was in Florence at a realtor's brunch.

Ashe set the ticking box down on Deborah's desk. His gut instincts told him that this wasn't a bomb, but his instincts had been wrong a few times and it had nearly cost him his life. He didn't take chances anymore. Not with other people's lives. Certainly not with Deborah's life.

Within five minutes Chief Burton and his bomb squad arrived. The employees of Vaughn & Posey stood across the street in front of the bank, their evacuation and the presence of several police vehicles garnering attention from passersby. A small crowd of spectators gathered on the corner.

Ashe stayed beside Deborah, who stood ramrod straight, her vision focused on her office building. She gripped Ashe's hand tightly, but he was certain she had no idea what she was doing.

A member of the bomb squad walked through the front door, holding the open box in his hands. "Somebody's got a real warped sense of humor, Chief. Take a look at this."

Ashe held on to Deborah's hand as she dashed across the street.

"Everybody can go back to work," Chief Burton said. "There's no bomb."

"What was ticking?" Deborah asked.

The chief held out the box. "Take a look, Ms. Vaughn."

Inside the hand-delivered package lay an ordinary alarm clock, tightly wound. Positioned on all four sides of the box, surrounding the ticking clock, were unlit sticks of dynamite. A small white card was stuck to the face of the clock, the message typed. "Next time, boom!"

Ashe could almost hear a man's insidious laughter. Buck Stansell's crazy, sharp laugh. Ashe remembered the man's diabolical sense of humor. Buck had not meant to harm Deborah, only to frighten her. If Buck had wanted Deborah dead, he would have killed her before Ashe had come into the picture.

But what would happen if Deborah couldn't be scared off, if she showed up in court to testify against Lon Sparks? With a man like Buck Stansell, anything was possible. All Ashe knew was that whatever happened, he was going to take care of Deborah.

"A clock!" Deborah balled her hands into fists. "A stupid alarm clock!"

"Looks like another warning," Chief Burton said. "I'll see that Charlie's people get a look at this. I doubt we'll be able to trace it to anybody, but we'll see what we can do. Maybe somebody at the messenger service will remember who sent it, but I've got my doubts. Anybody could've paid a kid off the street to run a package by the office.''

"It's not going to stop, is it?" Deborah looked to Ashe for an answer. He grasped her by the shoulders. She trembled.

"I'm not going to lie to you," he said. "The phone calls and letters aren't going to stop. But I'm screening them. You don't have to deal with them at all. And from now on, any UPS deliveries will come directly to me, too. You don't even have to know about them.''

"Unless you think it's another bomb and we have to evacuate the office again." Deborah wanted to walk into Ashe's arms, to lay her head on his chest and cry. Instead she pulled away from him, turning to her employees, still standing around outside on the sidewalk. "Let's get back to work." Then she held out her hand to Chief Burton, thanked him for arriving so promptly and took one last look at the gag gift she'd been sent.

She walked back into the building, her head held high. At that moment Ashe didn't think he'd ever been as enthralled by a woman's show of strength. He knew she'd been scared to death, had felt her trembling beneath his hands, but despite her anger and uncertainty, she was not defeated.

Ashe waited around outside for a few minutes until the police left and the crowd cleared. He found Deborah in her office, alone, her elbows propped up on her desk, her hands covering her face.

He closed the door behind him. Dropping her hands, she stared up at him, her eyes damp but without any real tears.

He walked over, knelt down beside her swivel chair and took her hands into his. "It's all right if you want to cry or scream or hit something. No-body can be strong all the time."

"I have to be," she said, her voice flat and even, masking her emotions. She looked down at her lap where he held her hands. "Mother and Allen have no one else but me. If I fall apart…if I…" Pausing, she swallowed. "I have to keep Vaughn & Posey going. So many people depend on this business. And since Mother's illness, she's become very fragile emotionally."

"Then put up a brave front for Miss Carol and Allen. Even let your employees go on thinking you're superwoman. But I've got some broad shoulders, Deborah. And they're here for you to lean on any time you feel the need."

She looked at him, her blue eyes softening just a fraction. "Part of the job, Mr. McLaughlin? I thought you were supposed to protect me. Giving comfort is extra, isn't it? How much more will that cost me?"

He stood and jerked her up into his arms in one swift move. She gasped as she fell against him and he trapped her body, holding her securely in his arms. He lowered his head until their breaths mingled.

She closed her eyes, blocking out the sight of him, telling herself she was a fool to succumb to his easy charm.

"The comfort is free, Ms. Vaughn." He whispered the words against her lips. "If you're woman enough to accept it."

Sucking in a deep breath, she opened her eyes. He released his hold on her and gave her a slight push away from him. Turning his back on her, he headed for the door.

"Ashe?"

"I'm just going to get a cup of coffee. I'm not leaving you, even if right now I'd like nothing better than to walk out that door and not come back."

"No one is stopping—"

He pivoted around, glaring at her. "No, that's not true. I don't want to walk out on you and never come back. What I want, more than anything, is to shove all that stuff off your desk, lift you up on it and—"

"I think you're confusing me with Whitney," Deborah said.

"No, honey, that's something I've never done. It's your legs I'd like to slide between and your body I'd like to claim, not your cousin's."

Ashe turned, walked out of the office and closed the door behind him.

Deborah stood beside her desk, trembling. Visions of her lying on top of her desk flashed through her mind. She shook her head trying to dislodge the thoughts of Ashe McLaughlin leaning over her body, lifting her hips and burying himself inside her.

She covered her mouth with her hand to still her cry, then bit down on the side of her finger as shivers of desire rippled through her.

Chapter 6

Deborah had thought about making a fire in her sitting room fireplace, but had neither the strength nor the determination. Although the October night was chilly, it wasn't really cool enough for a fire. She'd simply thought a cosy glowing fire would be soothing. Instead she had settled for a nice warm bath and a cup of cinnamon tea.

She curled up on the huge padded window seat beneath the stained glass window in her sitting room alcove. Her room was her haven. Since early childhood, she had escaped into this luxurious old room with its high ceilings and aged wooden floors. Many days she had sat where she sat now, watching the way the sun turned the colors in the stained glass window to sparkling jewels.

She had written silly, girlish poems about love and life and Ashe McLaughlin. She had long ago burned those poems. Even now she could feel the tears on her face, the tears she had shed the night she'd tossed those hopeless professions of love into the fireplace and watched her youthful dreams go up in smoke.

She shouldn't be dwelling on the past, not with so many problems facing her in the present. Between the constant harassing threats and Ashe's presence, her nerves were raw. She wanted to scream, to cry, to break something—anything— into a thousand pieces.

She wanted Ashe to go away; she wanted Ashe to never leave her. She fantasized about telling Ashe that Allen was his son; she lived in fear Ashe would discover the truth.

Deborah set her teacup on the mahogany tea table beside the window bench, pulled the cream crocheted afghan over her legs and rested her head against the window frame. She should have been in bed an hour ago, but she knew she wouldn't be able to sleep. The simple, orderly life she had worked out for herself had suddenly and irrevocably fallen apart. She had turned off on the wrong road, witnessed a murder and her life would never be the same again. Not only was her life being threatened by the most notorious hoodlums in the state, but the very man determined to protect her posed the greatest threat of all. How ironic, she thought, that she should fear Ashe McLaughlin even more than she feared Buck Stansell.

She heard a soft rap on her door. Her mother? Had she taken ill? Or Allen, who usually slept soundly the whole night through? No. Not her mother. Not Allen.

Ashe.

Dropping the afghan to the floor, she walked across the room, her heart hammering away in her chest. Just before opening the door, she readjusted her silk robe, tightening the belt around her waist.

Ashe McLaughlin stood in the hallway, one big hand braced against the doorpost. He still wore his charcoal gray slacks and his dove gray linen shirt, but the shirt was completely unbuttoned and the hem hung loose below his hips.

"May I come in? We need to talk."

"It's late, Ashe. After midnight. I'm tired." She didn't want him in her room, didn't want to be alone with him. "Can't this wait until morning?"

"It could, but since we're both awake, I see no reason to postpone our conversation." He dropped his hand from the doorpost, leaned toward her and looked her over from head to toe. "Are you going to let me in?"

If she said no, he would think she was afraid of him, that he still held some kind of power over her. She couldn't let him think she cared, that he… Oh, who was she kidding? Any fool could see that Ashe

McLaughlin made her act like a silly, lovesick schoolgirl.

"Come on in." She stepped back, allowing him entrance.

He followed her into the sitting room, glancing around, taking note of the lush femininity of the room. All muted cobalt blues and faded rose colors with splashes of rich cream. Ruffles and lace and dainty crocheted items whispered "Lady."

"Won't you sit down?" She indicated the antique rocker covered in a vibrant floral pattern.

Ashe eyed the delicate chair, wondering if it would hold his weight. Deborah sat on the wide, plush window seat. Without asking permission, he walked over and sat down beside her. She jumped, then glared at him.

"I was afraid I'd break that little rocker," he said, smiling.

"You could have sat in the arm chair, there by the fireplace." She indicated the wing chair, a wide-brimmed, lace hat hanging from one wing.

"I'd rather sit beside you." He knew he made her nervous, and he thought he knew why. No matter what had happened between them eleven years ago, no matter how betrayed either of them felt, the spark that had ignited a blazing fire between them that one night down by the river still burned inside both of them.

"Fine, sit beside me." She glanced over at the

tea service. "Would you care for some cinnamon tea?"

"No, thanks."

"What was so urgent that you couldn't wait until tomorrow to discuss it with me?" Feeling her robe slipping open across her thigh, she grabbed the blue silk and held it in place.

"Are you all right, Deborah?" he asked. "I mean really all right. You've had a rough day, and you barely said ten words at dinner. Miss Carol is worried. So is Allen."

"I'm fine, and I'll make sure Mother and Allen both know it. Now, if that's all you came to say—" she started to rise.

"Sit down."

She eased back down onto the bench.

"As you know, I paid a visit to Lee Roy and Johnny Joe, a couple of my cousins who work for Buck Stansell."

Her eyes, wide and overly bright, looked right at him. Damn her, she was working hard at being brave, at pretending she wasn't slowly falling apart. And he figured having him around wasn't helping her any. But he couldn't leave, couldn't let Sam Dundee send another agent to protect her. Deborah was his responsibility, his to protect, his to defend against whatever harm came her way.

"What happened?" Deborah asked. "I'm sure they didn't admit that Buck Stansell was harassing

me, trying to convince me that he'd have me killed
if I testify against Lon Sparks.''

''No, the boys didn't admit to anything. They
didn't have to. I know my cousins. I know their
kind. My father was one of them. They're what I
came from.''

Without hesitating, without thinking, Deborah
touched his hand. Comforting. Caring. So much
like the Deborah he'd known and liked.

''You were never anything like those people.
You didn't get into any real trouble when you were
a teenager. Everything you did, you did to improve
your life, to get away from your roots.''

He laid his open palm atop her small hand, trapping it between his big, hard hands. ''You never
looked down on me, never thought you were better
than I was, like so many people did. Even though
you were just a kid, you seemed to understand what
I wanted, what I needed.''

Deborah shivered, her stomach quivering,
warmth spreading through her like the morning
sunshine slowly bathing the horizon with its life-
giving light. She couldn't bear feeling this way,
longing to put her arms around Ashe, to tell him
that she had loved him so dearly, had wanted nothing more than for him to return her love. She'd
been a foolish girl; he'd been in love with her
cousin.

She pulled her hand out of his gentle clasp. ''So,

your…you…'' Her voice cracked. She cleared her throat. ''…your visit to your cousins didn't accomplish anything.''

Dear God, how he wanted to kiss her. Here in the feminine confines of her sitting room, surrounded by all her frills and lace. The smell of her fresh and lightly scented from her bath. Her skin glowing. Soft. Begging for his touch.

''No, you're wrong,'' he said. ''The visit did accomplish a few things. I made contact with the enemy camp. I found out Lee Roy and I still have a connection. And I sent a warning to Buck Stansell.'' He reached out; she retreated. He reached out farther and touched her cheek. She trembled, but didn't pull away from him. ''I laid claim to you. I told them that Buck should know you are my woman, and if he harms you, I'll seek revenge.''

''You…you…*claimed* me?'' She widened her eyes, staring at him in disbelief.

He ran the tips of his fingers down her cheek, caressing her throat, then circled her neck, urging her forward. ''I know Buck and his type. They're wild, they're ruthless, but they aren't stupid. The one thing they respect and understand is brute force. Another man's strength. They know who I am, the life I've lived. And they know that if I say I'll come after them if they harm you, I mean it.''

''But Ashe, I don't—''

''For as long as I'm your bodyguard, we will

pretend to be a couple. We're old friends who have become lovers. As far as Buck Stansell and the whole state of Alabama is concerned, you're my woman, and this isn't a job anymore. This is personal. In taking care of you, I'm simply defending my own against any harm. Do you understand what I'm saying?''

Yes, she understood. She understood only too well. Not only would she have to endure constant threats on her life and Ashe's daily presence in her life, but she would have to put on an act, playing the part of Ashe's lover.

''I can't do it,'' she said, trying to pull away from him.

He held her in his gentle yet firm grip, raking his thumb up and down the side of her neck. ''Why can't you?''

''I can't lie about something that important. I can't pretend with Mother and with Allen.''

''Tell your Mother the truth, and I don't think Allen will care if you have a boyfriend. He seems to think you need one.'' Ashe continued stroking the side of her neck.

''You had no right to tell anyone that I'm your woman! I'm not. I never have been and I never will be.''

He jerked her up against him, his lips a whisper away from hers. ''This pretense just might save your life or at least make Buck think twice about harming you. I don't give a damn about your objections—I'm more concerned about saving your life. From this moment on, for all intents and purposes, you're mine. Do I make myself clear?''

Deborah swallowed hard, then closed her eyes to block out the sight of Ashe's face. She couldn't pretend to be his woman. Dear Lord, didn't he understand anything about her? Years ago she had lived in a fantasy world where she dreamed Ashe would leave Whitney and come to her, claiming her, making her his. And on that one night, the night she conceived Allen, she had given herself to the man she loved, and afterward he had told her he didn't want her.

''You can't order me around. You can't make me do something I don't want to do.'' She clenched her teeth and stared him straight in the eye.

''You're so damned stubborn.''

His lips covered hers with hot, demanding urgency, the need to override her objections forefront in his mind. But his body's needs overcame his intention to bend her to his will. He didn't want to force her to do anything; he wanted her compliance.

Deborah fought the kiss for a few brief seconds, then succumbed to the power of his possession, giving herself over to the feel of his arm around her, pulling her closer and closer, his fingers threading through her hair, capturing her head in the palm of his hand.

Her breasts pressed against his hard chest. His tongue delved into her mouth. Slipping her arms around inside his shirt, she clung to him, her nails biting into the muscles of his naked back. Deborah and Ashe sought to appease the hunger gnawing inside them, their lips tasting the sweetness, their tongues seeking, their hands laying claim to the feast of their aroused bodies.

Ashe felt hard and hot as Deborah ran her hands over his chest, across his tiny, pebble hard nipples, lacing her fingers through his dark chest hair.

Ashe reached between their bodies, separating the folds of her silk robe, feeling for her breast. He eased the robe off her shoulder, then the thin strap of her gown, exposing her left breast, lifting it in his hand.

When he rubbed his fingers across her jutting nipple, she cried out. He took the sound into his mouth, deepening their kiss. She curled against him. He dragged her onto his lap, lowered his head and covered her nipple with his mouth, sucking greedily. All the while he stroked a fiery path down her back, stopping to caress her hip.

The taste of her filled him, urging him to sample more and more of her soft, sweet flesh. He hadn't meant for things to get so out of hand, but once he'd touched her, he couldn't stop himself, couldn't seem to control his desire.

Deborah's breath came in strong, fast pants as she clung to his shoulder with one hand and held his head to her breast with the other.

They wriggled and squirmed, arms embracing, hands caressing, lips savoring, legs entwined. Losing their balance in the fury of their passion, they toppled off the window bench and onto the floor. Ashe's leg rammed against the mahogany tea table, knocking it over, sending the tea service crashing onto the Oriental carpet.

Breathing erratically, Deborah glanced away from Ashe to the wreckage on the floor beside them. Reality intruded on the erotic dream. She shoved against Ashe's chest.

He wanted her to ignore everything around them, to concentrate on recapturing the raw, wild need that had claimed them, but he saw the hazy look of longing clear from her eyes.

She pulled up her gown to cover her breast and lifted herself into a sitting position on the floor. Ashe rose to his feet, offered her his hand and lifted her, pulling her back into his arms.

"You're Ashe McLaughlin's woman. I think we just proved that it won't be difficult for us to carry off the masquerade for as long as it's necessary."

He brushed her lips with his, then released her. Deborah staggered on her feet, but found her footing quickly, determined not to give in to the desire to scratch Ashe's eyes out.

Damn the man! He had gotten his way. He had proved that she was just as vulnerable to him as she'd been at seventeen.

"I'd like for you to go now," she said. "I'll explain things to Mother and I'll tell Allen what I think will pacify his curiosity."

"There's less than two weeks until the trial. I think we can pretend for that long. Then for another week or so, if Buck Stansell decides to retaliate for your testifying against Lon Sparks."

"I suppose there's always that possibility, isn't there? If that happens, then this nightmare could go on forever."

"Let's take it one day at a time. We'll get you through the trial, then worry about what might or might not happen afterward."

Deborah nodded. Ashe glanced down at the overturned table, the scattered tea service, the spilled tea.

"I'll clean up this mess," he said.

"No, please." She looked at him and wished she hadn't. His gaze said he still wanted her. "I'll take care of it. I'd like for you to leave. Now."

He walked out of her bedroom. She stood there trembling with unshed tears choking her. *I will not cry. I will not cry.* She knelt down on the floor, righted the tea table and picked up the silver ser-

vice. A dark stain marred the blue-and-cream perfection of the rug. She jumped up and ran into the
bathroom, wet a frayed hand towel and glanced into
the mirror above the sink.

Dear Lord. Her hair was in disarray, the long
strands fanned out around her face. Her cheeks
were flushed, her eyes overly bright. Her lips were
swollen. A pink rash covered her neck and the top
of her left breast, a result of Ashe's beard stubble.
She looked like a woman who'd been ravished.
Suddenly she felt like a woman who'd been ravished.

Tears gathered in her eyes. She laid her head
against the mirror and cried.

In the week since they had begun their pretense,
Ashe hadn't kissed her again, indeed he'd barely
touched her, except in front of others—a part of
their performance as lovers. In another week Lon
Sparks's trial would begin. But when it ended,
would the threats end, too, or would they turn
deadly? Ashe screened all of Deborah's calls and
her mail. The daily threats continued, meaningless
threats since Deborah never heard the messages or
read the letters. Two more little *gifts* had arrived,
both of these delivered by unknown messenger to
her home. One, a green garden snake, Ashe had
taken outside and released. The other had been
more ominous, one he'd made sure neither Deborah

nor Miss Carol saw. A newspaper photograph of Deborah, singed around the edges, a book of matches laid on top and the words "Your house might catch on fire" scrawled in red ink across the newspaper.

Nerve-racking threats to be sure, harassment to say the least, but not once had Deborah's life actually been in jeopardy. Was Buck Stansell playing some sort of sick game or was he trying to throw them off guard, waiting to act at the last moment?

"It's been a long time since you've been in the country club." Carol Vaughn slipped her arm through Ashe's. He looked away from the living room window where he'd been staring sightlessly outside while he waited for Deborah. He smiled at Miss Carol. "Eleven years."

"The night Whitney announced her engagement to George." Carol patted Ashe on his forearm. "She was such a selfish girl, but always so bubbly. Now she's a very sad, selfish woman."

"Are you trying to warn me about something, Miss Carol?"

"Do I need to warn you?"

"I haven't been carrying a torch for Whitney all these years, if that's what's troubling you."

"No, I didn't think you had. You wouldn't look at my daughter as if she were you favorite meal and you hadn't eaten in a long time, if you were in love with another woman."

Had he been that obvious? So apparent in his desire for Deborah that even her own mother had noticed? "Why, Miss Carol, what big eyes you have."

"And sharp teeth, too. If for one minute I thought you'd hurt Deborah again, I'd have no qualms about chewing you up into little pieces."

"And you could do it, too." Taking her hand in his, he walked her across the room and seated her on the sofa. "I never meant to hurt Deborah. I made a mistake, but I tried to keep from making an even bigger mistake. I was honest with her, and I paid dearly for that honesty."

"My husband adored Deborah. She was our only child. I didn't agree with what he did to you, and I told him so at the time. But Wallace could not be reasoned with on any subject, and certainly not when he felt Deborah had been wronged."

"I never made Deborah any promises eleven years ago, and I won't make any to her now. None that I can't keep." Ashe heard Deborah's and Allen's voices coming from the upstairs landing. "I'm attracted to Deborah and she's attracted to me. We're both adults now. If things become complicated, we'll deal with them."

Carol nodded meekly. Ashe couldn't understand the wary look in her blue eyes, that sad expression on her face. What was Miss Carol so afraid would happen?

Allen rushed down the stairs and into the living room. "Come see," he said. "Deborah's beautiful. She looks like one of those models on TV."

Ashe helped Miss Carol to her feet and they followed Allen into the hallway. All three of them looked up to the top of the stairs where Deborah stood.

For one split second Ashe couldn't breathe. He didn't think he'd ever seen anything as lovely as the woman who walked slowly down the stairs, the diamonds in her ears and around her throat dimmed by her radiance.

Allen glanced up at Ashe, then punched him in the side. "See, what'd I tell you?"

"You're right, pal. She's beautiful."

Deborah descended the staircase, butterflies wild in her stomach. How many times had she dreamed of a real date with Ashe McLaughlin? Now, it was a reality. Now, eleven years too late.

He stood at the bottom of the stairs, Allen to his left. The sight of her son at his father's side tugged at Deborah's heart. What would Ashe say if she told him the truth about Allen? Would he be glad? Or would he be sorry?

Ashe looked at Deborah, seeing her as if for the first time, all sparkling and vibrant, beautiful beyond description. How could any man see her and not want her?

The royal blue satin draped across her shoulders

in a shawl collar, narrowing to her tiny waist and flaring into a full, gathered skirt, ankle-length gown. Her satin shoes matched the dress to perfection, and when she stopped at the foot of the stairs, Ashe noticed that the deep rich color she wore turned her blue eyes to sapphires.

"You look lovely, my dear." Carol Vaughn kissed her daughter's cheek. "Please give my regrets to Whitney. I'm sure she'll understand that I'm not quite up to these late-night social affairs."

Deborah hugged her mother close. Her beautiful, brave mother, whose bout with cancer had taken its toll on all of them. "I dread going," Deborah whispered so low that only Carol heard her words. "I have no idea what Whitney will do. She's bound to make a play for Ashe."

Pulling out of Deborah's arms, Carol smiled. "You two run along now and have a wonderful time." Carol glanced at Ashe who hadn't taken his eyes off Deborah. "And don't feel that you need to come home early."

Allen rushed out of the hallway and into the library, returning quickly with a gold foil-wrapped gift. "Don't forget George's birthday present." Allen shook the small package. "What is it anyway?"

"It's a fourteen-karat gold money clip." Deborah took the gift. "Whitney mentioned that George had misplaced his money clip."

"Hocked it, no doubt." Carol nudged Ashe in

the center of his back. "I do believe you've taken Ashe's breath away with your loveliness."

"Yeah, he looks like somebody hit him in the head." Allen laughed. "Hey, man, have you got it bad or what?"

Ashe jabbed Allen playfully in the ribs, lifted him up off the floor with one arm and rubbed his fist across the top of the boy's head before placing him back on his feet. "You wouldn't make fun of a guy for mooning over his girl, would you?"

"Naw, as long as you don't kiss her in front of me." Putting his hand on his hip, Allen stood up straight and gave Ashe a hard look. "If I catch you kissing her, then, as the man of the house, I'd have to ask you what your intentions are, wouldn't I?"

"Yes, Allen, I suppose you would," Ashe said. "So, I'll tell you what, I'll try to make sure I kiss Deborah when you're not around."

"Will you two stop this." Deborah tried to hug Allen, but he wriggled away from her. "What's the matter? Have you gotten too big to give me a hug and a kiss?"

"No, that's not it." Grinning, Allen swiped his hand in front of him in a negative gesture. "I'm just afraid your boyfriend will get jealous and sock me."

Allen broke into peals of boyish laughter. Ashe chuckled. Carol covered her mouth to hide her giggle. Deborah shook her head in mock disgust.

"Let's go now, Ashe, before I wind up socking Allen," Deborah said.

Taking the long satin jacket from where Deborah carried it across her arm, Ashe wrapped it around her shoulders. He slipped his arm about her waist and escorted her out to her repaired and newly painted Cadillac waiting in the drive.

When he opened the door, he turned and lifted her hand to his lips. "You're the most beautiful thing I've ever seen."

He kissed her wrist. Chills shivered through her. She looked into his eyes. "Thank you."

He helped her into the car, rounded the Caddy and got behind the wheel. "No matter what happens tonight, there are a few things I want you to keep in mind."

"Such as?" Deborah smoothed the gathers in her skirt, her fingers gliding nervously over the heavy satin. She didn't look at Ashe.

"Such as I didn't come back to Sheffield to protect Whitney. I wouldn't have, for any amount of money. And I'm not staying in town because of her or issuing threats to dangerous men because of her."

"Did she hurt you so badly back then that you hate her now? You know they say there's only a fine line between love and hate. Maybe you still care about her more than you'd like to admit. After all, she was your first love and—"

Ashe grabbed Deborah so quickly that she didn't have time to think of resisting. His kiss came so hard and fast that it obliterated every thought from her mind, filling her with the heat of his anger, the determination of his desire. His mouth devoured hers, the kiss turning from bold strength to gentle power. Her hands crept up around his neck. He stroked her waist. The satin jacket fell from her shoulders leaving them bare. Ashe allowed his lips to retreat from hers, as he nibbled at her bottom lip and tasted her chin. He lowered his head to her shoulder, his mouth closing over her soft flesh.

Shutting her eyes and tossing back her head, Deborah moaned. ''Ashe...''

''Don't ever try to tell me how I feel.'' Lifting his head, he stared into her blue eyes. ''Whitney wasn't my first anything. I'd had a dozen girls before her. You should remember all the girls I dated. And as far as my being in love with her, I wasn't. I was infatuated with what she represented. She represented a dream. That night at the country club when she announced her engagement, I saw my dream come to an end.''

''Neither of us has ever been able to forget that night, have we? But for different reasons.''

He gripped her chin between his thumb and forefinger. ''If you think I've ever forgotten what it was like making love to you, then you're wrong.''

''I suppose you remember all of them, don't

you? Whitney, the dozen before her, and God only knows how many since.''

Ashe fell backward against the soft leather of the seat, shook his head and laughed. ''You're jealous! You are honest-to-goodness jealous.''

''I am not!'' Deborah jerked the satin jacket up around her shoulders.

''Somewhere deep down inside, Deborah Vaughn, you're the one who still cares. I still mean something to you, don't I?''

Yes, she wanted to scream. Yes, you mean something to me. You are my first and only lover. You are the father of my child, the child I can never claim as my own. Oh, yes, Ashe McLaughlin, you most definitely still mean something to me.

''I think you're taking the part of playing my lover far too seriously.'' Deborah turned around in the seat, focusing her attention on the front porch lights. ''We are pretending to care about each other. That's all.''

''That's not all,'' Ashe said. ''You asked me if I remember all the women I've had sex with. Well, yes, I do remember. Some more than others. But I didn't have sex with you, Deborah.'' There in the darkness his voice sounded deeper and darker and more sensuous than ever. ''I made love to you. I took all that sweet, innocent passion you offered and I drowned myself in your love. I had never been in so much pain, and I had never needed a woman's unselfish love the way I needed yours that night. Don't you think I know that I did all the taking and you did all the giving.''

''Please, Ashe, I don't want—''

''What? You don't want to hear the truth? You don't want to hear how much I wanted to keep on taking what you offered? How much guts it took for me to reject you? Hell, I knew I couldn't give a girl like you what you should have. I knew the best thing I could do for you was to get out of your life and stay out.''

''And that's exactly what you did.'' Deborah cringed at the accusatory tone of her own voice. ''You couldn't even stay in the same town with me, could you? You couldn't hang around long enough to find—''

Dear God, she'd been about to say *find out if you'd gotten me pregnant!*

''None of this matters now, does it?'' Pulling the shoulder harness across her, she snapped the seat belt in place. ''If we don't leave for the country club right now, we're going to be more than fashionably late.''

''Sooner or later we'll have to finish this conversation,'' Ashe said. ''I think we both have quite a lot to get off our chests.''

''It'll have to be later.''

''Fine.'' He turned on the overhead lights. ''You might want to check your makeup. I think most of

your lipstick is on my mouth.'' Pulling a handkerchief from his pocket, he wiped his face.

Deborah opened her evening bag, took out her
lipstick and glanced in the mirror to see how much
repair was needed. She worked quickly, trying not
to notice that she looked like a woman who'd just
been thoroughly kissed.

''I'm ready,'' she said.

Ashe backed the Cadillac out of the drive and
headed toward the country club.

''Ashe McLaughlin, you old dog. I never thought
I'd see you back in Sheffield.''

Keeping his arm firmly around Deborah's waist,
Ashe jerked his head around, seeking the familiar
voice. ''Peanut Haygood?''

The skinny teenage boy who'd lived down the
street from Ashe's grandmother had turned into a
heavyset, bearded man wearing a uniform and carrying a gun. By the looks of old Peanut, Ashe figured he was part of the private security for George
Jamison's big birthday bash.

''Peanut? Man, you've changed since the last
time I saw you.''

''Yeah, well, a guy grows up and fills out,'' Peanut said. ''I heard you were in town.'' He nodded
politely to Deborah. ''Nice to see you, Ms. Vaughn.
Sorry to hear about all your problems. One of these

days we're going to get the goods on Buck Stansell and put him away for life.''

''Are you on the police force?'' Deborah asked.

''Yes, ma'am. Over in Muscle Shoals.'' Peanut slapped Ashe on the back. ''Looks like you and me wound up in the same business, huh? You a Green Beret and me a policeman. Now you're a private security agent and I moonlight as a guard for these fancy shindigs at the country club.''

''Ashe, if you'll excuse me, I need to go to the ladies' room and then check my wrap.'' Forcing a smile, Deborah nodded toward the rest room.

''I'll be waiting right outside.'' Ashe followed her down the corridor, Peanut right behind him keeping up a steady stream of conversation.

From where he stood, Ashe could see the entrance to the ballroom. He spotted Whitney immediately. Her loud laughter echoed out into the hallway. She had her arm draped around a young man who seemed utterly fascinated by her.

''Who'd ever thought Deborah Vaughn would turn into such a looker, huh?'' Peanut jabbed Ashe in the ribs. ''You two were always friends, weren't you? Rumor was her daddy had you run out of town.''

''Rumors aren't always reliable,'' Ashe said.

''Well, Ms. Vaughn sure got herself into a mess with ol' Buck and his bunch of roughnecks. It's too bad she come up on Lon Sparks shooting Looney. Neither one of those boys was worth a cuss.''

"Do you think Buck would kill to protect Sparks or seek revenge if he goes to the pen?''

"I'd say Buck would be more likely to have Lon Sparks killed to keep him from talking than he would to kill Ms. Vaughn. Sparks is a liability to them now. Me and some of the boys at work have got us a theory.'' Peanut stretched his five feet nine inches and placed his hand atop the gun holster resting on his hip.

"What's your theory?''

"We think Buck is putting on an act of trying to scare Ms. Vaughn, trying to make Lon Sparks think he's protecting him. You get my drift?''

"Yeah, I get it. Buck always was one for playing games.'' Ashe knew he should be comforted at the thought that it was possible Buck Stansell had no intention of killing Deborah, but Ashe's gut instincts told him that he should take nothing for granted. No matter what Buck's intentions were, the man was dangerous, a highly explosive bad boy, who was capable of anything.

Ashe caught a glimpse of Whitney coming his way. She swayed her narrow hips, encased in silver lamé, as she sauntered out of the ballroom.

"Now there's a real piece of work," Peanut said. "Sexy as hell and so gorgeous she gives a man ideas. But not worth the cost of the lead it'd take to shoot her.''

''You seem to know an awful lot about Whitney Jamison.'' Ashe watched his old lover flirting outrageously with every man in her path as she made her way through the influx of late arrivals congested in the hallway.

''Hey, I've been moonlighting on this job for a good many years and I've seen quite a bit of Mrs. Jamison. She really works these social occasions, and I've rarely seen her leave with her husband, if you know what I mean.''

Ashe grinned. ''Not the faithful type?''

''Can't say I blame her, married to a loser like George Jamison. The man hasn't held a job in years. They live off her inheritance, you know. Her shares in that real estate firm Ms. Vaughn runs. And Georgie Porgie likes to gamble. They're always flying off to Vegas and Atlantic City and down to Biloxi.''

Whitney walked up to Ashe, slipped her arms around his neck and kissed him soundly on the mouth. Still draped around him, she smiled. ''Come dance with me, darling. If I remember correctly, you were a marvelous dancer.''

''You were the marvelous dancer,'' Ashe said. ''I just followed your lead.''

Whitney's throaty laughter rumbled from her chest. Her almost naked chest, Ashe noted. Her strapless silver lamé dress crisscrossed over her full breasts, just covering her tight nipples. "It's been a long time, hasn't it?" Whitney sighed. "Come on, let's see if we're still good together." She rubbed herself intimately against Ashe.

Peanut cleared his throat. Ashe stared at him. The guard gave his head a few sharp jerks in the direction of the ladies' room. Glancing over his shoulder, Ashe saw Deborah watching him.

Grasping Whitney's arms, he pulled them from around his neck and stepped backward, putting some distance between them. Whitney's gaze followed Ashe's. She laughed again, an almost hysterical giggle.

"You'll have to find yourself another partner," Ashe said. "I'm afraid my dance card is filled."

Whitney leaned over and whispered in Ashe's ear, "If you think my little cousin is going to give you what you need, then you'd better think again. She doesn't know the first thing about men, and most certainly nothing about a man like you."

"That's where you're wrong, Mrs. Jamison." Ashe walked over to Deborah, slipped his arm around her rigid body and pulled her up against his side. "Would you like to dance, honey?" he asked Deborah.

Unsmiling, every nerve in her body tense, Deborah glared at Ashe. "Perhaps, after I've wished

George a happy birthday and given him his present.'' She held up the shiny golden gift.

When Ashe guided Deborah past Whitney, Deborah paused. ''You look lovely tonight, Whitney. But then I'm sure you already know that. No doubt every man at the party has told you at least once.''

Whitney grinned, a rather shaky grin, one that didn't reach her eyes, one that didn't begin to compare with the smile spreading across Deborah's face.

''And you look adorable,'' Whitney said, giving Deborah a quick hug. ''And aren't you the lucky one, having Ashe McLaughlin as your escort. But then, I suppose Aunt Carol is paying him extra, isn't she?''

''And he's worth every cent.'' Deborah tugged on Ashe's arm. She led him away from her cousin, down the hallway and into the ballroom.

Ashe and Deborah heard Peanut Haygood's hardy chuckle, but neither turned around to see Whitney's reaction.

''When did you learn to play hardball?'' Ashe asked.

''When my father died and I had to take responsibility for his business as well as my mother and Allen.''

''Let's find George and give him his present.'' Ashe ran his hand up and down Deborah's arm. ''I want to dance with you.''

Deborah wasn't quite sure what she thought or how she felt. A mixture of anger and exhilaration rioted along her nerve endings. All the old jealousies she'd felt for her cousin had come racing to the forefront when she'd walked out of the ladies' room and seen Whitney wrapped around Ashe. But when she had won their verbal sparring match, she'd felt as if she were walking on air.

She couldn't help wondering what would happen if she spent the night in Ashe's arms, dancing with him here at the country club? Perhaps the safest course of action would be to give George his present, stay long enough to appease her social set's curiosity and make a quiet, discreet exit. If Whitney indulged in her usual weakness for champagne, there was a chance she might make a scene later on. And Deborah wanted to avoid a real confrontation that would put her in the spotlight.

The whole town knew she was the prosecution's star witness, and that her life was in danger. And she had no doubt that Ashe McLaughlin's constant presence at her side had set tongues wagging. What would they say once Ashe had shown everyone that their relationship was intimate?

She didn't give a damn what *they* would say. She never had. She'd always been a lot like her mother. Carol Allen Vaughn had known who she was—an Allen—and had never considered herself subject to the rules and regulations of the society biddies. And no one had ever dared question Carol's judgment or suggest her actions were inappropriate. In that respect, Deborah was her mother's daughter.

But Carol had given in to Wallace Vaughn's authority, always the dutiful wife. If only her mother had gone against her father's wishes. If only—

"Deborah, such a smashing dress!" George Jamison III smiled his widemouthed, white-toothed smile and gave his cousin-in-law a peck on the cheek. "For me?" George eyed the gold foil-wrapped gift.

"Oh, yes. This is for you." Deborah hadn't realized that while she'd been thinking, Ashe had led her straight to the birthday boy. Although boy was hardly the appropriate word for a balding man of forty. Then again, perhaps boy was the correct word to describe George, who, in many ways, was far more immature than Allen.

"I'll just put it here with my other goodies." George laid the gift on top of a stack of presents arranged on the table behind him. "I suppose Whitney greeted y'all at the door. She's such a marvelous hostess. And she does love a good party."

"Yes, she met us in the hallway, actually," Deborah said.

Ashe tightened his hold around Deborah's waist. "Happy birthday, George."

George glanced at Ashe, his long, thin nose slightly tilted upward. He made no move to offer

Ashe his hand. "McLaughlin." George's pale gray eyes met Ashe's vibrant hazel glare. "I was surprised to hear you'd come back to Sheffield to act as Deborah's bodyguard. Of course, we're all pleased that someone is looking out for her. I understand that you're highly qualified to handle brutes like Buck Stansell. Then, of course, it must be a help that you've had ties to those people all your life."

"Yes, it is a help." Ashe lifted the corners of his mouth just enough to hint at a smile, but he knew George Jamison would recognize the look in his eyes for what it was. Contempt. Dislike. Disgust.

"We can't stay too long," Deborah said. "I don't like to leave Mother alone."

"I quite understand." Glancing across the room, George waved at someone. "Do enjoy yourselves. I'm sure this is a bit of a treat for you, McLaughlin. Finally getting to come to the country club through the front door. Rather different from the last time you were here, isn't it?"

"George, you're being—" Deborah said.

"You're right." Catching sight of Whitney dancing with the young man she had cornered earlier, Ashe nodded in her direction. "Eleven years ago you and I were the only two guys Whitney was seeing."

"How dare you!" George's thin, white cheeks flushed pink.

Ashe led Deborah away from George, quickly ushering her through the crowd and onto the dance floor.

"That was a horrible thing to say to George," Deborah said.

"I was justified, don't you think?" Ashe pulled her close, leaning over to nuzzle her neck with his nose.

She gulped in a deep breath of air. "Yes, you were most definitely justified. George always has been a little snot! He's so immature."

"A little snot?" Ashe chuckled. "I guess that does aptly describe George, doesn't it?"

Deborah loved the feel of Ashe's arms around her, the security of his strength, the sensuality of his nearness. She didn't know what she had expected to happen tonight. Between Ashe and Whitney. Between Ashe and George. But she certainly hadn't expected to feel so light and free and thoroughly amused.

It suddenly hit her that neither she nor Ashe were the same two people who had left this country club eleven years ago. They had both grown up.

Ashe was no longer in awe of the wealthy social set that ruled the county. His dreams weren't wrapped up in a sexy package called Whitney

Vaughn. He wasn't an angry, outraged, spurned lover.

And Deborah no longer saw herself as a wall-flower beside her exquisite cousin. Any residue of leftover jealousy she might have once felt disappeared completely. She was strong. She was successful. She was attractive.

And Ashe McLaughlin wanted her!

They moved to the music, giving themselves over to the bluesy rendition of an old Glenn Miller song. They spent nearly an hour on the dance floor, wrapped in each other's arms. Occasionally Deborah noticed some curious stares and heard a few whispered innuendoes. None of it mattered, she told herself. She and Ashe were presenting themselves to the world as lovers. She could not allow herself to think otherwise. When the danger to her life ended, Ashe would be gone.

But during the duration of his stay, they could become lovers. She didn't doubt for one minute that Ashe wanted her. He had made that abundantly clear. The question was did she dare risk giving herself to him? Did she dare risk falling in love with him all over again? How could she become his lover and continue lying to him about Allen?

"Are you about ready to leave?" Ashe whispered, then kissed her ear.

Deborah shivered. "Yes. I think everyone has seen us and drawn their own conclusions."

"We don't have to go back to your house." Ashe ran his hand up and down her back. "We could find some place to be alone."

"No. I'm not… Just take me home. I can't handle a repeat performance of that night eleven years ago when we left the country club together."

"It wouldn't be the same. We aren't the same," he said. "We'd both know what we were getting into this time."

"That's the problem, isn't it? At least for me."

The music came to a end. Couples left the dance floor, while others waited for the next set to begin. Deborah pulled away from Ashe, intending to make a quick exit. Ashe jerked her into his arms, grasped the back of her head with his hand and kissed her, long, hard and devouring. Every rational thought went out of her head.

When she was weak and breathless, he ended the kiss, draped his arm around her shoulders and escorted her off the dance floor, past a glaring Whitney and her openmouthed guests.

"Every person in this room knows you're mine," he whispered as they walked out into the hall. "And since they're aware of my reputation, no one will doubt that I'm the kind of man who'd kill to defend his own."

Chapter 7

Deborah folded the blueprints and laid them aside. She couldn't seem to concentrate on the plans for Cotton Lane Estates, although she had promised Vaughn & Posey's backers a detailed report on their present subdivision project.

She lifted the cup of warm coffee to her lips and downed the sweet liquid. Clutching the coffee mug in her hands, she closed her eyes. In a few days, Lon Sparks's trial would begin and she'd be called on to testify. The waiting had been almost unbearable, not knowing what might or might not happen. She couldn't give in to her fears and allow the likes of Buck Stansell to frighten her into backing down from doing what she knew was right. But sometimes she wondered what her mother and Allen would do if anything happened to her. Her mother's health was so precarious, and Allen was still so young. What if he lost both her and her mother?

Ashe McLaughlin had a right to know he had a son. That's what her mother had told Deborah's father years ago and that's what she kept telling Deborah now. If anything were to happen to the two women in Allen's life, he would still have his father.

But how could she tell Ashe the truth? She and her mother had kept the true circumstances of Allen's birth a secret for ten years. What would Allen do if he suddenly discovered that the two people he loved and trusted most in the world had been lying to him his whole life?

No, she didn't dare risk losing Allen's love by telling Ashe the truth. She had no way of knowing how Ashe would react and whether or not he'd tell Allen everything.

Her mother had warned her that sooner or later Ashe would have to be told. Deborah had decided that it must be later, much later. She had to be strong. Just a little while longer. Ashe wouldn't stay in Sheffield if she wasn't in danger. He would walk out of their lives and never look back, the way he'd done eleven years ago. She could trust him with her life, but not with her heart—and not with Allen's future.

When she heard a soft knock at the door, Deborah opened her eyes. ''Yes?''

Annie Laurie eased the door open. "Mr. Shipman's on the phone. He says it's urgent he speak to you."

"Mr. Shipman? The principal at Allen's school?"

"Yes, that Mr. Shipman."

"Okay. Thanks, Annie Laurie." Deborah picked up the telephone and punched the Incoming Call button. "Hello, Mr. Shipman, this is Deborah Vaughn. Is something wrong?"

Ashe slipped by Annie Laurie and into Deborah's private office, closing the door behind him. Deborah glanced at him.

"Ms. Vaughn, you need to come to school and pick up Allen," Mr. Shipman said. "I'm afraid there's been a problem on the playground during PE class."

"Has Allen been in a fight?" Deborah asked.

Ashe lifted his eyebrows and shrugged his shoulders as if saying "Boys will be boys."

"Oh, no Ms. Vaughn, I didn't mean to imply that Allen had gotten himself into any trouble. Quite the contrary. It seems that when the fifth graders were playing softball during PE, a stranger approached Allen. Your brother won't tell us what the man said to him, but Allen seems terribly upset. I thought it best to phone you immediately."

"Yes, yes, you did the right thing, Mr. Shipman. I'll be right over." Deborah's heartbeat throbbed loudly in her ears, obliterating every other sound, even Ashe's voice. "Please, don't leave Allen alone. Make sure someone is with him until I pick him up." Deborah returned the phone to its cradle.

When Deborah didn't respond to his questions, Ashe grabbed her by the shoulders, shaking her gently. "What's going on? Has something happened to Allen?"

"A strange man approached Allen on the playground during PE. Mr. Shipman said the man upset Allen." Deborah clutched the lapels of Ashe's jacket. "What if— Oh, God, Ashe, what if Buck Stansell sent someone to hurt Allen?"

"Did anyone besides Allen get a good look at this man? Did they see whether he was on foot or driving?"

"I didn't think to ask, dammit." Releasing her hold on Ashe, Deborah walked around to the front of her desk. Yanking open the bottom drawer, she lifted out her leather bag and threw the straps over her shoulder. "I have to pick up Allen and take him home. I have to make sure he's all right. If anyone dares harm him, I'll—"

"I'll take care of anyone who threatens Allen, in the same way I'll handle anyone who threatens you." Ashe held out his hand. "Give me the keys to your Caddy. I'll drive. On the way over to the school, pull yourself together. Allen doesn't need to see how upset you are."

Deborah took a deep breath. "You're right. It's just that, in the back of my mind, I kept wondering if and when Buck Stansell would target Mother or Allen. Oh, Ashe, I can't let anything happen to Allen."

"Nothing is going to happen to Allen." He took her hand in his. "I promise."

Within five minutes they marched side by side into Richard Shipman's office where Allen sat, silent and unmoving, in a corner chair. The minute he saw Deborah, he ran into her open arms.

"Give us a few minutes alone with Allen," Ashe said to the principal, who immediately nodded agreement and exited his office.

"What happened, sweetheart?" Deborah asked, bending on her knees, hugging her child close, stroking his thick blond hair. "Tell us everything."

Allen clung to Deborah for several moments, then glanced over at Ashe. "You can't let them do anything to hurt her."

"Allen, will you tell me what happened?" Ashe reached down and patted Allen on the back.

Allen shook his head, released his tenacious hold on Deborah, but still clung to her hand as she stood. "He walked up to me on the playground. I was waiting my turn at bat. He said he knew my sister and that he wanted me to give her a message."

"Oh, Ashe!" Deborah clenched her teeth tightly together in an effort not to cry in front of Allen.

Laying his hand on Deborah's shoulder, Ashe gave her a reassuring squeeze. "Had you ever seen this man before?"

"No," Allen said.

"Come on, let's go sit down over here on the sofa." Deborah led Allen across the room to the small, leather sofa situated against the back wall between two oak filing cabinets. "I want you to answer all of Ashe's questions. He's here to help us. Do you understand?"

"What—what do you want to know?" Allen looked at Ashe.

"Would you recognize the man if you ever saw him again? Can you tell me what he looked like?"

"Yeah, I'd recognize him, all right. He was big and ugly and he smelled bad."

"Sounds like somebody Buck would sent around to frighten a child," Ashe said.

"He didn't scare me." Allen tightened his hold on Deborah's hand. "I told him off. If you don't believe me, just ask Tripper Smith. He heard me telling that guy he'd better leave my sister alone."

Ashe knelt down in front of Allen. "I know you're brave and that you'd fight for your sister."

Deborah forced a smile when she looked at Allen's pale little face. "Did the man try to hurt you?"

"Naw, he just said to give my sister a message. He said to tell you that if you show up in court

Monday, you'll be very sorry. And I told him that nothing he said or did would keep you from testifying against that murderer. And he said if you did, you were stupid. That's when I tried to hit him, but he just laughed and walked away."

"Did your teacher see the man, or any of the other kids beside this Tripper Smith?" Ashe asked.

"My teacher didn't see nothing, but several of the kids saw him. Tripper's the one who went and told Coach Watkins what had happened."

"Okay, Allen, why don't you and Deborah go do whatever is necessary to get you checked out of school for the day. I'll make a couple of phone calls and then we'll be ready to leave." Ashe wished he had the big, bad-smelling stranger in front of him right now. He'd teach Buck Stansell's messenger that it wasn't nice to go around frightening little boys, especially not a child under his protection.

"Are we going home?" Allen asked. "Do we have to tell Mother what happened? She'll just worry."

"We aren't going home," Ashe said. "I think you and Deborah and I should go somewhere for burgers and fries and then do something fun together this afternoon. How does that sound to you, Allen?"

"Sounds great to me." Allen looked at Deborah. "Can I really play hooky for the rest of the day?"

"You bet you can." Deborah stood. Allen

jumped up beside her. "We'll go get Allen checked out of school and wait for you in the office."

"I'll only be a few minutes." Ashe picked up the telephone and dialed the police department. "Allen, I know you don't want to worry your mother, but we'll have to tell her what happened when we go home."

Allen nodded. Deborah ushered him out of the principal's office, thankful that Ashe McLaughlin was taking charge of the situation, thankful that she hadn't had to face this alone. The thought that they had come together like a family—a mother, a father and their child—flashed through Deborah's mind. She couldn't allow herself the indulgence of such thoughts. Thinking of the three of them as a family could be dangerous.

"I can't eat another bite." Ashe shoved a French fry into Deborah's mouth. She slapped his hand away.

"I want one of those sundaes, don't you, Ashe?" Allen read the list of desserts off the wall sign behind the counter. "I want caramel with nuts."

"That's my favorite, too." Ashe slid out from behind the booth. "I'll order us both one. What do you want, Deborah?"

"Nothing! I've eaten enough for a couple of meals."

"Ah, she's just worried she'll get fat," Allen

said. "She used to be sort of plump a long time ago. Hey, you already know that. You knew Deborah even before I did."

"So I did." Ashe sauntered off to order their desserts, coming back with two caramel sundaes and a small chocolate ice-cream cone, which he handed to Deborah.

"Chocolate used to be your favorite," he said.

"It still is," she admitted, taking the cone and napkin he handed her. During the last months of her pregnancy, she had craved chocolate ice cream. Maybe that was the reason Allen hated the stuff. She'd gorged him on it before he'd been born.

She didn't realize she'd been sitting there smiling, a dazed look in her eyes until Ashe waved his hand in front of her face.

"Where did you go?" he asked. "You're a million miles away."

"Just thinking about chocolate ice cream," she said.

"Well, you'd better eat it before it melts." Allen lifted a spoonful of his sundae to his mouth. "Thanks for getting extra nuts, Ashe."

"Nothing's too good for us, pal." Ashe didn't think he'd ever felt about a kid the way he felt about Allen. He didn't understand it, couldn't explain it, but he felt connected to Allen Vaughn. Maybe it was because of his past history with the family, his respect for Miss Carol, his friendship with Deborah. Whatever the cause, he found himself wondering what it would be like to have a child of his own, a boy like Allen.

"Now who's gathering moss?" Deborah wondered what Ashe was thinking. The man was such a mystery to her. Once she'd thought she knew him, but she'd been wrong. He'd never been the man she thought he was.

"What can folks do on a weekday afternoon around here for fun?" Ashe asked. "How about a movie?"

"No matinees except on the weekend," Deborah said.

"What about miniature golf?" Allen wiped his mouth with his paper napkin. "I think it's still open every afternoon until Thanksgiving."

"How about it, Deborah, are you game for a round of golf?" Ashe smiled at her and she returned his smile. "You should do that more often, you know."

"What?" she asked.

"Smile like that. A guy would agree to anything you wanted if you smiled at him like that." The warmth of her smile brought back memories of the way she'd smiled at him, lying in his arms in the moonlight, down by the river. He had never forgotten that beautiful smile or the way it had made him feel just looking at her.

"Aw, are you getting all mushy?" Allen shook

his head. "Save all that love talk for when you're alone with her. I'm too young to hear stuff like that."

"Allen!" Deborah rolled her eyes heavenward.

"Eat your sundae," Ashe said. "And I'll keep in mind that you aren't old enough to learn from a master just yet. But in a few more years, you'll be begging me to share my secrets of seduction with you."

"Ashe! Of all things to say to a ten-year-old."

"Ah, lay off Ashe." Allen spoke with his mouth half full of sundae. He swallowed. "You just don't understand guy stuff."

"Oh, well, excuse me." Grinning, Deborah licked the dripping ice cream from around the edge of her cone. She glanced over at Ashe, who watched her intently, his vision focused on her mouth. She licked a circle around the chocolate ice cream, all the while watching Ashe watch her. This was a grown-up game she was playing, a subtle sexual game that Allen wouldn't notice. But Ashe noticed. He knew precisely what she was doing and why.

His jaw tightened. His eyes shone with the intensity of their gaze, fixed on her mouth, on her tongue. He gripped the edge of the table with one hand and laid his tightly clenched fist beside his half-eaten sundae.

She was arousing him and she knew it. She liked

the sense of power he gave her by his display of desire. If they were alone, instead of sitting in a fast-food restaurant with Allen, she wasn't sure she'd have the nerve to tempt Ashe.

"Are you any good at playing miniature golf?" Allen tossed his plastic spoon into his empty sundae bowl. "Hey, Ashe, are you listening to me?"

"What did you say, pal?"

"Are you good at playing miniature golf?" Allen repeated. "Deborah and Mother play real golf and they take me along. They're teaching me how to play. But right now, I still like miniature golf better."

"I can't say I've ever played miniature golf before," Ashe said. "Today you'll have to be my teacher."

"I like that idea. I don't think I've ever taught anybody anything before." Allen beamed with pleasure.

Deborah relaxed and finished off her ice-cream cone, thinking how easily a child can adapt, how quickly Allen had gone from a frightened, worried little boy into a secure, happy kid looking forward to a new experience.

Would he adapt so easily if someday she told him the truth—that she was his mother and Ashe was his father?

"Straight upstairs and into the bathtub for you, young man." Deborah gave Allen a gentle push up the stairs, then dropped down on the bottom step. When Allen dashed off, galloping up the stairs and down the hall, Ashe propped his foot on the step beside Deborah and leaned over, kissing the tip of her nose.

She stared up at him, bewilderment in her eyes. "What was that for?"

"For being so cute. Your hair is an absolute mess." He twirled a loose strand around his index finger. "Your shoes are ruined and you've got chocolate stains on your blouse."

They both glanced down to the dark circle on the silk that lay over the rise of her left breast. "I need to get out of this blouse and soak it before the stain sets in any worse than it already has."

Ashe released her hair, ran his finger down the side of her neck and over into the V of her blouse. "Need any help?"

Carol Vaughn cleared her throat. Ashe straightened. Deborah looked up at her mother who walked from the living room into the hallway.

"Is Allen all right?" Carol asked. "He didn't seem upset."

"He's practically forgotten about what happened," Deborah said. "Thanks to Ashe. We've eaten hamburgers and fries twice today, played God only knows how many rounds of miniature golf, went to see that ridiculous dog movie and bought Allen a brand-new computer game.''

"Should we take Allen out of school until the trial is over?'' Carol asked.

"No, that would only make matters worse for him.'' Getting up, Deborah walked over to her mother and placed her arm around her frail shoulders. "I think Ashe should act as Allen's bodyguard from now on instead of mine.''

"Oh, Deborah, no. Do you think Allen really is in danger?''

"Miss Carol, there's no way to know whether Allen is in real danger, but we don't dare take any chances,'' Ashe said. "I called the police, and Chief Burton has assured me that they'll send a patrol car around every day during Allen's PE time. And I spoke to Sheriff Blaylock, gave him a description of the man who confronted Allen on the playground.''

"Do you think there's any chance of catching the man?'' Carol slipped her thin arm around her daughter's waist.

"I doubt it,'' Ashe said. "My bet is that Buck got somebody from out of town and the guy's long gone by now.''

"I didn't want to think that Allen might be in danger,'' Carol said. "But it did cross my mind that these people might try to get to Deborah through her...her brother.''

"You could also be in danger, Miss Carol, especially when you're outside the house. With the security system we have in place now, it would be difficult for anyone to break in." Anyone who wasn't a highly trained professional, Ashe thought. He doubted any of Buck's local boys had the know-how to get past a sophisticated system, but it was possible.

"I'm not worried about myself, only my children. You must keep Deborah and Allen protected no matter what."

"Mother, don't fret this way. It isn't good for you."

"With your permission, Miss Carol, I'd like to bring in another man to guard Allen," Ashe said.

"Someone else from Dundee Security?" Carol asked.

"Yes, ma'am."

"Do you think that's necessary?" Carol looked to Deborah, who nodded and squeezed her mother's hand.

"All right, you do what you think best." Carol allowed Deborah to help her up the stairs. Pausing on the landing, she looked down at Ashe. "You have no idea how reassured I am by your presence here, Ashe McLaughlin, knowing that you have taken responsibility for Deborah and Allen."

Deborah's gaze met Ashe's. Looking away quickly, she assisted her mother to her room. Ashe couldn't quite figure out that strange look in Deborah's eyes, almost pleading. And sad. And even afraid. This wasn't the first time he'd sensed Deborah feared him, but he couldn't understand why. Not unless she still loved him. Dear God, was it possible? Of course not, no one kept loving someone eleven years after they'd been rejected.

Ashe went into the library, closed the door and dialed Simon Roarke's private number. Dundee himself would have been Ashe's first choice, but Sam seldom took on private cases any more. His other top choices were J.T. Blackwood, who was already involved in another case, and Simon Roarke.

He'd known Simon for nearly a year, had met him when he'd first hired on with Dundee Security. The two had liked each other immediately, finding they had enough in common to form a friendship. A couple of former career soldiers who'd been born and raised in Southern poverty.

"Roarke here." His voice sounded like gravel being dumped onto sheet metal.

"This is McLaughlin. I need you on the first plane out of Atlanta. Tonight if possible."

"What's up?"

"The woman I'm protecting has a ten-year-old brother. Today a stranger approached him on the school playground and gave him a message for his sister."

"The bastard!" Roarke said, the sound possessing the depth of a rottweiler's bark. "He didn't hurt the kid, did he?"

"Allen's fine. I just want to make sure he stays that way." Ashe knew that if Simon Roarke had one weakness, it was children. His only child had died years ago, and Simon had never fully recovered, had never escaped the demons of pain.

"I'll let Sam know where I'll be. He can fax me all the information on your case," Roarke said. "And I'll see you first thing in the morning."

Ashe stayed in the den for nearly thirty minutes after he finished talking to Roarke. He stood by the window, looking out into the darkness, not seeing what lay before him, only envisioning Deborah's smile. He wanted her to smile at him again the way she'd smiled at him that night so long ago. He hadn't realized how much he needed someone to love him.

Hell! He was a fool. Deborah didn't love him. She might desire him the way he desired her, but she wasn't a seventeen-year-old girl anymore. She didn't look at him through the eyes of love and see her Prince Charming. And he had no one to blame but himself. He had been the one to destroy her fairy-tale dreams.

She had offered him everything. And he'd been too young and stupid to realize what he was rejecting.

He made his way upstairs, turning off lights as he went. Allen's bedroom door stood open. The sound of his and Deborah's voices floated down the hall. Strange, how quickly he'd come to feel at home in the Vaughn household, how quickly he had come to think of Miss Carol and Allen, and yes, dammit, Deborah, as his own family.

He stood several feet away from Allen's room, looking through the open door. Deborah, fresh from a bath and wearing a navy blue silk robe, sat on the edge of Allen's bed. She pulled the covers up around his chest, then patted the edges into place. Lifting her hand, she reached out and touched Allen's face, the gesture so filled with love that it hit Ashe in the pit of his stomach with knockout force.

"We're going to be just fine, you know," Deborah said, cradling Allen's cheek with her hand. "I've been taking care of us for a long time now and haven't done such a bad job. Now Ashe is here, and he won't let anything happen to you or me or Mother."

"I like Ashe a lot, don't you? He's the kind of man any guy would like for a father." Allen threw his arms around Deborah, giving her a bear hug.

Deborah hugged him fiercely. Ashe noticed her shoulders trembling. He wanted to go to them, put his arms around Deborah and Allen and become a part of the love they shared. He wanted to tell them that he'd die to protect them.

Allen fell back into the bed, his eyes drooping as he yawned. "Since Ashe is too young for Mother, you could marry him. He'd make a pretty great brother-in-law."

"I'll keep that in mind, but don't expect anything. Ashe is our friend, but he has a life in Atlanta. Once the trial is over and things gets back to normal, Ashe will be leaving."

"I wish he would stay forever." Allen yawned, then closed his eyes. "Don't you wish he'd stay forever?"

Deborah kissed Allen on the forehead, turned out the lamp on the bedside table and walked out of Allen's room, leaving the door partially open. She saw Ashe standing in the hallway, staring directly at her, the oddest expression on his face.

"You didn't answer him," Ashe said. "Do you wish I'd stay forever?"

"Is anything forever, Ashe?" She walked toward him, then lowered her eyes and passed him, turning to go into her room.

Reaching out, Ashe grabbed her by the wrist. She halted. "I didn't use to think so. Now, I'm not so sure."

Deborah pulled her wrist out of his loose grasp. "Let me know when you're sure, Ashe." She went into her bedroom and closed the door.

Chapter 8

Completing the jury selection had taken all morning, so Deborah had remained at work until noon,
then gone home for lunch with her mother. Ashe
had told her there was no need for her to make an
appearance in court until she was called on to testify, but she had insisted on going.

Now she wished she hadn't. Local and state
newspaper and television reporters swarmed around
her like agitated bees, each person trying their best
to zero in on the prosecution's eye witness. Ashe
shielded her with his body, practically carrying her
past the horde of reporters and crowd of spectators.
She clung to her protector, closing her eyes against
the sight of clamoring people, the din of voices
rising higher and higher.

Seating her near the back of the courtroom, Ashe
stood at her side, like a guardian angel wielding a

flaming sword to keep danger at bay and the unwanted from trespassing on her private space.
When Judge Williams entered the courtroom, Deborah stood, taking Ashe's hand in hers. She sought
and found comfort in his presence. His power and
strength nourished her own, helping her face what
lay ahead.

There had been no question in her mind that she
would attend this first day of Lon Sparks's trial.
She thought it necessary to show the world, by her
presence, that she would not be intimidated by
Buck Stansell and his gang of hoodlums. Of course,
none of them were in attendance. They would stay
away, keeping up the pretense that they were not
involved, when the whole county knew they were.

One by one, the prosecution called their witnesses. First, the Leighton police, then Charlie
Blaylock and two of his deputies. The day's proceedings moved along quickly, Deborah sitting
tensely, Ashe at her side. At five o'clock, the court
session ended, the judge announcing a recess until
the following morning. Would they get to her that
soon? Deborah wondered. Would the trial actually
come to an end in a week's time? Unless the defense dragged things out, Deborah couldn't imagine
the trial lasting much longer.

When Ashe touched her, she jumped. Standing,
he offered her his hand. ''I'll get you to the car as

quickly as possible. Just stay right by my side. Don't look at or respond to the reporters.''

"Some of them kept watching me during the trial proceedings.'' She accepted Ashe's assistance. "I saw them looking at me during the testimony. Especially when Jerry Don Lansdell told how I came running into the Leighton police station that day. The defense lawyer, that Mr. Prater, had Jerry Don practically admitting that I was too hysterical to know what I was talking about, that I was a raving lunatic.''

"Don't worry about it. The jurors aren't stupid. They saw through what Sparks's lawyer was trying to do.'' Ashe slipped his arm around her. "When you're on the stand, you'll convince the jurors that you saw Lon Sparks murder Corey Looney. These people are not going to doubt your word, Deborah. You're a respected citizen with nothing to gain by lying.''

Deborah glanced at her diamond-studded wristwatch. "It's too late to make Allen's soccer game. It should be ending about now.''

"Then let's go home and let him tell us all about the game.'' Ashe led Deborah out of the crowded courtroom.

In the hallway, the same horde of insistent reporters swarmed around her. Deborah squared her shoulders. Ashe kept her protected, holding her close to his side.

"Ms. Vaughn, are you disturbed by the defense's accusation that you were too traumatized by the murder you witnessed to make a proper identification of the killer?" A lanky young reporter stuck a microphone into Deborah's face.

Ashe pierced the man with a sharp look, then shoved his way through the semicircle of inquisitors. They followed in hot pursuit. When Ashe and Deborah reached the stairs, he halted, turning around sharply.

"Ms. Vaughn has no comment, ladies and gentlemen, other than she will be in court to testify when called upon."

Ashe hurried her down the stairs, the reporters following, bombarding them with questions—everything from "Is it true Ms. Vaughn's ten-year-old brother had been attacked by a stranger on the school playground?" to "Is she romantically involved with her bodyguard?"

By the time Ashe and Deborah made their way to her Cadillac, parked across the street in the adjacent parking lot, Deborah wanted to scream. How on earth did celebrities endure their every move being a media event?

Ashe drove the Caddy out of the parking lot and headed up Water Street, making a right turn onto Main Street. Laying her head against the back of the leather seat, Deborah closed her eyes and let out a deep breath. Her face would be spread across the morning newspapers and appear on the evening newscasts. Right then and there, she decided not to turn on the television or even look at the paper.

A train caught them before they entered Sheffield. Ashe shifted the car into Park and glanced at Deborah. She looked like she was ready to scream or cry, maybe both. If only she had taken his advice and not gone to court today. Maybe now she would wait until time for her testimony before returning. She was so damn stubborn, so determined to show him and the rest of the world what a strong woman she was.

"When is Allen's next soccer game?" he asked.

"What?" She opened her eyes. "Oh. Day after tomorrow."

"If you're not on the witness stand, I think we should go to Allen's game."

"I try to make it to as many of his games as I possibly can. Except when she was very sick, Mother's never missed one. She's Allen biggest supporter."

"You haven't been worrying about Allen, have you?" Ashe noticed the last train car pass and the guard rails lifting. "I can assure you that Simon Roarke will guard him and your mother with his life. He's a good man, and highly trained."

"I'm sure you're right." Deborah rubbed her forehead with her fingertips. "But even good men who are highly trained can be taken out. No one, not even you, Ashe, is invincible.''

Shifting the gears into Drive, Ashe followed the line of backed up traffic over the railroad tracks and up Montgomery Avenue. ''It's all right, you know, if you want to cry or scream or hit something. I won't think you're weak if you do.''

''Thanks for your permission, but I don't need to do anything except get home and show my mother and my…my brother that I'm fine.''

''Hey, they already know you're strong and capable and in control. You don't have to try to be a paragon for them. My God, Deborah, what are you trying to prove by this woman of steel routine? And to whom?''

To you, she wanted to scream. To you, Ashe McLaughlin. I want you to know that I'm not the same silly little girl who threw herself at your feet. I want you to see me for the woman I am now. The woman your rejection helped create. A woman in charge of her own life. A woman capable of caring for others, without any help from a man.

Ashe turned into the Vaughn driveway and saw Simon Roarke pulling Carol Vaughn's silver Mercedes in right beside them. He parked in the three-car garage behind the house. The moment Deborah emerged from her Cadillac, Allen, in his gold-and-blue soccer uniform, raced around the cars and directly toward Deborah and Ashe.

"We won. I scored the winning goal." Allen jumped up and down in a boyish frenzy of triumph. "Tell them, Mr. Roarke. Tell them, Mother. I was awesome, wasn't I? You should have been there."

"Yes, I should have been," Deborah said. "Ashe and I will be at Wednesday's game if I don't have to testify that day."

Deborah caught the quick exchange of glances between Ashe and Simon Roarke. She wanted to ask them what was going on, but didn't dare in front of her mother and son. Besides, it might have meant nothing more than a coded recognition that all was well.

"Allen is quite an athlete," Roarke said in his gravelly voice. "They wouldn't have won the game without him."

"See. See." Full of youthful exuberance, Allen bounced around in the driveway. "Boy, Ashe, I wish you could have seen me make that goal."

A twinge of guilt tugged on Deborah's heartstrings. How was she going to handle Allen's growing dependency on Ashe? How would she be able to keep Ashe from disappointing their son? And that's the way she thought of Allen—as their son.

"Miss Carol should have videotaped it for us." Ashe winked at Carol, who stood near the entrance to the side patio.

"Oh, I could never watch the game and videotape it at the same time. I get too excited at these games,'' Carol said. ''I'd end up dropping the videocamera and breaking it.''

''Hey, what's Mazie fixing for supper tonight?'' Allen asked, running around the side of the garage, Roarke following him. ''I'm starving.''

''Pork chops, I think,'' Carol said, opening the gate to the side patio.

''I gotta go get Huckleberry out of the backyard now that we're home. I'll bet he's hungry, too.'' Allen bounded out of sight, Roarke on his heels.

Ashe and Deborah followed Carol through the gate and onto the side patio. A cool evening breeze swirled around them. Carol shivered.

''I think autumn weather is here to stay,'' she said.

''Yes, it seems—'' Deborah said.

A loud scream pierced the evening stillness. Allen's scream!

''Allen!'' Deborah cried, gripping Ashe by the sleeve, then breaking into a run.

Ashe grabbed her by the arm, stopping her. ''You and Miss Carol go into the house and lock the patio door. I'll see what's wrong.''

Deborah nodded agreement, then led her mother inside, locking the door behind them. ''Sit down in here and rest, Mother. I'll go see what's happened.''

Once she had seated her mother on the sofa,

Deborah raced through the house, meeting Mazie coming down the stairs.

"What was that screaming all about?" Mazie asked. "It sounded like Allen."

"It was," Deborah said. "Go see about Mother. She's in the living room."

Deborah rushed through the kitchen, flung open the back door and ran into the fenced backyard. Roarke stood facing Deborah, but his attention was riveted to the boy and man and dog on the ground. Deborah's heart stopped, her lungs filling with air as she sucked in a terrified breath.

Huckleberry lay on the ground, Allen on his knees beside him, trying to hug the big dog in his arms. Ashe hovered over Allen, his hand on Allen's shoulder as he talked in a low voice.

In the throes of a spasm, Huckleberry jerked. His spine arched, his head leaned backward, his legs twitched.

"What—what happened?" Deborah walked forward slowly.

"Looks like the dog's been poisoned," Roarke said.

"He's vomited," Ashe said, nodding toward the foul-smelling evidence. "If he has been poisoned, vomiting is a good sign. There's hope a vet might save him."

Tears streamed down Allen's face. He glanced

up at Deborah. "Why would anybody want to hurt Huckleberry?"

Why indeed? Ashe looked at Deborah and she knew. This was another warning from Buck Stansell.

"Come on, Allen." Ashe pried the boy's arms from around his dog, lifting him to his feet. "Go inside and get a quilt to wrap Huckleberry in. He's still alive. If we hurry we might be able to help him."

Allen nodded in numb silence, then flew through the open back door.

"Roarke, get the vet's phone number from Miss Carol and call and tell him to meet us." Kneeling, Ashe hoisted the big, stiff-legged Lab into his arms. "Deborah, go get the car started. Allen and I will bring Huckleberry around."

Deborah had the car ready when Allen opened the door and helped Ashe place Huckleberry on the backseat. Father and son leaped into the backseat beside the dog, Ashe pulling Allen onto his lap.

"Let's go," he said.

Deborah drove like a madman, running several red lights as she flew down Second Street. She prayed that nothing would prevent them from making it to Dr. Carradine's Pet Hospital in Muscle Shoals. She heard Ashe talking to Allen, reassuring him without giving him false hope.

"Talk to Huckleberry, son. Tell him we're taking care of him. Tell him he's a fine dog."

Tears gathered in Deborah's eyes. She swatted them away with the back of her left hand while she kept her right hand on the steering wheel. It was so unfair for this to happen to Huckleberry. He was an innocent animal, a child's pet. The rage inside her boiled. If she could have gotten her hands around Buck Stansell's neck, she didn't doubt that, at this precise moment, she had the strength to strangle the man.

When she swerved into Carradine's Pet Hospital, Dr. Carradine rushed out the front door and over to the car. Ashe got out, pulling Allen with him. Dr. Carradine leaned over inside the car.

"I'd say from the looks of Huckleberry that he has been poisoned. My guess is strychnine." Dr. Carradine lifted Huckleberry, straining himself in the process, his small, slender arms barely able to manage the dog's weight.

Ashe took Huckleberry from the vet the moment he emerged from the car.

"Bring him inside quickly. I'll anesthetize him. It'll stop the spasms."

Deborah took Allen's hand and they followed Ashe into the veterinary clinic. When they entered the lobby, Ashe turned to Deborah.

"You and Allen stay out here."

"No, I want to go with Huckleberry," Allen cried.

"You can help Huckleberry by letting me take care of him," Dr. Carradine said.

Allen clung to Deborah, tears pouring from his eyes, streaking his face, falling in huge drops from his nose and chin.

Ashe laid the big Lab on the examining table. Huckleberry panted wildly, then went into another spasm. Ashe watched while the doctor filled a syringe and plunged it deep into the dog's body. Poor animal. The veterinarian refilled the syringe and administered a second injection.

"What now?" Ashe wondered if there was any hope of saving Allen's pet.

"Wait and pray," Dr. Carradine said. "I've given him enough anesthesia to put him in a deep sleep. If we can keep him this way, he has a slight chance of pulling through. But I have to be honest with you. It doesn't look good."

"Huckleberry had been vomiting when we found him." Ashe looked down at the short, slender young veterinarian. "It's possible he didn't completely digest all the poison."

"Good. It's the best possible sign, and that's what we'll tell Allen. There's nothing to do now but wait. If Allen and Deborah want to come on back here and be with him, it'll be all right."

The moment they saw Ashe in the doorway leading to the examining room, Deborah and Allen hurried toward him.

"Huckleberry is resting," Ashe said. "He's sound asleep. Dr. Carradine says that since Huckleberry vomited, there's a good chance his body hasn't absorbed enough poison to kill him. We have hope he'll pull through."

Allen flung his arms around Ashe's waist. Ashe laid his hand on Allen's head, then leaned down and picked him up into his arms and carried him into the examining room. Deborah followed behind them, tears blurring her vision.

"Huckleberry needs to rest," Dr. Carradine said. "I'll continue to give him injections to keep him peaceful. We'll hope for the best."

Ashe set Allen on his feet beside the examining table, keeping his hand on the boy's shoulder. Allen reached out, stroking his pet's back.

"Y'all can go on home and I'll call if there's any change," the vet said.

"No, I can't leave Huckleberry. What if he wakes up and I'm not here?" Allen threw his arms around the comatose animal."

Ashe pulled Allen away from the dog, turned the child to face him and knelt down on one knee. "We aren't going anywhere until Huckleberry wakes up. You and Deborah and I will keep watch over him."

Deborah gulped down the sobs when she saw the

tentative little smile trembling on Allen's lips as he nodded his head.

Ashe glanced over at Dr. Carradine. "I'll bring in some chairs from the waiting room."

The doctor smiled. "I'll help you."

For what seemed like endless hours to Deborah, she and Ashe and Allen waited at Huckleberry's side, rising in fear each time the dog showed signs of going into another spasm. Dr. Carradine kept him medicated, and as the hours wore on, Deborah almost wished she, too, could be given an injection that would ease her pain. Watching the way Allen suffered tore at her heart the way nothing ever had. To watch her child hurting and know she could do nothing to ease his pain became unbearable.

Standing quickly, Deborah paced the floor. Allen had fallen asleep, his head resting in Ashe's lap. Deborah walked into the waiting room and looked out the windows. Evening had turned to night. The bright lights along Woodward Avenue sparkled like Christmas tree decorations. She glanced down at her watch. Ten-thirty.

Turning around, she walked back to the examining room, stopping in the doorway. Ashe was in the process of removing his jacket. He raised his leg just a fraction to give Allen's head a slight incline, then draped his jacket over the sleeping child. Covering her face with one hand, Deborah closed her eyes and said a silent prayer, asking God to save Huckleberry.

Ashe felt a hot fury rising inside him. A killing rage. Buck Stansell had no respect for animal life and little for human life. Buck's kind thought of animals as unfeeling, worthless creatures. Killing a dog would mean no more to him than flicking ashes off his cigarette.

Ashe adjusted his jacket around Allen, amazed how much he'd grown to care about Deborah's young brother. He had never been around children, had never allowed himself to think much about what it would be like to be a father. But he couldn't help wondering about how it would feel to have a son like Allen. The boy was intelligent and inquisitive and filled with a joy for life. He was sensitive and caring. In so many ways, Allen reminded Ashe of the young Deborah he had known and loved. Perhaps that was the reason he felt so close to Allen, so connected. Because he was so very much like Deborah.

Odd thing was, the boy reminded him of himself, too. Tall and lanky, with hands and feet almost too big for his body. He'd been the same as a kid. And cursed with being left-handed himself, he understood the adjustments Allen had had to make.

Ashe felt a twinge of sadness. Eleven years ago, he'd been thankful he hadn't gotten Deborah pregnant, but being around Allen so much these days had made him wonder if a child of theirs wouldn't have been a lot like Deborah's little brother.

For a couple of months after their passionate night down by the river, Ashe had worried about not having used any protection. But it had been an unfounded worry. By the time Wallace Vaughn had had him run out of town, Deborah would have known whether or not she was pregnant. And if she'd been carrying his child, she would have told him. Deborah had loved him, and she would have known that a child could have bound them together forever.

Deborah came in and sat down beside Ashe. Reaching out, he draped her shoulders with his arm and drew her close. She sighed.

"It's going to be all right, honey," Ashe said. "No way is God going to let that dog die and break Allen's heart."

She couldn't reply; instead she nodded and tried to smile. Closing her eyes, she relaxed against him.

Ashe sat there in the veterinarian's examining room, one arm holding Deborah possessively, the other laid protectively over Allen. As the hours passed, his leg fell asleep and his arms became stiff, but he didn't readjust his position. Both Allen and Deborah slept, as did Huckleberry.

Ashe closed his eyes for a few minutes, resting, then reopened them quickly when he heard movement from the examining table. Huckleberry opened his eyes and raised his head. No longer was his big body grossly contorted, but lay relaxed on the table.

Ashe gave Deborah a gentle shake. Opening her eyes, she glanced up at him. "Huckleberry's awake. Take a look."

"Oh, my God!" She jumped up out of the chair and ran toward the dog, taking his huge face in her hands. "Hey, there, big boy. You sure had us worried."

Ashe shook Allen, who groaned in his sleep. Ashe shook him again.

"What?"

"Wake up, son. Huckleberry wants to see you." Ashe lifted Allen in his arms and carried the boy across the room, sitting him down on the examining table beside his dog. "Go get Dr. Carradine," Ashe told Deborah.

She rushed out of the room. Allen hugged Huckleberry, who, though still groggy, raised his head and tried to sit up. "He's going to be all right!" Allen repeated the words several times, as if to convince himself.

Deborah returned with Dr. Carradine, who took a good look at Huckleberry and smiled. "Looks like we got lucky. I think Huckleberry will soon be as good as new."

The dog struggled to get up. Ashe lifted him off the table and set him on the floor. He staggered around slowly, like a drunken sailor. Sitting on the floor, Allen called his pet to him. The Lab padded over to the boy, who threw his arms around the big dog and hugged him.

"Why don't you folks go on home and get some rest," Dr. Carradine said. "Leave Huckleberry here until—" he glanced down at his watch "—it's after midnight. Well, I was going to say until tomorrow afternoon. Pick him up anytime after 2:00 p.m. today."

"If he's all right, why can't I take him home now?" Allen asked.

"Because Huckleberry needs some rest and so do you, young man." Dr. Carradine glanced at Deborah. "And so does your sister and Mr. McLaughlin. I have a feeling that if you take Huckleberry home now, all three of you would stay up the rest of the night with him."

"Come on, pal." Ashe leaned down to give Huckleberry a pat on the head. "Let's go home. Huckleberry is in good hands with Dr. Carradine. And I promise we'll pick him up at two o'clock."

Allen agreed reluctantly, giving Huckleberry a farewell hug before leaving.

Ashe carried Allen, who'd gone to sleep on the drive home, from the car into the house. The boy roused from his sleep and smiled at Ashe.

Allen yawned. "I'm not a baby. I can walk."

"Sure you can, pal," Ashe said.

He set Allen on his feet, then he and Deborah followed the child upstairs and into his room. Deborah spread back the covers. Allen's eyelids drooped. Curling up in the middle of the bed, he made no objections when Deborah removed his shoes, jeans and shirt. By the time she had stripped him down to his white cotton briefs, he had fallen fast asleep.

"He's all tired out," Ashe said. "He's been through almost as much as Huckleberry."

Deborah pulled up the covers, then sat down on the side of the bed. Allen was the dearest, most precious thing in her life. There wasn't a day that passed when she didn't want to tell him she was his mother, to claim him as her own. But she had agreed to this charade when she'd been eighteen and not strong enough to stand up to her father. He had told her she had two choices, either give Allen up for adoption or allow him to be raised as her brother.

If only she'd had the strength to tell her father to go to hell. If only she'd taken her child and found Ashe McLaughlin and forced him to face his responsibility as a father. But she'd done what was expected of her. She'd taken what others would consider the easy way out.

Deborah smoothed the loose strands of Allen's

thick blond hair away from his face. Leaning over, she kissed his forehead, then stood.

Ashe watched her, the way she looked at Allen, the way she touched him. No one could doubt the depth of her love for the boy. If he didn't know better, he'd swear she was his mother instead of his sister. But then motherly love was not limited to mothers. Indeed his grandmother had loved and cared for him in a way his own mother never had.

But what if Deborah was Allen's mother? Was it possible? No, don't even consider the possibility, he warned himself. Idiotic thoughts like that could be dangerous to his sanity. He was letting his imagination run away with him.

Allen was Deborah's brother, Miss Carol's change-of-life baby. Any other explanation was out of the question. There was no way Deborah could have been pregnant and not told him. She wouldn't have kept something that important a secret.

Deborah, although lovely beyond words, looked tired. Drained. Sad. On the verge of renewed tears.

"Come on, honey, you need to get some rest." Turning off the light, he guided her out of Allen's room and down the hall.

"I need a bath before I go to bed," she said. "I'm filthy."

He walked her into her sitting room and gently shoved her down in the rocking chair. "Sit still and rest. I'll get your bath ready for you."

When she started to protest, Ashe laid his index finger over her lips, silencing her. She stared up at him, her eyes filled with such deep emotion that Ashe wanted to lift her into his arms. But he didn't. Instead he entered her bathroom and turned on the gold taps, letting the warm water flow into her claw-foot bathtub. Rummaging around in the antique chest beside the vanity, he found some perfumed bath oil and splashed it into the water flow. He laid out two huge, fluffy, blue towels and a crochet-edged wash cloth.

In Deborah's bedroom, he turned down her bed and then found her gown, neatly folded in a top dresser drawer. Pale pink silk, spaghetti straps, heavy white lace across the bodice and hem. After spreading the gown out across the foot of her bed, he flung the matching robe over his arm.

When he returned to the sitting room, she was rocking back and forth slowly, her eyes opening and closing, her chin nodding farther and farther toward her chest.

Before she could protest, he lifted her out of the rocker and into his arms. Her eyes flew open. She grabbed him around the neck to balance herself.

"What are you doing?" She stared at him, wide-eyed.

"Taking you to the bathroom."

"I'm perfectly capable of walking, you know."

"I like carrying you," he said. "It gives me an excuse to hold you in my arms."

She relaxed, allowing him to carry her. She felt completely safe and secure wrapped in Ashe's strong arms. When they passed through her bedroom, she noticed he had turned down her bed and laid out her gown. The gesture touched her, making her feel cherished and cared for in a way she couldn't remember being cared for since she was a child.

"Ashe?"

"Hmm?"

"Thank you for being so wonderful with Allen."

"It was easy. Allen is a great kid. He reminds me so much of you, Deborah. The way you were at his age."

And he reminds me of you, she wanted to say. Every time I look at him, I see you. The way he smiles. The way he rests the side of his face in his hand when he's pondering something. The expression on his face when he's trying to talk me into allowing him to do something he knows is against the rules.

Once in the bathroom, Ashe lowered Deborah to her feet, sliding her slowly down his body, his big hands holding her hips in place against him.

She felt his arousal, knew he wanted her. And heaven help her, she wanted him.

She pulled away, turning her back to him.

"Thank you for everything." Bending over the tub, she turned off the faucet. "I can handle things from here on out. Good night, Ashe."

He whirled her around. She gasped when she saw the look of longing in his eyes. "Are you sending me away?"

"Yes, please, Ashe. Go."

"All right. If you're sure that's what you want."

"Yes, I'm sure." She really didn't want him to leave. She wanted him to stay, to undress her, to bathe her, to dry her damp skin and carry her to her bed.

Ashe ran the tip of his index finger down her cheek, then stepped back. "If you need me, you know where I'll be." He laid her pink silk robe on the vanity stool.

Looking down at the bathtub, she nodded. Ashe turned and left her alone. She closed the door behind him, and took a deep breath. She undressed quickly, throwing her clothes into a heap on the floor, then stepped into the bathtub and buried herself in the soft, scented water. Leaning her head back against the wall behind the tub, she closed her eyes and picked up the washcloth. Soaping the cloth, she ran it over her face, then rinsed by splashing water in her face. She slid the cloth down one arm and then the other. Lowering the soapy cloth to her breasts, her hand froze when the material made contact with her nipple, which jutted out to a peak.

She was aroused and aching. Aching to be with Ashe. Aching to open her arms and her body and take him in. But she didn't dare. For if she opened her heart to him, she would be lost.

Hurriedly, she bathed, washed her hair and dried off, praying she would be able to find forgetfulness in sleep.

Chapter 9

Ashe stood at the window of his bedroom that looked down over the patio. The moonlight illuminated the autumn flowers and shrubs so lovingly cared for by the Vaughns' weekly gardener. Ashe sloshed around the brandy in his glass, took a sip and set the liquor down on the ornate antique table to the left of the window. He scratched his naked chest, then ran his hand across his stomach.

He couldn't remember the last time he'd ached so badly for a woman, and certainly not for one particular woman. Deborah Vaughn had insinuated herself into his mind so firmly that he couldn't shake her. She had become his first thought in the morning and his last thought at night. Not Deborah Vaughn his client, but Deborah the woman.

He'd made a mistake coming back to Sheffield, seeing Deborah again. He had walked away from her once, rejected her because he hadn't loved her the way she'd loved him. Now he wanted her as he had never wanted another woman. He burned with the need to possess her.

Ashe slipped on his leather loafers. Buttoning his open shirt, he walked out into the hall. He'd tried for nearly an hour to relax, to stop thinking about Deborah, to quit remembering how she'd felt in his arms when he'd carried her to her bath. But he couldn't forget.

He walked down the hallway, stopping at Allen's open door. Looking inside, he saw the boy sleeping soundly, his upper body uncovered. Ashe crept silently into the room and pulled the sheet and blanket up to cover Allen's shoulders. The little fellow had been through quite an ordeal. Ashe balled his hands into fists. Buck Stansell didn't deserve to live. But his kind always landed on their feet, always found a way to slip through the cracks in the legal system.

After leaving Allen's room, Ashe eased the door to Miss Carol's room ajar and peered inside. She slept peacefully. Deborah had told him that often her mother had to rely on sleeping pills in order to rest.

He opened Deborah's bedroom door. More than anything he wanted to find her awake, waiting for him, her arms open, imploring him to come to her.

What he found was an empty bed, Deborah nowhere in sight. Where the hell was she?

He made his way down the stairs, checking each room, one by one, until he entered the library. A table lamp burned softly, casting gentle shadows over the woman sitting alone on the leather sofa, her feet curled beneath her. When he stepped inside the room, she turned her head and looked at him.

"Couldn't you sleep, either?" she asked.

"No."

Did she have any idea how beautiful she was, how irresistible she looked? Like a porcelain figure, all flawless creamy skin and pink silk clinging to her round curves, her long blond hair cascading down her back and over her shoulders.

He grew hard just looking at her, just smelling the scent of her bath oil clinging to her skin. He stood inside the open door. Waiting. Wanting. Needing.

"I can't believe I'm still wide awake." She looked at him with hunger in her eyes, and wondered if he realized how much she wanted him. "I'm exhausted and yet I feel as if I've had an extra dose of adrenaline."

"Yeah, me, too."

She stretched her back, leaning into the sofa. Ashe caught his breath, the sight of her almost more than he could bear. Her firm breasts strained against the silk of her gown. Her full hips pressed into the soft leather cushions.

"I fixed myself a drink." She nodded to the partially full glass on the end table. "It didn't help."

"I did the same thing," he said. "I came down about thirty minutes ago and swiped some of your brandy."

"Obviously it didn't help you go to sleep." She clenched her hands, then unclenched them, repeating the process several times. She wished he hadn't come downstairs and found her alone and restless. He'd know she couldn't stop thinking about him, couldn't make herself forget the feel of his arms around her, the strength of his arousal pressing against her.

"Since neither of us can sleep, how about taking a ride?" Holding his breath, he waited for her reply.

"A ride?" She scooted to the edge of the sofa, knowing there was more at stake than just a moonlight drive. "That sounds like a great idea." Standing, she smiled at him, then rushed past him and out into the hallway. "Give me a minute to put on some clothes," she said softly, then ran up the stairs.

He checked his back pocket for his wallet, then thought about his gun and holster lying on his nightstand. He hurried upstairs, retrieved his gun and put on his jacket, then walked down the hall to Simon Roarke's bedroom. He knocked softly. Within seconds Roarke cracked the door and peered out at him.

"What's up?"

"Deborah and I are going for a ride," Ashe said. "I wanted you to know I'd be out of the house for a while."

"Yeah, sure. No problem." Simon grinned, something the man didn't do often.

"Don't go reading anything into this." Ashe turned to leave.

Opening the door, Roarke laid his hand on Ashe's shoulder, gripping him firmly. "She's the one, isn't she?"

Ashe stiffened at his friend's words. "The one what?"

"The one you told me about that night six months ago when we both got stinking drunk and wound up crying all over each other."

Ashe didn't like to remember that night; he'd thought Roarke would never remind him. "Yeah, she's the one."

Pulling away, Ashe ran his hand through his hair, straightened his jacket and headed downstairs. He paced the marble-floored entrance hall until Deborah descended the stairs wearing a pair of olive green cotton twill pants and a baggy cotton sweater in an olive-and-cream stripe.

"Let's go," she said, her chest rising and falling with quick, panting little breaths.

"You want to take your Caddy or my rental car?"

She tossed him a set of keys. "The Caddy."

He slipped his arm around her waist and they rushed outside, the cool night air assaulting them the minute they opened the door.

"I should get you a set of keys to the Caddy," she said as he helped her inside.

He leaned down, giving her a quick kiss, then closed the passenger door and raced around to the other side of the car.

He knew where he was going to take her; he'd known the minute he'd suggested the ride. It hadn't been a premeditated idea, just something that hit him in a flash. In the dark confines of the car, he could hear her breathing, could smell that heady scent of flowery bath oil mixed with the musty scent of woman. He started the Caddy and backed out of the drive.

She waited for him to ask her where she wanted to go. He didn't ask. It didn't take her long to realize the direction in which he was headed. Dear God, no! Surely he wasn't taking her there. Was he that insensitive? Didn't he realize she'd never been back since that night?

The road leading down to the river was dark, lonesome and flanked on both sides by heavily wooded areas. Deborah closed her eyes, shutting out the sight, clenching her teeth in an effort not to scream. How could he do this to her!

"Please take me home." Her voice wavered slightly.

"I thought you wanted to take a ride." He kept his gaze focused on the view ahead of him.

"I don't want to go down to the river."

"Why not?"

"You know damn well why not."

"I want you to tell me." He glanced at her and wished he hadn't. Her face was barely visible in the moonlight, but he could feel the tension in her body and make out the anger etched on her features.

"Take me home, Ashe. Now!"

He continued driving toward the river. "It's time we talked. Really talked. We need to clear up a few things before we make love."

"Before we make… Why, you arrogant bastard! You think you're going to take me down to the river and screw me again and then walk out of my life and never look back. Well, you'd better think again. I'm not some lovesick teenager who believes in fairy tales."

"No, you're not." He pulled the Cadillac off the road and onto a narrow dirt lane surrounded by trees. "You're a woman who wants to be made love to very badly, and I'm the man who is dying to love you."

When he reached out to touch her, she jerked away from him. "Don't. I don't want you. Do you hear me? I *do not* want you."

"Honey, stop lying to yourself. Do you think I like knowing I'm so hung up on you I can't think about anything else? Do you honestly think you're the only one with bad memories about that night?"

"Oh, I know all about your bad memories!" Whipping around in the seat, she faced him. "You let your anger with Whitney and your need for a woman overcome your better judgment, and you screwed me. Then afterward you were filled with regret."

He jerked her into his arms, lowered his head and whispered against her lips. "Stop saying I screwed you, dammit! It wasn't like that and you know it. I made love to you, Deborah."

Struggling to free herself, she laughed in his face. "You didn't make love to me, you sc—"

He kissed her hard and fast, adeptly silencing her. She pulled away as much as he would allow and glared at him.

"Maybe I wasn't in love with you," he admitted. "But I did love you. I'd loved you since we were kids. You were one of my best friends."

The tears welled up inside her; her chest ached from restraint. This was what she didn't want—

what she couldn't bear. "All right. We made love. But you regretted it. You said it could never happen again."

"I cared too much about you to hurt you by pretending there could be more for us. I felt like a heel, but I did what I thought was best for you."

She took a deep breath. "I hated you after that night, you know. But all the while I swore to myself I despised you, I kept praying you'd come and tell me you loved me. I was such a fool."

"And when two months went by and I didn't come to you, you decided to get revenge. All that love turned to hate so quickly."

"What are you talking about? I admit I thought about how I'd like to toss you into a pool of piranhas, but that's as far as my seeking revenge went." She scooted away from him when he loosened his hold on her. "Besides, you didn't stick around long enough for me to plot any elaborate revenge schemes."

"You don't call siccing your daddy on me revenge?"

Her eyes widened. She opened her mouth on a silent gasp, then shook her head. "What—what do you mean, siccing my daddy on you?"

"Are you pretending you've forgotten or are you trying to tell me you honestly don't know what I'm talking about?"

"I have no idea what you're talking about," she said.

"Then let me refresh your memory." Turning sideways, Ashe leaned his back against the door, crossed his arms over his chest and rested his head on the side window. "About two months after our night down here—" moving his head from side to side, he glanced out at the starlit sky, the dark waters of the Tennessee River and the towering trees tipped with moonlight "—the police chief hauled my rear end downtown. And who do you think was waiting for us when we got to the police station?"

Deborah's stomach did a nervous flip-flop. "Daddy?"

"Bingo! Wallace Vaughn himself, fit to be tied and ready to string me up for raping his little girl."

"Raping!" The blood soared through Deborah, her heartbeat wild, the pounding beat deafening to her own ears.

"Yeah, that was my reaction," Ashe said, uncertain whether to accept Deborah's shock at face value or remain suspicious. "But the D.A. was there with your daddy and he assured me that they weren't kidding. They were accusing me of rape, and when I told them that the charge would never stick, they both laughed in my face."

"I had no idea Daddy could have done anything so—"

"You didn't go crying to your Daddy?" All

these years he had been so sure Deborah had lied to her father, that she had made him believe that, at the very least, Ashe had seduced her, and at the worst, had taken her by brute force.

"I didn't tell my father anything." Deborah scooted to the far side of the car, her back up against the door, she and Ashe glaring at each other in the semidarkness.

"Why the hell lie to me now?" He wanted to shake her until her teeth rattled. God, help him, he never thought he would feel such bitter anger again, that confronting her with what she'd done would resurrect the hatred he'd felt—for Wallace Vaughn, for the whole town of Sheffield, and, yes, for Deborah herself.

Deborah lifted her feet up on tiptoes, tensing her legs as she ran her hands up and down the tops of her thighs. "I never told Daddy about our…about our making love that night. I told my mother." *I had to tell her. I was seventeen and pregnant by a man who didn't love me or want me. I didn't know what else to do.*

"You told Miss Carol?"

"I needed someone to talk to about what had happened." *About the fact that I was carrying your child.* "Who else would I have gone to other than my own mother?"

"Did you tell your mother that I'd forced you?"

Cold shivers covered Ashe like a blanket of frost spreading across the earth on a winter night.

"No. I told my mother the truth, all of it. She'd known, of course, that I'd left the country club with you that night and she knew why."

"I'm surprised your father didn't hunt us down."

"He didn't know I was with you. He didn't see me leave," Deborah said. "Mother told him I was spending the night with a girlfriend after the engagement party."

"I know Miss Carol often kept the complete truth from your father in order to maintain peace, so why did she feel it necessary to tell him about what had happened between you and me that night?"

Because I was pregnant! "I was very upset, very unhappy. Mother thought she was doing the right thing by telling Daddy. She couldn't have known what he'd do. And I never knew anything about what he did. Obviously, Daddy realized what a mistake he'd made. You were never arrested. If you had been, I would have told the truth. I would have made them understand that what happened that night was my fault, not yours."

"Deborah?"

"Well, it was, wasn't it? I mean, I did throw myself at you and practically beg you to make love to me, didn't I?"

"If I'd been more of a man and less a boy that night, I'd have turned you down and saved us both a lot of misery."

"And that's what the memory of that night has been for you, hasn't it, a misery?" Deborah shut her eyes, capturing her tears beneath closed lids.

Dear God, no! The results had been a misery, but not that night. Never that night! "No, honey, that's not true. The memory of that night is bittersweet for me."

"More bitter than sweet." Swallowing her tears, she lowered her head, wrapped one arm across her stomach and cupped the side of her face in her other hand. "That's why you left town, wasn't it? To get away from me?"

"I left town because your father and the D.A. gave me no other choice." Ashe slid across the seat, grabbed Deborah by the shoulders and shook her gently several times. "Look at me, dammit." With her head still bowed, she raised her eyes to meet his. "Your father told me that if I didn't leave town and never come back, he'd make sure I did time for rape. He wanted me out of your life for good."

"No, he wouldn't have… He knew. Oh, Ashe, he knew."

"He knew what?" Ashe gripped her shoulders, tightening his hold when she didn't immediately respond.

"He knew I was—" She'd almost said *pregnant with your baby.* "He knew I loved you, that I would never have testified against you, that I would have made a fool of myself to protect you."

A searing pain ripped through Ashe, the hot, cauterizing pain of truth, killing the festering infection of lies and suspicions, preventing him from clinging to past resentments.

"Dear God, Deborah. All these years I've thought..." He pulled her into his arms. She trembled, and he knew she was on the verge of tears, that she was holding them in check, being strong. He stroked her back; she laid her head on his chest.

She had not betrayed him. She hadn't even told her father, only her mother. She had never accused him of forcing her or seducing her. Lies. All lies. Wallace Vaughn's lies to force Ashe out of Deborah's life. Had the old man been that afraid that sooner or later Ashe would destroy Deborah's life?

Ashe found himself kissing the side of her face, along her hairline, one hand continuing to stroke her back while he threaded the fingers of his other hand through her hair, caressing her tenderly.

"Have you hated me all these years, Ashe?" she asked, her voice a whisper against his chest.

"I've hated you. I've hated myself. Hell, I've hated just about everyone and everything associated with my past." When she gazed up at him, he dotted her forehead with kisses. "But I never hated what we shared that night, the feelings inside me when we made love. It had never been like that for me before.'' He swallowed hard. ''And it's never been that way for me again. Not ever.''

''Oh, Ashe.'' She slipped her arms around him, burrowing her body into his, seeking and finding a closer joining.

He took her mouth like a dying man clinging to life, as if without the taste of her he could not go on. She accepted the kiss, returning it full measure, her hands clawing at his back, inching their way up beneath his jacket, yanking his shirt from his slacks, making contact with his naked flesh. Ashe thrust his tongue deeper into her mouth, their tongues mating furiously.

Breathless, their lips separated, but they clung to each other, Deborah unbuttoning Ashe's shirt, Ashe lifting Deborah's sweater up and under her arms.

''I've wanted you since that first day I came back to town.'' He nuzzled her neck with his nose as he lifted his hand to her lace-covered breast. ''I've called myself every kind of fool, but nothing's eased this ache inside me.''

She curled her index finger around a swirl of dark chest hair, then leaned over to kiss one tiny nipple. Ashe groaned. ''I hated you for making me want you again,'' she said. ''I swore no one would ever hurt me the way you did, and here I am throwing myself at you again as if I were seventeen.''

"No, honey, no." He took her face in both his hands, looking deep into her eyes, smiling his irresistible smile. "This works both ways. I want you and you want me. Neither of us are kids. We're two responsible adults who are as frustrated as hell."

She laughed. "Ashe, I don't know if I can handle this, what I'm feeling. It scares me. It scares me more now than it did when I was seventeen." She circled his neck with her arms, pressing her cheek against his. "When I was seventeen I was so in love with you that nothing we did seemed wrong. I didn't know the first thing about sex. Now...well, now I'm aching with wanting you. It's different now. It's—"

"It's right this time, honey," he said against her lips. "No fairy tales, no declarations of undying love, just a man and a woman who want each other desperately. Mutual desire."

"Yes." She nodded. "Mutual desire." You're wrong, she wanted to shout. It isn't all that different now. I'm still in love with you and you still don't return that love.

"Let's vanquish all those bad memories," he said. "Let's lay the past to rest. Tonight."

His kiss was less frantic this time, more tender and giving, yet as hot and needy as the one before. There was no way to make him understand that she could never lay the past to rest, that Allen was the embodiment of that night so long ago when a young and foolish girl had given herself to a man who didn't love her.

Ashe held her in his arms, burying his face in her neck, breathing in the sweet fragrance of her hair. "We can't make love back at your house and I know you don't want to make love here, in the car, the way we did that night. Where can we go, honey? A motel room seems cheap and I want this night to be special for you—for us."

"You're wrong about my not wanting to make love here and now, in the car," she said. "I do."

"Why would you want to—"

"I'm not sure I can explain how I feel, but... Well, it would somehow validate that first time. I know it sounds crazy, but... I need for us to make love here, now, in the car, the way we did that night when... Please, Ashe, make love to me."

"That's exactly what you said to me that night." And damn his rotten soul, he hadn't been able to resist her. She had been the sweetest temptation he'd ever known—and she still was.

"I guess I'm still begging." A lone tear escaped her eye and trickled down her cheek.

Ashe kissed the teardrop. "No, Deborah, I'm the one doing the begging this time. I'm the one who'll die if I can't have you. I'm the one willing to do anything to make you happy, to see you smile, to make your forget."

He actually remembered every word she'd said to him that night when she'd told him she wanted to make him happy, wanted to make him forget Whitney, wanted to make him smile again. She had pleaded with him to make love to her, saying she'd die if he didn't.

"You remember what I said."

"Every word." He lifted her sweater up and off, tossing it into the back seat, then unhooked her bra and eased it off her shoulders. "And I remember how you looked and how you felt." He covered both breasts with his hands and planted a row of kisses from her collarbone to her shoulder. "And the smell of you. My sweet, innocent Deborah."

He licked the tip of her breast; she moaned. He unsnapped and unzipped her slacks; she shoved his jacket off his shoulders. Ashe removed his shoulder holster, laying it on the dashboard before removing his shirt.

She kissed his chest, tiny, loving nicks. He tugged her slacks down and off her legs, throwing them on top of her sweater. She shivered when he dipped his hand beneath the elastic of her silky panties and cupped her buttocks, lifting her up and over him as he slid down onto the seat, his head braced against the armrest on the door.

While he suckled at her breasts, his fingers delved between the delicate folds of her body, finding the sensitive, hidden peak. She unzipped his trousers and reached inside to cover his arousal with the palm of her hand. Their kisses grew hotter, harder, longer, as they moved to the rhythm of nature's mating music, their bodies straining for closer and closer contact.

Lifting his hips, Ashe removed his wallet, then tugged his trousers downward and kicked them into the floorboard. "I'm dying," he groaned. "I wanted to wait, to take more time, to—"

Leaning over him, she covered his mouth, silencing him with the fury of her kiss. He ran his hands up and down, over her shoulders, down her back, pulling at her panties until she helped him remove them. He eased her over and onto her back, drawing her body beneath his as he ripped off his briefs, sheathed himself and positioned her for his possession.

"Now, honey? Now!" He was fast losing control.

"Yes, now!"

He plunged into her, lifting her hips, delving deep and hard. She gripped his shoulders, rising to meet his demands. Sliding her legs up his until she reached his hips, she whispered his name over and over, telling him with the tone of her voice and little moans of pleasure that she was near the brink. He didn't want this to end, wanted it to go on forever, but knew he couldn't last much longer. The pleasure was too great, too intense to slow the upward spiral toward completion.

"It's too good, honey. Too good."

He felt her tightening around him. She clasped him like a tight fist. Crying out, she quivered in his arms as spasm after spasm of fulfillment racked her body. His release came hard and fast, shaking him to the core of his being.

He cried out, losing himself in her, kissing her as they shivered from the aftershocks of such a powerful loving.

Lifting himself, Ashe pulled Deborah up off the seat and into his arms, holding her against him, listening to her rapid breathing.

"I want to make love to you again," he told her. "Tonight. Tomorrow. The day after tomorrow."

She didn't say anything; she couldn't. She knew he was telling her that, this time, there would be no rejection and no regrets. She lifted her face to him, glorying in the feel of his arms around her, the passion in his consuming kiss.

Dawn spread a honeyed pink glow across the horizon. When Ashe parked the Caddy in the driveway, Deborah awoke. Lifting her head from his shoulder, she smiled.

"It's 5:40," he said. "Mazie is going to be up and about any time now."

"Think she'll catch us sneaking in?"

"Would you care if she does?" Ashe opened the car door and assisted Deborah. Wrapping his arm around her, he led her to the front door.

"She'd probably be shocked. She's not used to me sneaking into the house at all hours."

Ashe unlocked the door. They walked into the entrance hall, arm in arm. "What do you usually do, stay overnight at your lover's house?"

Shadowy morning light coming through the windows illuminated the stairs. Deborah stopped dead still in the middle of the staircase.

"I haven't had any lovers," she said, then pulled out of Ashe's arms and ran up to the landing.

He caught her just as she flung open her sitting room door, whirling her around to face him, pulling her into his arms. "What do you mean you haven't had any lovers?"

"There's never been anyone else. Only you." Lowering her head, she looked down at the floor.

He lifted her chin in the curve of his thumb and forefinger. "Honey, I—"

"I never fell in love again, that's all. I hoped that sooner or later the right guy would come along and I'd be ready, but it just didn't happen."

"Just Mr. Wrong again, huh?"

"No, Ashe, not Mr. Wrong. Just not Mr. Right." She slipped her arms around his neck and kissed him, then stepped back and smiled. "This time we're lovers. Remember? Mutual desire?"

"You'd better get in your room and lock me out or we'll be right in the middle of some mutual desire any minute now."

"Good night, then." She laughed. "Or should I say good morning."

"Next time, we're going to have to find some place else to make love." He rubbed the small of his back. "I'm too old to do it in a car, even a big Caddy."

"Next time," she whispered to herself. Next time. She knew she would never be able to resist him and that for him this was only an affair. But not for her. She was already so in love with Ashe McLaughlin she couldn't bear for him to leave her.

He kissed her with a passion that told her that even if he wasn't in love with her, leaving her was as difficult for him as it was for her. Releasing her, he shoved her into her room and closed the door. She took a deep breath, turned and raced into her bedroom, falling in a heap on her bed. Hugging herself, she rolled into a ball and closed her eyes.

This was what she had dreaded since the moment she'd walked in and saw Ashe talking to her mother in the living room. And, if she was honest with herself, this was what she had wanted to happen. No matter how hard she had tried to deny it, she still loved Ashe McLaughlin. She had never truly stopped loving him.

What on earth was she going to do now? She

had rushed headlong into an affair with her son's father. How could she continue lying to Ashe, keeping the truth about his child from him? The longer she waited to tell him, the more difficult it would be—for both of them. But did she dare tell him? Would he understand? Or would he hate her for keeping his son from him all these years?

Chapter 10

"Please, tell us, Ms. Vaughn, what happened when you took that wrong turn off Cotton Lane?" the district attorney asked.

"I realized I'd gotten off on the wrong road and was looking for a place to turn around." Deborah sat straight, her hands folded in her lap. "I noticed a truck pulled off the road. One man jumped out of the truck, but I couldn't see his face. There were two other men behind the truck, one holding a gun to the other's head."

Deborah's stomach tightened into a knot; she gripped her damp hands together. Glancing out into the courtroom she sought Ashe. Their gazes met and held. She took a deep breath.

"Are you all right, Ms. Vaughn?" District Attorney Jim Bitterman spoke softly, his voice a light tenor, a distinct contrast to his rugged, almost ugly face and wiry, muscular body.

"Yes." Deborah kept her vision focused on Ashe for several seconds longer, gaining strength from his presence.

"Will you continue, please?"

"The man holding the gun was Lon Sparks."

"Objection, your honor," the defense attorney, Leland Prater shouted, rising from his seat and moving his short, rotund body around the desk. "Ms. Vaughn was not acquainted with Mr. Sparks and therefore could hardly have recognized him."

"Ms. Vaughn later identified Mr. Sparks from a photograph, your honor," Jim Bitterman said.

"Overruled," Judge Heath said.

"Please continue." District Attorney Bitterman stood directly in front of Deborah. "Tell the jury what you saw."

"Lon Sparks shot the man in the head." Deborah closed her eyes momentarily, the memory of that dreadful sight closing in around her, filling her with the sense of fear she'd known in those horrific seconds when she'd witnessed the murder.

Jim Bitterman allowed her to continue recalling the events at her own pace. Leland Prater, long known as an old bag of wind and one of the most crooked lawyers in the area, objected every chance he got, deliberately unnerving Deborah as much as possible. But she did not waver in her testimony, not even when Prater cross-examined her.

She'd been warned, by Jim and by Ashe, that Prater's strategy would be to bring her to tears, show her to be a highly emotional, hysterical woman, who had allowed her hysteria and fear to wrongly identify Lon Sparks.

Not one tear fell from her eyes. Not one shrill word escaped her lips. When her nerves rioted, she took deep breaths and looked to Ashe, seeking and finding the strength she needed to do the job she and she alone could do.

When she was dismissed, Deborah stepped down and walked slowly toward Ashe, who stood and waited for her. He slipped his arm around her and led her out of the courtroom. Even the bevy of reporters flinging questions at her did not disturb the serenity she felt as Ashe led her downstairs and out of the courthouse.

Neither of them said a word until they were safely inside Deborah's car. Ashe buckled her seat belt, kissed her on the nose and smiled at her.

"It's over." She sighed. "It's really over."

"Yeah, honey, it's over." But Ashe wasn't sure. Not one incident of harassment had occurred since Huckleberry's poisoning two days ago, and that made Ashe all the more suspicious. Buck Stansell should have escalated his threats the closer the day came for Deborah to testify. But he hadn't. He hadn't done anything. Did that mean he was waiting to take revenge? Hell!

Deborah checked her watch. "We have time to make the last half of Allen's soccer game, don't we?"

"That's where I'm headed." Ashe maneuvered the Caddy out of the parking lot and onto Water Street.

Leaning against the cushioned headrest, Deborah closed her eyes. Ashe reached out and took her hand, squeezing it tightly. She smiled, but didn't open her eyes or speak. She felt such a great sense of relief.

She had done the right thing, despite being afraid. She had faced the devil—and won! Now, all she had to face were her own personal demons, the biggest lie in her life. She'd had the courage to stand up against Buck Stansell and his gang, but did she have the guts to tell Ashe the truth about Allen? She knew now that she'd been wrong to keep his son's existence a secret from him all these years. Despite her own feelings, her deep sense of betrayal and rejection, she should have contacted Ashe long ago. Mama Mattie would have given her his phone number or address if only she'd asked.

But what would telling Ashe the truth now do to their new relationship? Although he had promised her nothing permanent, had made no commitment to her, she knew he truly cared about her. She, and she alone, was the woman he wanted. Would it be so wrong to wait, to take what time she had left with Ashe and savor the joy she felt, the mutual passion and desire?

"Are you sure you're up to this?" Ashe parked the Cadillac behind a row of cars lined up along the shoulder of Avalon Avenue, west of the railroad tracks that separated Muscle Shoals from Tuscumbia and Sheffield.

"The worst is over. Right? There's no reason why I can't resume my normal activities, is there?"

"Deborah..." Dear God, he didn't want to tell her that he thought the worst might not be over, that the worst might be yet to come. But he would not lie to her. "We can't be sure what Buck Stansell might do if Lon Sparks is convicted."

"You're saying it isn't over." She clutched her shoulder bag to her stomach. "You think he might try to kill me after the trial ends, don't you?"

"There's no way to know." Ashe grasped her shoulder, urging her to turn to him. "But my guess is that you're safe until the jury reaches a verdict."

She leaned toward him, wanting to fall into his arms, wanting and needing his comfort and reassurance. But this was hardly the time or the place. "Then I'm going to try not to think about it, for now. I don't know how much more Mother and Allen can take. I can't bear to think what it would have done to Allen if Huckleberry had died."

"Don't think about it. Huckleberry is as good as new," Ashe said. "Come on, let's go cheer for the home team."

Deborah and Ashe joined Carol Vaughn and Simon Roarke on the sidelines of a tense soccer game between two sets of ten-to twelve-year-olds. Carol had built herself a comfortable nest around her folding lawn chair. She sat with a plaid blanket wrapped about her legs, a thermos of hot coffee at her side. Roarke stood directly behind her chair, his gaze moving around the crowd, then back to the soccer game where Allen Vaughn raced down the field, his long, strong legs moving with agile grace.

Roarke stepped aside when Deborah laid her hand on her mother's shoulder. Ashe nodded, motioning to Roarke.

"How's the game going?" Deborah asked.

"We're ahead," Carol said. "Two to one."

Deborah glanced at the sky. "It's getting cloudy and the wind's up. I hope it doesn't start raining."

"Where's your coat?" Carol asked.

"I didn't wear one today. Just my suit. But don't worry, I'm fine."

"Mothers worry."

"I'm okay. Really. Everything is going to be all right."

Ashe and Roarke moved away from the crowd, close enough to keep an eye on everyone and yet far enough away to have a private discussion.

"We're going to be staying for at least another couple of weeks," Ashe said. "If we're lucky, this will be over when the trail ends, but my gut instincts tell me not to count on it."

"A man could do a lot worse than living around here, spending the rest of his life in a small town." Roarke's dark gaze came to a halt on Allen Vaughn as the boy kicked the ball past the goalie and scored a point for his team.

Ashe slapped Roarke on the back. "Did you see that? Damn that boy's good. He's big and fast and strong and a real fighter. Look at his face. Good God, how I know that feeling. He's lightheaded from the victory."

"He reminds me of you," Roarke said.

"What?"

"Allen Vaughn reminds me of you."

"Hell, he's just like Deborah. They could be twins."

"I know he looks like Deborah, but the more I'm around the kid, the more he reminds me of you."

"What the hell are you talking about?" Ashe watched Allen, seeing nothing except his blond hair, his blue eyes, his strong physical resemblance to Deborah.

"When did you leave Sheffield and join the army?"

"When did I... Eleven years ago."

"When exactly?"

"In July."

Grunting, Roarke nodded. "Allen Vaughn was born in February. Seven months after you left town."

"So?"

"Has it never once crossed your mind that you might have gotten Deborah pregnant, that Allen could be your son?"

Ashe's body rebelled, tensing every muscle, bringing every nerve to full alert, knotting his stomach painfully. "She would have told me. Deborah never would have kept something like that from me. She was in love with me. If she'd been pregnant with my child, she would have come running to me."

"Are you sure?"

"Yes, dammit, I'm sure!"

"Then forget I said anything."

"I sure as hell will." Ashe glared at his friend, a man he had come to like and respect since their first meeting over a year ago. Roarke stood eye to eye with Ashe, the two equal in height and size, broad-shouldered, long-legged. Roarke, like Ashe himself, a former warrior, still in his prime.

"You want me to give Sam a call tonight and let him know we'll be staying...indefinitely?" Roarke asked.

"No. This is my case. I'll call Sam." Ashe

watched Allen, inspecting his every move with an
analytical eye, searching for evidence to substan-
tiate Roarke's suspicion. ''I'll let him know we
could be here for a few more weeks. Once I know
Deborah is safe, we'll head back to Atlanta.''

Dammit! Why couldn't Roarke have kept his
suspicions to himself? They were totally unfounded. They had to be! Not getting Deborah
pregnant that long-ago night was the one and only
thing Ashe hadn't had to feel guilty about all these
years. Allen Vaughn was Deborah's brother, not
her son. Most certainly not *his* son. No way in hell!

Dinner had been a double celebration. Deborah's
court appearance was over and Allen Vaughn had
once again scored the winning goal that led his
team to victory.

Deborah and Ashe had allowed her family to believe the danger was over; indeed, Deborah convinced herself that there was hope all the threats
and harassment had come to an end.

She had sensed a tension in Ashe she hadn't noticed before tonight. He kept watching Allen and
his close scrutiny unnerved her. Did he suspect
something? Or was he simply worrying that Buck
Stansell still posed a threat to her family, that Allen
might be the target of the man's revenge?

But then Ashe would look at her and his eyes
would warm, his expression telling her plainly that

he was remembering their lovemaking in the early morning hours. Yesterday. Less than forty-eight hours ago.

"I'm afraid I must say good-night." Carol rose from her chair in the library. "Come along, Allen. It's a half hour past your bedtime."

"How about coming up with me, Ashe?" Allen asked. "You said you wanted to see my science test."

"You bet I do. I want to see what you did to get 105% on that test instead of just a plain old 100%." Ashe laid his hand on Allen's shoulder and the two followed Miss Carol.

"Are you staying down here for a while?" Carol asked her daughter.

"Yes, I think I'll fix myself a drink and relax a bit before I come up."

"Don't forget to say good-night," Allen called out from the hallway.

"I won't forget."

Alone in the library, Deborah kicked off her shoes and tucked her feet up on the sofa. Suddenly she felt the man's presence before she heard him clear his throat. Jerking her head around, she saw Simon Roarke standing in the doorway.

"Come on in, Mr. Roarke," Deborah said. "Would you care for a drink?"

"No, thanks." He walked over to the liquor cart. "May I fix something for you?"

"Just a little brandy."

Roarke poured the liquor and handed it to Deborah. "This about right?"

"Perfect." Deborah looked up at Simon Roarke, thinking, and not for the first time, that there was a hint of sadness in his eyes. "Please, sit down and talk to me."

"What do you want to talk about, Ms. Vaughn?"

"Call me Deborah. And I'd like to ask you about your friendship with Ashe."

Roarke sat in the wing chair to Deborah's left. "We've known each other a year. We have similar backgrounds and found we worked well together and enjoyed spending some of our off time together."

"You were in the army, too?"

"Yeah."

"How long have you worked for the Dundee Agency?"

"Over two years."

"You aren't married?"

"No."

"Girlfriend?" Deborah asked.

"Neither Ashe nor I are in a committed relationship, if that's what you're asking. I'm sure he's told you that."

Deborah smiled. "I'm not very good at this, am I? Cross-examining you to get information about Ashe isn't something I'd ordinarily do, but—"

"But you're curious about Ashe. Why don't you just ask him what you want to know?"

"Yes, that would be the logical thing to do, wouldn't it?" Deborah slid her feet off the sofa and back into her shoes. "Did he tell you that we knew each other, years ago?"

"Yes."

"You aren't making this easy for me, Mr. Roarke."

"Just Roarke," he said. "I'm afraid I can't tell you what you want to know. I'm not sure Ashe can tell you. He probably doesn't even know himself."

"Is it that obvious?" Deborah clasped her knees with her fingertips. "I made a mistake about the way Ashe felt about me once, and I don't want to make another mistake."

"You're talking to the wrong man. I can't speak for Ashe." Roarke grunted, then chuckled softly. "Hell, I'm a failure when it comes to figuring out the way other people feel and think. I'm thirty-five. I'm alone, and I'll be alone the rest of my life. Ashe is different. He's not so far gone, the right woman couldn't save him."

Deborah took a sip of the brandy, then set the glass aside. "I like you, Roarke. I—"

"Allen is waiting for you to come up." Ashe stood in the doorway, a rather comical look of jealousy on his face.

Deborah couldn't suppress a gurgle of laughter from escaping.

Standing, Roarke took a couple of steps, leaned over, lifted Deborah's hand and kissed it. "I like you, too, Deborah." He walked past Ashe without glancing his way.

"What the hell was that all about?" Ashe asked.

"I was pumping Roarke for information about you."

"That's not what it sounded like when I walked in. Sounded more like a mutual admiration society."

Deborah stood and walked over to Ashe, slipped her arm around his neck and pressed her body into his. "I like your friend Roarke." She rubbed herself against Ashe. "But not the same way I like you."

Ashe jerked her up against him and his lips covered hers, claiming her with demanding possession. Breathing hard, they ended the kiss, but held each other close.

"I want to make love to you," he said. "Is there any way we can slip off somewhere? Anywhere?"

"Let me go up and say good night to Allen, then I'll meet you in the pool house in thirty minutes."

"The pool house? Out back?"

"Yes. We'll have all the privacy we want out there."

Ashe laughed. "I don't know if I can wait thirty minutes."

"Let's make it twenty minutes," she said, pulling out of his arms.

"You aren't afraid someone will find us out, using the pool house as a rendezvous?"

"I really don't care, do you?"

"No, honey, I don't give a damn who knows we're lovers."

Deborah saw the light in the pool house from where she stood on the back patio. Soft, shimmering light. Candles? Had Ashe found the candles left over from the last pool party they'd given back in the summer, the one for her mother's garden club friends?

She straightened her green satin robe, readjusted the quilted lapels and tightened the sash belt. She told herself not to be nervous, that she had no reason to be. After all, it wasn't as if she were a seventeen-year-old virgin.

Who was she kidding? She might not be a totally inexperienced teenager, but she was hardly accustomed to late night rendezvous in the pool house with a virile, amorous lover. She couldn't believe she was actually going to do this. But then she had never dreamed that she and Ashe would become lovers. Truly lovers.

She walked slowly toward the pool house, her

heart hammering, her nerves quivering, her body filled with anticipation. Music met her as she hesitated in the doorway. An instrumental version of ''The Shadow of Your Smile'' surrounded her. Apparently he'd found the tape player and the stack of her mother's favorite tunes on cassettes. He stood inside waiting for her, two glasses of wine in his hand. He held out one to her when she entered the small octagon-shaped shelter, centered directly behind the swimming pool.

Ashe had changed into a pair of faded jeans and a zippered fleece jacket. He looked incredible. All muscle and firm flesh, tanned and lean and waiting for her.

She accepted the wine. He nodded toward the padded poolside chaise longue that had been stored for the winter. Seating herself, she glanced around inside the twelve-by-twelve-foot room. A dozen fat pink and yellow candles, half consumed on a previous occasion, circled the inner perimeter, casting a mellow, romantic glow over the room.

''To the most beautiful woman in the world.'' Ashe saluted her with his glass.

Her smile wavered, but she managed to keep it in place after she took a sip of the white wine. ''You're beautiful, too, you know. You always were. The most beautiful boy, the most beautiful man. I never could see anyone else except you.''

Hurriedly she downed the remainder of the wine.

The tune changed to "What Are You Doing for the Rest of Your Life?" She'd heard her mother hum these old tunes for as long as she could remember. They were such romantic songs, meant to be shared by lovers.

Ashe took her empty glass. "Want a refill?"

"No." She looked up at him. "I don't dare drink any more. I'm already drunk from just looking at you."

He set their glasses on a small round glass and metal table, then took Deborah's hands and lifted her to her feet. Drawing her into his arms, he rubbed his cheek against hers and danced her slowly around the room.

"You don't have any idea what your honesty does to me, do you?" He caught her open mouth before she could reply, thrusting his tongue inside, loving the taste of the wine that lingered in her mouth.

When he ended the kiss, he smiled when he saw her face. Eyes closed, face flushed, she was so beautiful it tore at his heart to look at her. "I can't believe how much I want you."

"Oh, Ashe, I never dreamed this could happen, that you and I… But it's real, isn't it? We're here, together. Lovers."

"Lovers, in every sense of the word." Reaching down, he loosened her sash belt until her robe fell open. Seeing that she was naked beneath the green satin, he swallowed hard. "My God, Deborah!"

Her shaky fingers grasped the metal pull on his jacket zipper and opened the hooded blue sweatshirt. She laid her hand on his chest. He covered her hand with his.

"I don't really know anything about this. I don't have any experience. Teach me, Ashe. Show me what you want."

"Take off my jacket," he said.

She obeyed, sliding it off his shoulders and tossing it on the floor. "Now what?"

"Remove my jeans."

Without hesitation, she unsnapped, unzipped and tugged off his jeans. He kicked his shoes off and to one side, then spread the satin robe away from her body, allowing it to fall to her feet.

They stood, only inches separating them, naked and unashamed, passion wild within them both. He took her hands in his, lifted them for a kiss, then placed them on his chest before lifting her in his arms.

Ashe was magnificent. Big, tall and lean. He carried her back to the chaise, but set her on her feet.

"Night before last we were so hungry for each other, we didn't take the time to savor the moment. Not the first time nor the second time. Tonight, I want to learn every inch of your body, and I want you to know every inch of mine."

"Whatever you want, Ashe." She moved closer, her breasts brushing against his hair-rough chest. She gulped down a sigh as shivers of pleasure shimmied through her.

"No, honey. Whatever you want." He cupped her buttocks, bringing her completely up against him, letting her feel his arousal, telling her, even without words, how much he wanted her.

"I just want you, Ashe." She slid her hands up his chest and around his neck. "I just want you."

He kissed her until she was breathless, then he painted a trail of warm, moist kisses across her shoulder and down to one breast. All the while he caressed her hip with his other hand. She quivered, then cried out when he suckled her breast. Her knees weakened. He stayed at her breast long enough to have her panting, then knelt on bended knee and delved his tongue into her navel at the precise moment his fingers found the soft inner folds of her body. Her knees gave way and she would have fallen if she hadn't caught Ashe by the shoulders, bracing herself.

He covered her stomach in kisses, then moved back and forth from one thigh to the other, kissing, licking, nipping her tender flesh. She moaned with the pleasure, shivering as she dug her nails into his shoulders.

Lifting her, he laid her on the chaise and came

down over her, one knee resting on the side of the cushion, his other foot on the floor.

"Touch me, Deborah. Feel me."

She sucked in a deep breath, then began a timid exploration of his chest and belly. Garnering her courage and enticed by his glorious body, she ran her fingers over his hardness. He groaned, but she knew the sound was one of pleasure and not pain. She circled him. He covered her hand, teaching her the movements that pleased him. But as quickly as he'd instructed her, he pulled her hand away and laid it on his hip.

"I can't take much of that, honey."

Lowering his head, he captured her nipple in his mouth, teasing it, then sucking greedily. She arched her back up off the chaise. He delved his fingers between her satiny folds, finding her most sensitive spot. She writhed beneath him as he fondled her. Within minutes she shuddered and he swallowed her cries of completion in a tongue-thrusting kiss. As the last wave of pleasure shook her, Ashe lifted her hips and entered her. One sure, swift move that joined their bodies and began the mating dance.

Slowly. Precisely. In and out. Hands roamed. Lips kissed. Bodies united in pleasure. Soon the rhythm changed, the waltz became a wild fandango. Slow. Quick. Slow. Quick. Deborah clung to Ashe as the tension in her body mounted. He thrust into her harder and faster, sweat forming on his body.

She called his name over and over again as her pleasure climbed upward, closer and closer to the apex. Ashe's movements became frantic, his need for this woman growing hotter and hotter.

She cried out in the moment of release, spiraling out of control and into oblivion. Ashe thrust once, twice more, and followed her over the precipice. His own hardy male cry blended with her feminine ones, their breaths ragged, their bodies coated with perspiration.

Ashe maneuvered Deborah so that they fit together on the chaise, their bodies stuck together with the moisture of their lovemaking.

"We're going to stay here all night," he told her.

"Yes. I know." She kissed him, taking the initiative, smothering him with all the passion she'd buried deep within her eleven years ago when he had walked out of her life.

But he was back and for however long Ashe McLaughlin stayed in her life, she planned to be his lover. Maybe nothing lasted forever. Maybe they didn't have a future. But for tonight, she would pretend. Tomorrow was a million miles away. Nothing mattered tonight, nothing except loving and being loved by Ashe.

Deborah opened the door to her bedroom. Ashe circled her waist with his arm, pulling her back against his chest, nuzzling her neck with his nose.

"Get in your room. It's nearly six. Mother will be up and about soon," Deborah said, but turned in his arms, kissing him.

He shoved her away, turned her around and swatted her behind. "See you downstairs for breakfast in about an hour."

Deborah stood in the open doorway, watching until Ashe disappeared down the hall and into his room. Smiling, she walked into her sitting room, humming "Goin' Out of My Head," the tune that had been playing on the cassette when she and Ashe had made love right before returning to the house.

"Good morning," Carol Vaughn said.

Deborah came fully alert, stared across the room and saw her mother perched on the edge of the window seat. "Mother!"

"Come in and close the door. I think we need to have a little talk, don't you?"

"How long have you been waiting in here?" Deborah closed the door and walked across the room, sitting down beside her mother.

"Only a few minutes." Carol took Deborah's hand. "I awoke early. I'd had a difficult time sleeping all night. The sedatives don't last very long. I walked around and just happened to stop by the windows and saw light coming from the pool house. I checked your room and found it empty, then I knocked on Ashe's door. Mr. Roarke heard me and came out to see what was going on.''

"Did you tell Roarke that Ashe and I were missing?"

"I told him that y'all had obviously spent the night in the pool house," Carol said. "I rather think I embarrassed the man."

"Oh, Mother, really."

"I was awake and heard the two of you on the stairs, so I came over here to wait for you."

"I'm a big girl now. I don't need your approval to spend the night with a man."

"No, of course you don't." Carol patted Deborah's hand, then released it. "But if you and Ashe have begun an affair, then I can't help being concerned. For you and for Allen."

"Mother, I—"

"Shh. I deliberately brought Ashe back here because I knew you'd never gotten over him, that there had been no one else." Glancing down at her hands, Carol twisted her diamond ring and her gold wedding band about on her finger. "I admit I played God in your life, but I want you to be happy."

"I'm glad Ashe came back into my life. We've cleared up several misconceptions we had concerning each other."

"He told you what your father did, didn't he?"

"Yes, he told me."

"Deborah, your father thought he was doing the best thing for you. I disagreed, but you know how your father was. He wouldn't listen to me."

"I don't blame you, Mother. I don't even blame Daddy." Deborah hugged Carol. "It's all right. Really it is. We can't change what happened. Besides, I'm the one who has kept Allen's parentage a secret. I could have gotten in touch with Ashe at any time and we both know it."

No, Deborah blamed no one except herself. If she had been a little older and less dependent on her parents, she never would have agreed to her father's plan to send her and her mother away to Europe for the last few months of Deborah's pregnancy. A chubby girl who had been able to disguise her pregnant state with loose, baggy clothes, even at six months, Deborah hadn't had a problem keeping her pregnancy a secret. And once they had returned to Sheffield with Allen, no one had dared to openly question his parentage.

"I lied to Mattie," Carol said. "She asked me once, when Allen was just a baby, if he was your child. Yours and Ashe's."

"You never told me that she suspected Allen wasn't yours and Daddy's."

"I lied to her. I convinced her that her suspicions were wrong. She never questioned me again."

"If she'd known, she would have told Ashe."

"She does know, Deborah." Carol kept her eyes downcast. "I told her the truth when I asked her for Ashe's telephone number in Atlanta."

"Mother!"

Carol's chin quivered as she looked directly at her daughter. "She has promised not to tell Ashe, to give you time to tell him the truth." Carol clutched Deborah's hand. "You must tell Ashe. You can't keep putting it off, not now the two of you are lovers."

"Mother, I'm not sure telling Ashe would be the best thing to do, under the circumstances."

"What circumstances?"

"Ashe and I have made each other no promises. He hasn't committed himself to me for any longer than his business here will take. Once I'm no longer in danger, he's going back to Atlanta."

"I see."

"If I tell him about Allen, I have no idea what he might do. He could tell Allen. He could demand joint custody. Or he could make a commitment to me because of Allen and not because he loves me." Jumping up off the window seat, Deborah walked around the room. She stopped abruptly, then turned to face her mother. "I'm afraid to tell him. I'm afraid I'll lose him all over again."

"Deborah, dear child, you musn't—"

"I know. I know. I'm not fooling myself. It's

just that I want whatever time we have together to go on being as wonderful as it was tonight.''

"You must tell the man he has a son." Carol shook her head. "You can't lie to Ashe if you love him."

"I didn't say I loved him."

"You didn't have to. I see it in your eyes. I hear it in your voice."

"I can't tell him. Not yet."

"I go back to the doctor for a checkup and more tests soon," Carol said. "If you haven't told Ashe by then—"

"No, Mother, you musn't tell him."

"Then you tell him. We should have told him long ago. Besides, if you don't tell him before he leaves Sheffield, Mattie will tell him."

"But what if he tells Allen?"

Carol stood, walked across the room and laid her hand on Deborah's shoulder. "Ashe isn't going to do anything to hurt Allen. Don't you know him any better than that?"

"Give me some time, Mother. Please, just let me do this my way and in my own good time."

"Don't wait too long. My heart tells me that you'll be sorry if you do."

Ashe came out of the shower, dried off and stepped into a pair of clean briefs. He didn't know when he'd ever felt so good, so glad to be alive.

Deborah. Sweet, beautiful Deborah.

She was, in so many ways, the same innocent, loving girl she'd been eleven years ago; but then she was also a woman of strength and courage and incredible passion.

Whoever she was, part innocent girl, part bewitching woman, Deborah Vaughn was honest and trustworthy. She would never lie to him. Never!

He had tried to put Roarke's suspicions out of his mind, and for those magic hours he'd spent with Deborah he'd been able to do just that. But now he had to face them again.

There was no way Allen Vaughn could be his son. Deborah would have told him if she'd been pregnant. She'd have come running to him. She'd been so crazy in love with him that she would have…

She would have come to him after he'd rejected her, after he'd told her that he didn't love her the way she loved him?

Allen isn't your son, he told himself. He looks just like Deborah. He's her brother, dammit. Her brother!

Besides, Mama Mattie would have told him if she'd thought Allen was his child.

Don't do this to yourself! Don't look for similarities between you and Allen. Don't let Roarke's outrageous suspicions spoil what you and Deborah have found together this time.

Miss Carol never would have dared you to come back to Sheffield and face the past if Allen was your son.

Ashe dressed hurriedly, then rushed downstairs, eager to see Deborah again. He would not look at Allen Vaughn and search for a truth that didn't exist. He trusted Deborah. His heart told him she wouldn't lie to him. And just this once, he intended to listen to his heart.

Chapter 11

The trial had lasted eight days, everyone saying the case was pretty well cut and dried since the prosecution had a reliable eyewitness to the murder. After three and a half hours of deliberation, the jury had rendered a guilty verdict, surprising no one. Five days later, the judge had sentenced Lon Sparks to life in prison, and Deborah Vaughn had been free from threats and harassment for nearly two weeks.

Ashe had been waiting for Buck Stansell to strike, but nothing had happened, not even a wrong number telephone call. He'd thought about paying Buck a visit, but decided against it. Why take a chance on stirring a hornet's nest? He had talked to his cousin Lee Roy, who'd said little, except that *people* weren't overly concerned with an insignificant guy like Lon Sparks, that the man wasn't worth enough to cause trouble over.

Roarke had suggested it might be time to think about returning to Atlanta, but Ashe kept putting him off. How could he take a chance on leaving Deborah undefended? She'd come to mean far more to him than she should. He had allowed himself to become too involved with her, with Allen and Miss Carol. This was a job, but not like any other. These were people he cared about, a family he'd started thinking of as his.

Maybe he had reached the age when he needed to settle down, to start considering marriage and children. He wasn't sure. He and Deborah were attracted to each other, always had been, although he'd fought that attraction when they'd been younger. Maybe somewhere deep down inside him, he'd always thought he wasn't quite good enough for Deborah. Not just because her parents were wealthy and socially prominent and he'd come from white trash hoodlums, but because he'd never been innocent or pure or good, and Deborah had been all those things. Even now, at twenty-eight, she still personified everything right with the world.

And he still wasn't good enough for her.

Ashe paced the floor in the doctor's office, waiting for Deborah and Miss Carol. He'd told himself that he would hang around Sheffield until they knew the test results. It was as good an excuse as any. This way he could justify his reluctance to leave, to Deborah and her family, as well as to himself.

Sitting, he flipped through several magazines, then stood and paced the floor again. He glanced at the wall clock, checking it against his watch. Nearly an hour. Dammit, how long did it take for a doctor to explain test results?

Just when his patience came to an end, Deborah and Miss Carol emerged from the office, solemn expressions on their faces. Deborah's arm draped her mother's slender shoulders.

"We're ready to go home, now, Ashe," Deborah said.

Ashe didn't ask any questions, didn't say a word, simply nodded his head and led the ladies outside and assisted them into the car.

Miss Carol, sitting in the front seat beside Ashe, reached over and touched his arm lightly. "Can you stay awhile longer?"

"Yes, ma'am, of course I can stay." He pulled the car out of the parking lot and onto the main thoroughfare.

"Deborah and Allen will need you," Carol said.

"Mother, please don't—" Deborah said.

"Hush up." Carol swatted her hand in the air. "Ashe is like family and I want him here. Even if you think you can handle this alone, I believe you'll need a strong man at your side."

"I take it the tests results weren't good." Ashe kept his gaze fixed straight ahead.

"The cancer has returned and Dr. Mason has scheduled surgery for the first of next week." Carol opened her purse, took out a lace handkerchief and wiped her hands, then returned the handkerchief to her purse.

"I'm sorry, Miss Carol."

"No need for all this gloom and doom." Carol sat up straight, squaring her shoulders as if preparing herself to do battle. "I licked this thing once and I can do it again. But I'll rest easier knowing Deborah won't be alone, that you'll be at her side."

"You hired me, Miss Carol. I won't leave Sheffield as long as you need me."

"Thank you, Ashe." She patted him on the arm.

Little more was said on the short drive home. Indeed, what more could be said? Ashe wondered. Life certainly didn't play fair. Not when it heaped more trouble on one family than it could bear. But then, Deborah and Miss Carol were both strong women. They were fighters despite their genteel backgrounds.

Sirens blasted, shrill and menacing in the quite, lazy atmosphere of Sheffield's main street.

"Oh, my." Carol shivered. "I do so hate the sound of those things. Sirens always mean bad news."

"Look at that black smoke," Deborah said. "It's coming straight up Montgomery Avenue."

"My goodness, you don't suppose it's one of our neighbors' homes, do you?" Miss Carol leaned toward the windshield, her gaze riveted to the billowing smoke filling the blue sky.

The closer they came to home, the darker the smoke, the louder the sirens. A sudden sick feeling hit Ashe in the pit of his stomach. Allen was still at school. Roarke would be with him. Ashe blew out a breath.

Before they reached the Vaughn driveway, they saw one fire truck parked at the back of the house and another just turning in behind it. "It's our garage!" Deborah gripped the back of her mother's seat. "It's on fire!"

Ashe pulled the Cadillac up to the curb, stopped and jumped out. "Stay here." He ran across the front yard.

"Stay in the car, Mother. I'll come back and check on you in just a few minutes."

"But Ashe said for both of us to stay here," Carol said.

"Ashe isn't my boss."

Deborah jumped out of the car, catching up with Ashe at the back corner of the house, where he stood watching the firemen do their job. He grabbed her around the waist, pulling her to his side.

"It's just the garage," he said. "And it looks like they're getting the fire under control."

"Mazie? Where's Mazie? Is she all right?"

"She's at the grocery store. Remember? This is Wednesday morning, her midweek trip to pick up supplies."

"Oh, yes, of course."

Deborah leaned against Ashe, watching while the firefighters extinguished the blaze, leaving a charred three-car garage, a blackened Mercedes, a soot-covered BMW and swirling clouds of gray smoke spiraling heavenward.

Fire Chief Greg Wilbanks nodded, removed his hat and wiped his face with the back of his hand. "Damn curious blaze. Whoever set this baby didn't try to hide the fact that it was out-and-out arson."

"What do you mean?" Deborah asked.

"The place was doused with gasoline and torched. We found two empty gas cans at the back of the house." Greg looked at Ashe. "I've called Chief Burton. I'd say your job isn't finished, Mr. McLaughlin. Looks like somebody's out to get himself a little revenge."

"Ashe?" Deborah grabbed his arm. "Do you think that—"

"I don't think anything," he said.

"But Greg said—"

"I know what he said. There's no point jumping to conclusions. We'll take every precaution, but we're not going to panic.'' He grasped her by the shoulders. ''Go tell Miss Carol that everything's all right. The fire's out. Tell her the truth, but play it down. There's no need to worry her any more than can be helped.''

''You're right.'' She slipped her arms around Ashe's waist and sighed when he hugged her close. Pulling away, she tried to smile. ''I'll take Mother in the front door. There's no need for her to see this until later.''

''Don't read anything into this,'' Ashe said. ''Not yet. Let me handle things. I'm not going anywhere, not until you're completely out of danger. Trust me, honey.''

''I do trust you. With all my heart.''

Ashe watched her walk away, a tight knot forming in the pit of his stomach. She expected a great deal from him. Was it more than he could deliver? Would he let her down again, or could he be the man Deborah wanted and needed?

Ashe approached Greg Wilbanks. ''When Chief Burton arrives, tell him I'd prefer he not bother Miss Carol or Deborah. I'll talk to him. And once you've filed your report on this fire, I'd like a copy.''

''As Miss Carol's representative?'' Greg asked.

''Yeah, as Miss Carol's representative.''

''No problem.''

Going in the back door, Ashe met Carol and Deborah in the hallway.

"I'm taking Mother upstairs to rest," Deborah told him, then turned to assist her mother. "I'll fix you some tea and bring it up in just a little while."

"Tea would be nice." Halting on the landing, Carol grabbed Deborah's arm. "Let him do whatever he has to do to put an end to this."

"Mother, what are saying?"

"I'm saying that Ashe knows how to deal with those people. However he chooses to handle the situation, I don't want you trying to persuade him otherwise."

"Ashe is not a hired assassin, Mother. He's not going to kill Buck Stansell."

"You two go on," Ashe called out from the downstairs hallway. "I'll fix you both some tea and bring it up."

"Thank you," Miss Carol smiled.

"Mother!" Deborah glared at Carol. "Do you honestly think Ashe would murder someone?"

"Not murder, my dear, kill. There is a difference. And Ashe McLaughlin has been trained to kill. There is no doubt in my mind that he would kill anyone who'd harm you."

"I don't want him to have to kill to protect me, but… Perhaps Buck Stansell wasn't responsible for the fire. Besides, no one was harmed."

Downstairs, Ashe put on the water to boil, set

two cups on a tray and laid two Earl Grey tea bags in each cup. Lifting the phone out of the wall cradle, he dialed Roarke's cellular phone number.

"Roarke, here."

"Keep a very close eye on Allen."

"What's wrong?"

"We've had a fire here," Ashe said. "Someone doused the garage with gasoline. They left the cans for the firemen to find."

"Looks like we'll be hanging around Sheffield for a while longer than we thought."

"Yeah. I'd say Buck Stansell is back to playing games with us. The question is just how deadly will his games become."

Deborah took care of her morning phone calls, dictated several letters and closed a deal on the old Hartman farm before her ten-thirty coffee break. She had wanted to stay home with her mother, whom she worried would fret the day away there at the house with only Mazie, the eternal pessimist, as company. But her mother had insisted she didn't need a baby-sitter, so Deborah had found an alternative plan.

She glanced in the outer office where Ashe sat with his long legs stretched out, his big feet propped up on a desk in the corner, situated where he could see directly into Deborah's office. He had begun work on his second crossword puzzle book since his arrival in Sheffield.

Deborah dialed the telephone, hoping her plan for keeping her mother occupied would work out.

"Hello."

"Mama Mattie," Deborah said. "I have a favor to ask of you."

"What is it, child?"

"Mother's at the house all alone with Mazie, and I'm afraid, after the doctor's news and the fire in the garage yesterday, she'll spend the day fretting."

"You need say no more. I've just baked an apple cinnamon coffee cake. I'll take it over and spend the rest of the day with Miss Carol."

"Thanks so much, Mama Mattie."

"It'll be my pleasure." Deborah hung up the phone and glanced back at Ashe, who looked up from his puzzle and grinned at her. She lifted her hand to her mouth in a drinking gesture. Ashe nodded agreement. They met at the coffeepot, one of three set up on a table in a small, open room directly across from the office rest room.

"Good morning." Holding a mug of hot coffee in one hand, he cupped her hip with the other and brought her close enough for him to kiss.

She returned the kiss, then pulled away, turning to pour her coffee. "Get your hand off my hip, Mr. McLaughlin. This is an office, not a bedroom," she teased.

"I'm glad you told me," he said. "I was planning on backing you up against the wall over there and ravishing you. But since this is an office, I don't suppose ravishing the boss lady is allowed."

"Most definitely not."

"You've had a busy morning."

"I've accomplished a great deal."

They carried their coffee back into the outer office, pausing just outside Deborah's private domain.

"Ashe, have there been any threatening phone calls or a letter today?" she asked.

"No, honey, not a one."

"I'd thought that since…well since the fire yesterday, the harassment might start all over again."

He nudged her through her office door. "There may not be a connection. But…" He didn't want to alarm her.

"But what?"

"If Buck Stansell was behind yesterday's fire, I'd say phone calls and letters are a thing of the past. Simple harassment will no longer be the order of the day."

"I see. You're saying things will get nasty."

"They could."

"Do you think Allen and Mother are in danger?"

"Possibly."

"Oh, Ashe." The coffee sloshed over the edge of her mug. Quickly holding the mug outward so the liquid could run down the sides, she averted being burned.

Just as Ashe started to close the door to Deborah's office, a string of loud, piercing blasts sounded. The front office windows shattered. Glass blew across the room. The office staff screamed and dived for cover under their desks. Ashe knocked Deborah to the floor, covering her body with his as he drew his gun.

"Crawl to the left," he told her.

She obeyed silently, not questioning Ashe's order for one minute. Standing, he lifted her to her knees and sat her in the corner behind a row of metal file cabinets.

"Stay put."

She nodded. He made his way to the outer office where he found the staff in hiding. The front of the office wall consisted of a line of long windows, all of which had been destroyed by a barrage of bullets.

Annie Laurie looked up from beneath her desk, her eyes wide with fright. "Ashe? Oh, my God, what happened?"

"Everyone stay put," Ashe said.

Cracking his office door a fraction, Neil Posey peered outside. "Is everyone all right?" he asked. "Is Annie Laurie okay? Was Deborah hurt?"

"As far as I know the only damage is to the windows," Ashe said as he made his way to the bullet-riddled front door. He walked out onto the sidewalk. People were staring at him and at the Vaughn & Posey building. In the distance he heard a police siren and knew, the police station being only a few blocks away, the authorities would arrive at any moment. Returning inside, he made his way toward Deborah's office.

"It's all right," Ashe said. "Whoever did all this damage is long gone."

One by one the staff of Vaughn & Posey emerged from under their desks.

Neil opened his office door. "Annie Laurie, are you sure you're all right?"

"I'm fine, Mr. Posey. Just scared to death."

Ashe found Deborah still sitting in the corner behind the filing cabinets. She stared up at him, her eyes dry, her face pale.

"It's okay, honey." Reaching down, he lifted her to her feet. She shook uncontrollably. "Deborah?"

She clung to him, her trembling growing worse. "Was anyone hurt?"

"Everybody's fine. Nothing's hurt but the building."

"I can't let the people who work for me be at risk because of me."

Ashe stroked her back, trying to soothe her. "You can't blame yourself for this."

"Yes, I can. And I do. I'm Buck Stansell's target. If I hadn't been here at the office, then he wouldn't have sent someone *here* to shoot up the place."

"Don't start blaming yourself for something that isn't your fault." Dammit, she was shaking like a leaf. He wasn't getting through to her.

He grabbed her by the shoulders and shook her soundly. She glared at him, then nodded her head. Ashe pulled her back into his arms, and that's how the police chief found them.

"Deborah, Chief Burton is here," Annie Laurie called out from the doorway.

Deborah turned in Ashe's arms, but made no move away from him. He kept his arms tightly around her.

"They sure as hell made a mess of things," Chief Burton said. "A couple of witnesses across the street said they saw one man drive by real slow, coming to a stop right out front before he pulled out what they thought looked like some sort of automatic weapon. Of course, they can't identify the weapon. Said it happened too fast. He was driving a new Chevy."

"The car was probably stolen," Ashe said.

"Could've been. Anyway, I just wanted to ask if either of you saw anything that could help us."

"No," Ashe said. "We didn't see anything."

"Nobody in the office seemed to have seen a thing. Just heard the shooting." The police chief looked directly at Deborah. "Ms. Vaughn, you might want to think about staying at home for a few days, that is, unless you plan on closing down the business."

"No, I do not plan on closing Vaughn & Posey." She stiffened her spine. Sliding his hand up and around, Ashe caressed her back, then placed his arm around her shoulders. "However, I will consider staying at home. I don't want to put my employees' lives at risk."

"I'm taking Ms. Vaughn home, now," Ashe said. "If you need to question us further, you'll know where to find us."

"Fine," Chief Burton said. "I don't think we'll need either of you any more today."

"I need to make arrangements to have the building cleaned and repair work started immediately." Deborah allowed Ashe to lead her across the shattered glass and splintered wood covering the outer office floor.

She stopped at Annie Laurie's desk; the two women hugged each other. Deborah turned to face her employees. "I'm sorry this had to happen. I'm so relieved no one was injured." She glanced over at Neil, whose round, normally pink face was a pale gray. "Let everyone go home for the rest of the day. I'll have someone come in and clean up. Rearrange things so work can continue tomorrow.

Make use of my office. I'll be working at home. Temporarily.''

"Certainly, Deborah. We'll carry on," Neil said.

Ashe hurried her outside and into her car. "Just hang on, honey. I'll take you home.''

"I dread telling Mother, but I have no choice. You know someone may have already called her.''

"Miss Carol will handle this okay. She's a strong woman, just like her daughter.''

When they arrived at the Vaughn home, they found Mattie Trotter waiting on the front porch. The minute Deborah approached her, she opened her arms.

Going into Mattie's arms, Deborah sighed. "Oh, Mama Mattie, this has become a nightmare. I thought it was over, that the worst had been Huckleberry's poisoning.''

"It'll be all right," Mattie said, glancing over Deborah's shoulder at Ashe. "Ashe isn't going to let anything happen to you.''

"Someone called already, didn't they?" Deborah asked. "Mother knows.''

"Miss Carol is fine. She's lying down in the library, taking a little nap." Mattie winked at Deborah as she slipped her arm around her waist and led her inside. "I put a few drops of brandy in her tea.''

"Where's Mazie?" Deborah looked around in

the hallway. "I can't believe she's not out here foretelling the end of the world for us all."

"I sent that silly woman to town on an errand," Mattie said. "I had to get her out of the house. She was driving me crazy and upsetting Miss Carol. She should be gone a couple of hours. And Allen won't be home from school until after three."

"Thanks." Deborah swayed, her head spinning. Mama Mattie motioned to Ashe, who lifted Deborah in his arms.

"Put me down!"

"Take her on upstairs and tend to her." Mattie pointed to the closed library door. "I'll go sit with Miss Carol and finish reading that new Grisham book. If we need y'all, I'll let you know."

Ashe carried Deborah up the stairs and into her sitting room, but didn't put her down. With her arms around his neck, she stared into his eyes and knew he was going to kiss her. She didn't resist, indeed she welcomed the kiss, needing it desperately. Quick. Hard. And possessive. Deborah sighed.

He carried her over to the window bench and sat down, placing her in his lap. She laid her head on his shoulder.

"Do you want a drink?" he asked. She shook her head from side to side. "A bath?" Another negative shake. "A nap?"

"All I want is for you to hold me," she said, clinging to him.

He hugged her fiercely. "Nobody was hurt."

"This time. But what about the next time or the time after that? You can't guarantee me that some innocent person won't be harmed because of me."

"Not because of you, honey! Dammit, why do you insist on blaming yourself?"

"Maybe I should go away. Far away. That way the people I love would be safe."

"Not necessarily," Ashe said. "Running away isn't the answer if Buck Stansell is out for revenge. If you leave town, he might target Miss Carol or Allen."

"Oh, God, Ashe, Mother has enough to deal with already." Deborah grasped the lapels of Ashe's jacket. "Promise me that you won't let anything happen to Allen."

"I won't let anything happen to Allen." He kissed her forehead, then smoothed the loose strands of her hair away from her face. "You love Allen a great deal, don't you?"

"He's the most important person in the world to me. I—I... He's just a little boy."

Ashe caressed Deborah's face, cupping her cheek in his palm. "I'll take care of you and Allen. And Miss Carol."

Gulping in air, Deborah looked at Ashe pleadingly. She needed him, needed his tender loving care, needed his strength, his power.

He stood with her in his arms and carried her into the bedroom, laying her on her bed. He came down over her, turning her to one side as he eased his body onto the bed. Facing her, he removed her jacket, then unbuttoned her blouse. Slowly, carefully, stroking and caressing her as he uncovered more and more of her body, Ashe undressed her completely.

She was a bundle of nerves, her emotions raw. She needed soothing, needed to forget, at least for a few hours, the nightmare her life had become. He hated the feeling of helplessness, knowing he hadn't been able to prevent the drive-by shooting at her office. But he could give her the reassurance and care she needed now. And soon, very soon, he would have to confront her enemy.

Ashe made love to her with his hands and mouth, whispering endearing words of comfort and admiration. Never before had he felt so totally possessive about a woman, wanting her and her alone in a way that bordered on obsession. How had this happened? When had Deborah become the focal point of his existence?

Every touch, every word was meant for her pleasure, but with each touch, each kiss, each heated word, he became lost in the fury of a passion over which he was fast losing control.

He caressed her breasts, loving the way her tight nipples felt beneath his fingertips, loving her hot little cries. He kissed her inner thighs. She sighed, squirming when his tongue turned inward for further exploration.

She moaned and writhed, her body straining for release as Ashe pleasured her, his lips and fingers masterful in their ministrations, bringing her to the very brink, then pausing, only to return her to that moment just before satisfaction.

She cried out, begging him not to prolong the agony, clinging to him, pleading for fulfillment. His words grew more erotic, more suggestive, as he carried her to the edge. With one final stroke of his tongue, he flung her into ecstasy.

Covering her mouth in a heated kiss, he devoured her cries of pleasure. Pulling her close, he reached down and lifted the hand-crocheted afghan and covered her. He lay there holding her while she dozed off to sleep and the noonday sun began its western descent.

His heart beat like a racing stallion. Sweat coated his body. He ached with the need for release. But this time had been for Deborah, not for him. She had needed the powerful fulfillment, and what Deborah needed was far more important to him than what he needed.

When Ashe had sent Buck Stansell a warning, declaring Deborah Vaughn his personal property, it had been a ruse. Now it was a fact. If he had to destroy Buck Stansell to keep Deborah safe, he'd do it. No one was going to harm his woman.

Chapter 12

Deborah set up a temporary office in the library, moving in a computer and borrowing Annie Laurie for the first day. She would do whatever was necessary to protect her employees. That might mean staying away from Vaughn & Posey for a few weeks, but it also meant business as usual. Too many people depended upon the real estate firm for their livelihoods, including Deborah's family. She had no idea whether or not Whitney had any money left in her trust fund, but she doubted it. Not after nearly eleven years of marriage to George Jamison. That meant Whitney, too, depended upon revenue from Vaughn & Posey to keep her and her worthless husband from bankruptcy.

Ashe McLaughlin's return to Sheffield was a mixed blessing. He and Roarke guarded the family night and day. Anyone wanting to harm her or Allen or her mother would have to go through two highly trained professionals. But her personal relationship with Ashe had her confused and uncertain.

She could not deny that she was in love with him. Always had been. Always would be. But the lie about Allen stood between them as surely as Ashe's inability to make a commitment. If she knew Ashe loved her, if she knew he wanted to spend the rest of his life with her, telling Ashe the truth about Allen would not be as difficult. But he hadn't said he loved her and certainly had made her no promises beyond defending her with his life.

"Where do these go?" Ashe stood in the doorway, a stack of file folders in his arms.

"What are those?" she asked.

"They're printouts of all your current files on your present listings." Annie Laurie scurried past Ashe, dragging a swivel desk chair behind her.

Deborah smiled at Ashe; he returned her smile. She couldn't stop looking at him, couldn't stop remembering how it felt when they made love. She was as giddy and light-headed as a teenager in love for the first time. And the crazy thing was she honestly thought Ashe was acting the same way.

He looked incredible this afternoon, but then he always did. Tall, muscular and lean. Gray slacks. Navy blue jacket. Light blue shirt, worn unbuttoned and without a tie. She could see the top curls of dark hair above his open shirt.

They hadn't made love since yesterday and she ached to be with him.

Annie Laurie cleared her throat. "We could take a break. It's after one and we haven't stopped for lunch."

"Good idea." Ashe laid the file folders to the left of the computer atop the antique mahogany desk. "Why don't you two do whatever it is you need to do and I'll tell Mazie we're ready for some of her famous chili. I've been smelling the stuff for hours now."

"Check on Mother, will you?" Deborah asked. "She's been busy all morning working on that cross-stitch piece she wants to finish before she goes in the hospital."

"I'll see if she wants to join us for lunch or have something in her room," Ashe said.

Deborah looked around the library and wondered if it would ever return to normal once she went back to Vaughn & Posey's downtown office. Together she and Annie Laurie had managed to keep everything fairly neat, but office clutter had certainly changed the charming old room's atmosphere.

Deborah fell into the huge, tufted leather chair behind the desk. Her father's desk. Her grandfather's desk.

"So, Neil finally came to his senses and asked you out." Folding her arms behind her, Deborah placed her hands at the back of her head and stretched. "You'll need to leave here early enough to go home and change and—"

"It really isn't a date, Deborah. We're just having dinner and Neil is going to help me study. If I can't pass the test, I'll never become a Realtor. There is no need for me to leave early. Neil's picking me up here after work."

"Neil could have helped you study without taking you out for dinner," Deborah said. "My goodness, Annie Laurie, give the man a little encouragement. I think everyone, except Neil, knows how you feel about him."

"I can hardly throw myself at Neil when he's in love with you." Annie Laurie plopped herself down in the swivel chair she'd placed at the edge of the desk.

"Neil is not in love with me. It's just that he's had a sort of crush on me for years. I've made it perfectly clear that we can never be more than friends."

"I guess none of us can help who we love, can we? I'm in love with Neil, he's in love with you and you're in love with Ashe."

"I see you have this all figured out." In Annie Laurie's version of their love lives, they were beginning to sound like a modern day Southern ver-

sion of *A Midsummer Night's Dream.* "But if actions speak louder than words, as Mama Mattie
says, then I'd say you're the woman Neil cares for
the most. After all, I'm not the one he checked on
first yesterday after the gunman's drive-by attack."

"He couldn't have gotten to you without going
through Ashe and Neil certainly would never try to
confront Ashe."

"I'm telling you that if you want Neil, you're
going to have to let him know. And I mean in no
uncertain terms. Seduce the man."

Annie Laurie gasped. "Why Deborah Luellen
Vaughn, what sort of advice is that? Are you saying
that if I sleep with Neil, he'll fall madly in love
with me?"

"No. I'm saying he's already in love with you,
but just doesn't know it. Besides, a man Neil's age
isn't going to be seduced unless he wants to be.
And I'm telling you, he's ready for you."

"You and Ashe are having an affair, aren't
you?" Annie Laurie kept her head bowed, but
risked a quick glance in Deborah's direction. "I
know it's none of my business, but you've been a
good friend to me and I don't want to see you get
hurt."

Deborah sighed, then smacked her lips lightly.
"Yes, Ashe and I are having an affair. And I know
only too well that I could wind up getting hurt
again. But I've been in love with him for as long

as I can remember. I've never wanted anyone else.''

''I know exactly how you feel.''

''Then don't wait around. Go get what you want. Neil isn't going anywhere, and take my word for it, you're exactly what Neil needs and what he wants, whether he knows it or not.''

Ashe knocked on the doorpost, announcing his presence. ''Chili is served in the kitchen. Coffee? Tea? Cola?''

''Tea,'' Deborah said.

''I'll go wash up and help Mazie get everything on the table.'' Annie Laurie stood. ''Is Miss Carol joining us?''

''Yes, she said for me to come up and get her when we're ready to eat,'' Ashe said.

''I'll bring her down after I help Mazie.'' Annie Laurie rushed out of the library.

''What's wrong with her?'' Ashe asked.

''I think my advice on her love life upset her.''

''What kind of advice did you give her?''

''I told her to seduce Neil.''

Ashe bellowed with laughter. ''Good God, woman! I'd say you're sending two virgins into uncharted waters. How the hell will they know what to do?''

''I think they'll figure it out.'' When Ashe walked around the desk, Deborah slipped her arms around his neck.

"Annie Laurie and Neil? How long has this been going on? I thought the guy had a thing for you." Ashe pulled her up against him.

"He thinks he has a thing for me. But given the right encouragement, he'll realize Annie Laurie is the only woman for him." Deborah nuzzled the side of Ashe's neck with her nose. "Besides, Annie Laurie's so in love with Neil she can't see straight. A man would have to be a complete fool to reject that kind of love."

The moment she said the words, she wished them back. She tensed in Ashe's arms.

Taking her chin in one hand, he tilted her face. "It's all right, honey. I know you were talking about Neil, but the shoe certainly fit me once, too, didn't it?" He kissed her. Quick. Hard. Passionate. With his forehead resting on hers, he held her close. "I know what a fool I was eleven years ago. I didn't appreciate what I had. I was too young to know what I wanted or needed."

And now? she wanted to ask. Did he know what he wanted and needed now? "We can't change the past. Either of us."

"We aren't a couple of kids anymore, are we, Deborah? We can handle a love affair without either of us getting hurt this time."

"Yes, of course, we can." She nudged him with her hip. "I'm starving. Let's go eat."

*   *   *

Neil arrived at six-thirty, late and haggard, fuming about the workmen Deborah had hired to clear away the rubble from the office and fussing at the price their contractor was charging them to repair the damage.

Deborah tried to soothe his ruffled tail feathers, but he calmed very little, even after Deborah assured him their insurance would cover most of the costs.

She finally shooed Neil and Annie Laurie out of the house, suggesting the perfect restaurant for their dinner. When she and Ashe turned to close the front door, they realized Neil couldn't get his car started.

Getting out of his car, Neil walked back toward the house, leaving Annie Laurie waiting patiently in the car.

''I've been having trouble with the darn thing for weeks now, but haven't had time to take it in for a check-up.''

''Leave it here.'' Deborah and Ashe met Neil on the porch steps. ''Take my Caddy and you two go on for dinner. Keep it for the night. We'll call the garage in the morning and have them come get your car.''

''I couldn't possible take your Cadillac.''

''I insist. I'll go get the keys.''

When she turned to go inside, Ashe grabbed her by the wrist. ''I've got the extra set of keys you gave me.'' He pulled the keys out of his pocket and tossed them to Neil, who caught them, then almost dropped them from his shaky hand.

"I appreciate this," Neil said. "I'll drive safely."

Ashe and Deborah waved goodbye. Arm in arm, they returned inside to spend the evening with Allen, Miss Carol and Roarke, both of them counting the minutes until bedtime when they could meet at the pool house and make love.

Although the company was pleasant, Ashe wished the time would pass more quickly. He had wanted to drag Deborah off to some secluded spot all day. As the minutes ticked away, he grew more and more restless.

Deborah only partially heard most of what was said during and after dinner, her mind was so completely consumed with Ashe. All she could think about was being alone with him, loving and being loved.

There was no other man like Ashe—not for her. She had always been fascinated by him, even when she'd been a young girl. Indeed, she wondered if his years as a Green Beret hadn't enhanced the very basic male drives that had been born a part of him.

They watched each other, their eyes speaking the words they dared not utter in the presence of others. Deborah had no idea a man could make love to a woman without touching her. Ashe McLaughlin could. And did.

She felt herself growing moist and hot, her body responding to his every glance. She checked her watch for the hundredth time, wishing her mother and Allen would go to bed early. Roarke had excused himself thirty minutes earlier to take a walk around the block as he did each night.

The phone call came three hours after dinner. Ashe took the call, saying very little, but Deborah immediately knew something was terribly wrong.

Ashe replaced the receiver, a solemn expression on his face. His gaze met Deborah's; terror seized her.

"What happened?" she asked.

"There's been an accident," he said.

"What sort of accident?" Carol Vaughn glanced at Allen, who had stopped watching television and looked straight at Ashe.

"A car accident. Neil and Annie Laurie. They've been taken to the hospital in Florence." Ashe's gut instincts told him the car wreck had been no accident. Neil had been driving Deborah's car.

"Oh, dear Lord, no!" Miss Carol clutched her hands together.

"They're both alive. That's all I know." Ashe looked at Deborah. "I think we should go to the hospital immediately."

"Yes, of course we should," she said.

"I'll let Roarke know we're leaving." He turned

to Carol. "We'll go by and get Mama Mattie. Pray for them, Miss Carol. Pray for all of us."

Carol nodded, then placed her arm around Allen's shoulders when he started after Ashe and Deborah. "Did somebody do something to Deborah's car? Were they trying to hurt her?" Allen asked.

Ashe halted in the doorway. Deborah rushed over to Allen, pulling him into her arms.

"No, darling, of course not," Deborah kissed Allen's cheek. "Please don't worry about me."

"We don't know what happened," Ashe said. "I'll talk to the police and find out. But Deborah's right. Don't worry about her. I'll take care of her."

Allen hugged Deborah, then released her, waving goodbye as she and Ashe left.

No one, not even Ashe McLaughlin, could make Neil Posey leave Annie Laurie's side, and the doctors allowed him to stay when he told them he was Annie Laurie's fiancé.

When Deborah, Ashe and Mattie Trotter had first arrived at the hospital, Neil had been incoherent, his eyes glazed with tears as he sat holding Annie Laurie's hand. Neil had suffered a few cuts and bruises, but nothing serious. Annie Laurie was unconscious. A concussion, they'd been told. If she came around soon, there should be nothing to

worry about; however, if she remained unconscious…

Hour after hour passed without any change in
Annie Laurie. Mattie Trotter dozed in the big chair
in the corner of the room. Still holding Annie Laurie's hand in his, Neil had laid his head on the side
of her bed.

Easing open the door, Ashe glanced around the
room, saw his grandmother and Neil sleeping and
Deborah looking out the window, watching the
sunrise. He set the cardboard carton containing dis-
posable coffee cups on the meal tray, removed the
lids from two cups, picked them up and walked
over to Deborah.

"Thanks." Deborah took the coffee. "A few
more minutes and you would have found me in the
other chair over there asleep, too."

"Why the hell doesn't she wake up?" Ashe
squeezed the cup he held, pressing a bit of the dark
liquid over the edge and onto his hand. "Damn!
Good thing this stuff isn't very hot."

"I wish we knew exactly what caused the wreck.
I can't believe a careful driver like Neil would have
simply lost control of the car." Deborah sipped her
coffee.

"Thank God they were both wearing their seat
belts. If that pole hadn't crashed through the windshield and sideswiped Annie Laurie on the side of
her head, she'd be okay." Ashe drank half his cup

of coffee, then set the container down on the windowsill.

"I keep wondering what caused the accident. Neil is such a careful driver. He said the brakes didn't work, that coming off the hill on Court Street, he realized he couldn't slow down, couldn't stop."

"I think he probably panicked," Ashe said. "He realized he was going to slam into the back end of the car in front of him and possibly cause a pileup, so he tried to take the car off the road."

"I have my car serviced often. There's no reason the brakes shouldn't have worked." Deborah clutched her coffee cup in both hands.

"We both know there's a good chance someone tampered with your Caddy." Ashe balled his hands into fists. All night he had fought the desire to smash heads together, to run out of the hospital and hunt down Buck Stansell. But he would wait. Wait until he knew for sure.

A tall, skinny nurse walked into the room. Covering her lips with her index finger, she signaled Deborah and Ashe to be quiet. Silently she went about her business, checking on Annie Laurie, then nodding goodbye as she left.

"Are you hungry?" Ashe asked. "We could go down for breakfast soon."

"Let's wait awhile, until Mama Mattie wakes up. She needs some rest."

A soft knock sounded at the door. Ashe walked over and opened the door a fraction. Detective Morrow, from the Florence police, stood in the hallway.

"Could I speak to you, Mr. McLaughlin? The chief said to let you know what we've found out. He's talked to Chief Burton over in Sheffield and also to Sheriff Blaylock. They both said to fill you in."

Ashe stepped into the hallway, closing the door behind him. "Let's have it."

"The wreck wasn't an accident. Ms. Vaughn's Cadillac had been tampered with. There was no brake fluid. It had all leaked out. Looks like somebody intended for Ms. Vaughn to wreck her car."

Deborah stood with the door cracked enough to overhear what the detective said. Biting down on her bottom lip, she closed her eyes and said a silent prayer. A prayer to end this madness, to keep those she loved safe.

Ashe thanked Detective Morrow. "I'd like to see a copy of your mechanic's complete report as soon as possible." He shook hands with the policeman, then glanced at Deborah.

She opened the door, walked over to Ashe and tilted her chin defiantly. "So now we know for sure."

"Yeah, we know Buck isn't through playing games, and the games are getting more and more deadly.'' Ashe looked at her, his eyes hard, his face tense. ''I think it's time ol' Buck and I have a little talk. Face-to-face.''

''No, Ashe. Please.'' Deborah grabbed him by the arm. ''You can't go off alone and confront a man like Buck Stansell. He could have you murdered on the spot.''

''Yeah, he could, but he won't.'' Ashe put his arm around Deborah, hugging her to his side. ''You forget that I know Buck and his kind. He's had me checked out thoroughly and he isn't about to bring down any more investigations on him and his boys right now. Lon Sparks has kept his mouth shut, but there isn't any doubt who was behind Looney's murder.''

''But Ashe, you should let the police handle Buck Stansell. Talk to Charlie Blaylock. Let him talk to Buck.''

''Honey, you don't understand. There is nothing to link your car's brake failure to Buck Stansell. Sheriff Blaylock has no legal reason to question Buck.'' He kissed Deborah quickly, then gave her a gentle shove away from him. ''I don't need a legal reason. Your safety is the only reason I need. If I don't hunt Buck down after what happened with your car last night, he'll be wondering why.''

Mama Mattie rushed out the door, waving her hands and laughing. ''She's awake. She's talking to Neil. Come see. Oh, thank you Lord, she's all right!''

Deborah and Ashe went inside, stopping at the foot of Annie Laurie's bed. Sitting on the side of the bed, Neil held Annie Laurie in his arms, tears streaming down his face.

"Guess what?" Annie Laurie smiled, her bruised face beaming. "Neil just told me that he and I are going to get married."

Everyone laughed. Mama Mattie fluffed Annie Laurie's pillow, then went around the room hugging everyone.

Neil glanced at Deborah and smiled. "Funny how it takes something like this to make a man realize who he loves and how much he loves her."

"I think this is wonderful," Deborah said. "As soon as Annie Laurie is out of this dreadful place, we'll start planning an engagement party."

"Well, I think first we need to let the nurses know that Annie Laurie has regained consciousness," Ashe said. "The doctors will want to examine her."

"I'll go with you." Deborah gave Annie Laurie and Neil loving hugs, then put her arm around Mama Mattie's waist. "Why don't we leave these two alone until the doctors storm in here? We could go have breakfast."

"Sounds good to me."

Mattie followed Ashe and Deborah out into the

hallway. After stopping by the nurses' station to alert the staff that Annie Laurie was conscious, the three headed for the elevators. The elevator doors opened and Roarke stepped out, Carol and Allen at his side.

"Mother! Allen! What are y'all doing here?"

Ashe eyed Roarke, who nodded toward Allen, but didn't say anything.

"Allen has been frantic," Carol said. "None of us got any rest last night. He's convinced himself that someone tampered with your car, that you aren't safe."

Deborah drew Allen into her arms, hugging him with fierce motherly protectiveness. "Oh, darling, Ashe isn't going to let anybody hurt me."

Pulling out of Deborah's arms, Allen turned to Ashe. "They think I'm nothing but a baby. They won't tell me the truth. But you will, won't you, Ashe?"

Everyone moved away from the elevators and into the hallway. Deborah held her breath. Ashe knelt on one knee and put his hand on Allen's shoulder.

"Somebody tampered with the brakes on Deborah's car. They wanted to hurt her. But she's okay. And so is Neil and Annie Laurie."

"But what if Deborah had been driving the car, what if—" Allen beat his fists against Ashe's chest. "I hate Buck Stansell. I'd like to tell him what I think of him. I'd tell him if he hurts Deborah, I'll kill him!''

Ashe drew Allen into his arms. Deborah's eyes glazed with tears, but she saw the look in her mother's eyes, the look that said *He's his father's son. End this lie. Tell Ashe the truth.*

''That's exactly what I'm going to do, go see Buck Stansell.'' Ashe patted Allen on the back, then stood and looked at Roarke. ''You take care of things for me. I have to go talk to a man about revenge.''

''No, Ashe!'' Deborah reached for Ashe, but Roarke grabbed her, physically restraining her while Ashe entered the elevator and punched the Down button.

Ashe caught Lee Roy and Johnny Joe just as they were leaving. He pulled his car up in the drive, blocking their departure. Both men stayed in their vehicle when Ashe got out and walked over to them. Lee Roy stepped out of his car and faced Ashe.

''You're out bright and early, cousin.'' Lee Roy grinned, the look on his face as innocent as a new-born baby's.

''I've been up all night.'' Ashe stood several feet away, his gaze focused on Lee Roy.

''I'm surprised you'd leave your woman alone, even to pay a visit on your relatives.''

"This isn't a social call."

"Yeah, I figured as much."

"I want to see Buck. I don't think sending him another message can get my point across like a personal visit."

Johnny Joe opened the passenger side door, got out and placed his elbows on top of the car. "We heard about that wreck last night. Sure was a shame. Guess Miss Deborah Vaughn was lucky she loaned her car out to somebody else."

"Annie Laurie is family." Ashe didn't move a muscle, didn't even glance Johnny Joe's way. "Lucky for everyone involved, she's going to be all right."

"We wouldn't want to see Annie Laurie come to no harm." Lee Roy grunted. "Hell, we've always been fond of that girl, even though she's no blood kin to us, her being on your mama's side of the family and all."

"I want to see Buck," Ashe repeated. "Today."

"Well, Buck's a busy man," Lee Roy said. "It'll take time to arrange things. You understand."

"Then you get things arranged."

"Buck'll be agreeable to seeing you. He ain't got nothing but the best to say about you, you know. He respects you. And he wouldn't have allowed nothing really bad to happen to your woman."

"Bad things *are* happening. If he's seeking revenge against Deborah for testifying, then he'd better think again. Revenge works both ways.''

"Hellfire, Ashe, Buck ain't no fool. He might have given orders to throw a scare into Deborah Vaughn, just for the principle of it, you know. But Lon Sparks ain't nothing but a speck of dirt on Buck's shoe. Not worth the trouble. Buck don't want to cross you.''

"I need to hear Buck say that.'' Ashe turned, walked over to his rental car and opened the door. His gaze focused on the ground, Ashe laid one hand against the side window. "I'll be back this evening, around six. Tell Buck I won't wait any longer than that.''

Johnny Joe jerked a .38 revolver out of the back of his belt, aimed it just to the left of Ashe and fired, hitting a nearby tree limb. Ashe didn't blink an eye.

"God a'mighty,'' Johnny Joe said. "Did you see that? He didn't move!''

"You damned fool.'' Lee Roy shook his head. "Sorry about that, Ashe. You know Johnny Joe ain't never had a lick of sense.''

Ashe looked up and grinned. "Being foolhardy runs in the family, doesn't it? Remind Buck of that inherited trait. Tell him that when it comes to defending my own, I'm not much concerned with the consequences, just the results.''

"Ain't nobody in our gang been behind what's

happened to your woman since the trial ended,'' Lee Roy said. ''I know you ain't going to believe me, but I'll warn you that you'd better start looking elsewhere. There's somebody else wanting to see Deborah Vaughn dead. It ain't none of us. You'd better start checking out some of her highfalutin friends and relatives. See who's got something to gain if she dies.''

''I'll keep that in mind.'' Ashe slid behind the wheel of his rented car. ''I'll be back at six.''

Chapter 13

Ashe parked outside the Sweet Nothings club, a huge blue metal building. From where he sat inside his car, he heard the loud, lonely wail of a guitar. So this was Evie Lovelady's place, huh? Ashe's old teenage girlfriend was now Buck Stansell's private property.

Lee Roy had told Ashe that meeting with Buck would clear up everything and show Ashe that none of *their* bunch was responsible for Deborah's most recent misfortunes. Ashe hadn't mentioned anything to Deborah about Lee Roy's insinuations that someone other than Buck Stansell might have reasons for wanting her dead. She'd been through enough in the last couple of months to last a lifetime, and now Miss Carol faced a second surgery for cancer. There was no point in worrying Deborah with something until he was absolutely sure.

Ashe got out, locked his car and entered the nightspot. Typical Southern honky-tonk. Nothing more. Nothing less. Loud music. Smoky air. Fun-loving rednecks and good old girls ready for a hot time on the town. A country band belted out the latest heartbreaking tunes.

Ashe glanced around, looking for the right person to ask about Buck Stansell. A tall, willowy brunette approached him.

"Long time no see, stranger." Evie slid her arm around Ashe's waist, dropping one hand to cup his buttock. She gave him a quick little squeeze, released him and laughed. "Tight as ever."

"You're looking good, Evie. How've you been?" Ashe grinned at his old girlfriend, one he and Lee Roy had both dated. The scent of her expensive perfume overwhelmed him. Damn, had she taken a bath in the stuff?

"I've been just fine, sugar. Got my own business now, and I hooked me the top dog in these parts." She held up her left hand, showing Ashe the three-carat diamond on her finger. "Of course, I haven't forgotten old friends and our good times together."

"Yeah, we had some good times, didn't we," Ashe said. "But we were just kids fooling around. We're grown up now and life's not fun and games anymore."

"Come on, sugar." Keeping her arm around

Ashe's waist, Evie nudged him with her hip. "Let me get you a drink."

"I didn't come here to drink. I came to see Buck."

"Yeah, I know. He's waiting in back for you. I just wanted to be friendly and make you feel welcome, let you know I hadn't forgotten what good friends we used to be."

Ashe followed Evie around the edges of the enormous room, past the dance floor and down a narrow corridor. "You were friends with a lot of guys, before me and after me."

"You're right about that," she said. "I used to be a real good time girl. Now I'm a one-man woman. And Buck's that man."

"Lucky Buck."

Evie smiled. She was almost pretty, Ashe thought. Her eyes were too big, her lips too thin and her cheeks scarred by teen acne, scars she covered with heavy layers of makeup.

"He's waiting on you." Evie opened the last door on the left. "Just remember that Buck thinks of you as family. Your old man and his were tight." She crossed her index and middle fingers. "He's not going to lie to you. If your woman was marked, he'd tell you."

Ashe looked straight into Evie's eyes and knew she believed what she'd told him. Hell, maybe she was right. These men, men like his father and uncle and cousins, might be thieves, drug dealers and murderers, but they did adhere to a certain code of behavior when it came to their own people. And it was possible that they still considered Ashe one of their own.

"Take care of yourself, Evie." Ashe kissed her on the cheek.

She punched him playfully on the arm, stuck her head inside the office and waved at her husband. "Ashe is here, sugar."

Ashe entered Buck's private domain. Evie closed the door, leaving Ashe alone with the man he'd come to question. The man he'd come to warn. The man he would have to kill if all else failed.

"Come on in, Ashe." Buck Stansell pushed back his big black velvet chair and stood. Tall and husky, with a thick mustache and the beginnings of a beer belly, Buck looked every inch the successful no-class gentleman with money that he was. "You haven't got a drink. Didn't Evie offer you something?"

"She offered," Ashe said.

"Evie's still looking good, isn't she? She's held up well. You know she's thirty-five and had three kids. Two of 'em mine." Buck's loud, hardy laughter filled the room.

"Yeah, Evie looks good."

"She's having herself the time of her life running this place. Named it herself. Sweet Nothings.

I try to keep her happy. We do that, don't we, Ashe, try to keep our women happy?''

"And safe." Ashe glanced around the office. Expensive bad taste. Money could buy just about everything except good breeding and an innate sense of style.

"That goes without saying." Buck walked around the huge, ornate desk and sat down on the edge. "I had to put a scare into Deborah Vaughn before Lon was convicted. Had to keep up appearances and let Lon think I was doing what I could for him.''

"You never meant to harm Deborah or her family?" Ashe asked.

"To be honest with you, I did consider having her taken care of, but once you showed up, I had second thoughts. Lon Sparks is small potatoes. An idiot who made the mistake of doing his business in front of a witness. Guess I should have just gotten rid of him. It might have been easier, but I have a reputation for taking care of my own. You understand how it is?''

"You want me to believe that you're not after Deborah for revenge."

"Why should I need revenge? Lon hasn't got the guts to double-cross me. Besides, he trusts me more than he does the law. He knows I'll keep my promises, one way or the other. He'd rather do time in the pen than spend the rest of his life looking over

his shoulder, wondering what day might be his last.
As long as he's in prison and keeps his mouth shut,
he stays alive. He knows how things work. And he
understands I've done all I intend to do on his behalf.''

"Since the trial ended, the Vaughns' garage was
set on fire, a gunman destroyed the front of Vaughn
& Posey Realty and somebody tampered with the
brakes on Deborah's Cadillac.'' Ashe stood, his
legs slightly apart, his arms at his sides, his jacket
hanging open. "If you want me to believe you had
nothing to do with these incidents, then you're going to have to prove it to me.''

"Look, old friend, I've given you some leeway
because of who your daddy was, because of the
man you've become, but I can be pushed only so
far.''

"I haven't even begun to push you, Buck, if you
have any plans to kill Deborah. There are only a
few things in this world worth killing for and even
fewer worth dying for. To me, Deborah Vaughn is
both. Do you understand?''

"I understood just fine when Lee Roy told me
that she was your woman.'' Buck rose off the edge
of his desk, straightened the jacket of his three-
piece gray pinstriped suit, and ran his hand across
the top of his head, smoothing the strands of his
slick, brown hair.

"All right, let's say I believe you. If you're telling the truth, then someone else has put out a contract on Deborah. Who?"

"I don't know anything about a contract, but...for a friend, I could find out."

"For a friend?" Ashe wasn't sure what to believe, but his gut instincts told him that he just might have to trust Buck Stansell. "Okay, Buck, old friend. Although the local and state authorities may be interested in your illegal dealings, my only concern is Deborah Vaughn. As long as she's safe, I have no reason to cause you any grief."

"You give me your word and I'll give you mine." Buck stuck out his broad, square hand, each finger sporting an expensive ring.

"As long as Deborah and her family are safe, you have nothing to fear from me," Ashe said.

"You stay out of my business and, as proof of my innocence and a show of my friendship, I'll make some inquiries and find out who's behind Deborah Vaughn's recent problems."

Ashe took Buck's hand, exchanging a powerful, macho shake, sealing a deal with the devil, a deal to keep Deborah safe. Ashe knew only too well the kind of man Buck Stansell was, the kind of man his own father had been. Among these redneck hooligans there was a certain code of honor, so Ashe was willing to give Buck the benefit of the doubt. For the time being.

He knew better than to trust Buck completely,

knew he'd better watch his back. If Buck thought Ashe posed a threat to his organization, his old friend would have no qualms about killing him. A guy like Buck might even ask Lee Roy to do the job for him, and get some sort of perverse pleasure from seeing which cousin would come out alive.

No, Ashe trusted Buck Stansell only so far. Now wasn't the time to bring the man down. He'd leave that to the authorities. Unless Buck lied to him. Then he'd take care of Buck himself.

Ashe made several calls after he left the Sweet Nothings club, one to Sam Dundee to ask him to initiate an investigation of the people in Deborah's life, those who might benefit from her death. Buck Stansell could be lying about his innocence in the garage fire, the drive-by shooting, and the brakes tampering. If he was telling the truth, then someone else had a motive; someone else wanted Deborah out of the way. But who? And why?

He spoke with the Florence police again, then met with Sheriff Blaylock and Sheffield police chief Ed Burton. He couldn't fault the local authorities. They'd done their jobs the best they could. Ashe especially liked Burton. He respected the man. The two of them had spent the past few hours going over all the leads, all the possibilities.

Ashe had expected the entire Vaughn household to be in bed when he arrived, after all it was nearly eleven. Tapping in the numbers for the security alarm at the back of the house, Ashe unlocked and opened the door. Only the tiny night-light on the refrigerator's ice and water dispenser burned, creating a dim glow in the room.

Wearing a floor-length maroon red robe, Deborah stood in his path, blocking him from entering. Dear God, she looked good enough to eat, all soft and silky, lush and delicious. His first instinct was to reach out and grab her.

"I thought you'd be in bed." He took a step inside the kitchen. Deborah stood right in front of him, not moving an inch. "You didn't get any sleep last night. You should be resting, honey."

"How am I supposed to rest with you out till nearly midnight? Allen asked about you at supper and Mother's been worried."

What was this? She was fit to be tied. What was her problem? He didn't want to argue; he wanted to make love.

"Before I left, I told you I wouldn't be in until late." When he reached out to take her by the shoulders and draw her into his arms, she backed away from him, her blue eyes cold, their expression daring him to touch her.

"I had business to take care of," he said. "The business of keeping you safe, of making sure nothing happens to you or Allen or Miss Carol."

"Roarke was protecting us. Just what were you doing?"

"What the hell's wrong with you, Deborah? Why are you so angry?"

"I'm not angry." He took several steps toward her; she backed farther and farther away. "I was worried. You left here to go see Buck Stansell. You told us you'd be late, but you've been gone nearly five hours. For all I knew, you'd been killed or—"

Ashe charged across the room, drew her into his arms and held her close. "I'm fine, honey. You shouldn't have worried about me. I told you that I know how to handle Buck Stansell and his type."

Hell, she'd been worried about him. He should have called to let her know he was all right. But he wasn't used to having anyone worry about him.

Deborah clung to Ashe, running her hands up and down his arms, clutching him as she laid her head on his chest. She knew she was acting irrationally, but she couldn't help herself. With each passing minute that she had waited for Ashe, she'd grown more tense, more worried, more concerned that Buck Stansell might have killed him.

Smelling his jacket, she jerked her head up and looked at him, then pulled out of his arms. He'd been with a woman, someone who bathed in her perfume.

Deborah glared at him, her small hands tightening into fists. She'd been worried sick about him

and he'd been with another woman! Damn him!
She'd been a fool to trust Ashe McLaughlin, to
believe she was the only woman in his life.

"You smell like a very expensive French
whore!"

Ashe laughed. "Actually, I smell like a fairly
cheap Alabama whore."

He had left the house hours ago, on a mission to
confront Buck Stansell. She'd been half out of her
mind with worry. When hours passed and he didn't
return, didn't call, she had imagined all sorts of
terrible things, but she certainly hadn't thought that
he was with another woman.

"I've spent the last two hours crazy with worry,
scared to death that something had happened to
you, and you've been with some woman!"

Ashe covered his mouth to conceal his chuckle.
He'd never seen Deborah this jealous, not even
over Whitney. Did she honestly think that he'd
been fooling around with someone else? Didn't she
realize that he couldn't see anyone except her, that
she was the only woman he wanted, that thoughts
of her filled his every waking moment?

"Don't you dare stand there and laugh about it!"

"Your life is in danger," Ashe said. "There
could be a contract out on you and what are you
worried about? You're worried about whether or
not I've been out messing around with another
woman."

Dammit, he couldn't believe this! She honestly thought he'd touch another woman when he could have her.

"I don't care who you...you...mess around with!"

Ashe came toward her, taking slow, determined steps. He shoved Deborah against the kitchen wall, then braced his hands on each side of her head. "I'm only going to say this once, so listen very carefully. I have not been having sex with another woman. I don't want or need another woman. There has been no one else in my life since the day I came back to Sheffield."

Deborah's breasts rose and fell with her labored breathing. She stared Ashe right in the eye, her gaze hard, her lips trembling, her cheeks flushed. "Then I suppose what I smell on you is some sort of new aftershave."

Ashe leaned down, touching her lips with his. When she turned her head, he reached out and grabbed her chin in his hand, forcing her to face him. "What you smell is Evie Lovelady's perfume. She wrapped herself around me when I arrived at the Sweet Nothings club tonight to meet with Buck."

"Evie Lovelady?" Deborah spat the woman's name out between clenched teeth. "You and she used to be quite an item if I recall correctly."

"Evie and most of the guys I hung out with used

to be an item. Now she's a happily married woman with three kids. She's Buck's wife.''

"So you had to get reacquainted with Evie before your meeting with Buck Stansell." Deborah tried to pull out of Ashe's grip. He leaned forward, trapping her against the wall with his body. "Let me go. I've had enough!"

Ashe rubbed his body against Deborah's, then released his hold on her chin, only to pull her into his arms. "I had no idea I'd come home to this. A jealous woman ready to scratch out my eyes."

"I'm not jealous. I have no reason to be, do I? We haven't made a commitment to each other. We haven't promised each other anything." She couldn't bear having him this close, his hard body pressed intimately against her, his arms holding her tightly. "Just let me go, Ashe. I'm tired and I need some rest. Unless Buck Stansell confessed to trying to kill me and has promised to leave me alone, I think any discussion about your visit with him can wait till morning."

Her jealousy aroused him as much as it irritated and amused him. He had no intention of letting her go to bed angry and hurt and filled with jealous rage.

Ashe lowered his hands to her buttocks, lifting her up and against his arousal. "I've been with Ed Burton for the last couple of hours, discussing my visit with Buck and going over the best way to end this nightmare for you and your family.''

"You've been with the police?" She gasped when he began inching her robe and gown upward, gathering more and more of the material in his hands.

He hadn't been in bed with Evie Lovelady. He hadn't been enjoying himself with another woman while she sat at home worrying about him. She should have trusted Ashe. She should have known he wouldn't betray her.

"Buck claims he ended his harassment of you when Lon Sparks was convicted. He says someone else is after you.'' Ashe buried his face against her neck, nibbling, licking, kissing.

She squirmed in his arms. "You—you don't believe him, do—do you?" She could hardly breathe. The blood rushed to her head, her knees weakened, her body moistened.

"I'm not sure."

He reached under the bunched material he held against her buttocks and stroked her tenderly, then ran his hand up her back, loosening the tie belt of her robe. Nuzzling her soft flesh with his nose, he parted the robe in front, uncovering the rise of her breasts exposed by the low cut nightgown. He took her tight nipple in his mouth, biting her gently through the maroon silk and ecru lace bodice. Deborah moaned with sweet pleasure.

He wanted her. Wanted her bad. He hurt with the need to take her. Here. Now. Hard and fast.

"We'll discuss this tomorrow," he said, his breath ragged. If he didn't take her soon, he'd die.

"Tomorrow," she agreed, reaching for his jacket, tugging it off his shoulders.

He covered her mouth, thrusting his tongue inside. She clung to his arms, holding onto his jacket sleeves, which she'd managed to bring down to his elbows. He shrugged out of the jacket, letting it fall to the floor. Deborah unbuttoned his shirt, quickly, ripping off the last two buttons in her haste. Ashe removed her silk robe, then pulled her gown down to her waist. He teased her aching nipples with the tips of his fingers. Closing her eyes, she threw her head back and sighed, deep in her throat.

"Deborah," he moaned her name. "Honey…how I want you."

She reached out to touch his chest, moving her hand back and forth from one pebble hard nipple to the other, curling her fingers in his hair. Lowering her head, she licked one nipple and then the other. She stroked his shoulder holster, then reached around and under his shirt to caress his back, her nails biting into his flesh as she urged him to take her.

Clutching the sides of her gown, he eased it down her hips. It fell into a dark red circle at her feet. He lifted her breasts in his hands, as if testing their weight, then put his mouth on her, suckling her while she unbuckled his belt and lowered his zipper.

Deborah clung to his shoulder, her body aching with desperate need. Her breasts felt heavy, almost painful. Her body clenched and released, dampening, throbbing, ready for the ultimate pleasure.

When Ashe touched her most sensitive spot, she cried out, then covered her mouth with her hand, realizing she should be quiet. Somewhere in the back of her desire-crazed mind, she knew they were not alone in the house, that they were insane for taking such a risk.

He took her hand and placed it around him, telling her without words what he wanted. They stroked and petted each other, then Ashe removed her sheathing hand and whipped her around to face the wall. She shivered. He lifted her hair off her neck and kissed her, then covered her shoulders and back with kisses and stinging little nips which he followed with moist tongue caresses.

When he dropped to his knees behind her, Deborah squirmed and tried to turn around. He held her in place, his hand parting her thighs, his fingers seeking and finding the secret heart of her femininity. All the while he fondled her, he lavished attention on her buttocks, kissing every inch of her sweet, womanly flesh.

Deborah became wild with her need, pleading in

soft, almost incoherent words for him to end the torture and take her. When he turned her to face him, she grasped his shoulders and urged him to stand. Instead, he buried his face against her stomach, then nuzzled her intimately and spread her thighs farther apart. While his mouth brought her to the brink of fulfillment, his hands tormented her nipples.

The moment she fell apart, shattering her into a thousand pieces as if she'd been a glass doll, Ashe lifted her in his arms, carried her a few steps over to the kitchen table and set her down. Before she had a chance to catch her breath, he parted her thighs and plunged into her. He filled her completely. The aftershocks of her first release surged within her, gripping him as he invaded her hard and fast, with a fury born of a desire he could not control. The tension built again, higher and higher, and Deborah clung to him. He groaned, then shook from head to toe as he thrust into her one last time, emptying himself as unbearable pleasure claimed them both.

They kissed, again and again. He left her on the table while he picked up their scattered clothes. Her gown and robe. His jacket. Tossing the items over his arm, he lifted her and carried her out of the kitchen, down the hall and up the stairs.

He deposited her in her bed, kissed her on the tip of her nose and looked into her blue, blue eyes.

"Stay the night with me." She clung to him, her arms still draped around his neck.

"And what if Miss Carol or Allen find me in here in the morning?"

"Lock the door."

He smiled and nodded his head. "I'll go back to my room before daylight."

He tossed their clothes on the foot of the bed, pulled out of her embrace and locked the bedroom door. Returning to her side, Ashe lay down and took her into his arms. Tomorrow he would tell her about his meeting with Buck Stansell. Tomorrow they would discuss the possibility that someone else might have a reason to want her dead. But tonight they would keep the rest of the world at bay, they would forget everything and everyone except each other.

He could think of nothing but making love to her all night long, taking her again and again, hearing her wild little cries of pleasure and the way she repeated his name.

For now, this heady, wild passion would be enough. And now was all that mattered.

Chapter 14

Deborah sat in the hospital waiting room, her head resting on Ashe's shoulder, her eyes closed as she ended a prayer pleading with God to spare her mother's life and keep them all safe and well. The doctors had warned them after the first surgery that, although they had every reason to believe all the malignant tissue had been removed, there was always a chance the cancer could return. Now they faced a second cancer, a second surgery.

As if her mother's life hanging in the balance wasn't enough to worry about, Deborah now had to face the possibility that someone other than Buck Stansell was behind the recent threats on her life. Ashe had told her that he had considered waiting until after her mother's surgery before burdening her with Buck's denials and accusations. But with her life, and possibly Allen's, in danger from an unknown source, Ashe felt it necessary she be informed.

Ashe. Ashe. He was like a tower of strength, an endless source of comfort and protection. She could not imagine her life without him. She loved him more now than she ever had, and he had become such an integral part of her life, of all their lives, especially Allen's.

Allen hero-worshiped Ashe, adored him the way so many ten-year-olds adored their fathers. But neither Ashe nor Allen knew their true relationship, and Deborah's guilt at keeping the truth from them ate away at her conscience and broke her heart by slow degrees.

"Ms. Vaughn?" Missy Jenkins, a young LPN for whom Deborah had found a house a few months earlier, stood in the waiting room doorway.

"May we see Mother now?" Deborah asked.

"Yes. She'll be going in to surgery in about thirty-five minutes, if the doctor's schedule doesn't change." Missy's smile made her rather homely face brighten to a certain degree of cuteness. "She'll be getting groggy soon, so you'd better go on in."

Ashe stood, assisted Deborah to her feet and kept his arm around her waist as they walked down the hall. Deborah eased open the door to Carol's private room. Her mother looked so thin and pale lying there on pristine white sheets, an IV connected to her arm.

Carol opened her eyes and smiled. "Good morning, my dears. Come in. They've given me something and I'll be a babbling idiot soon."

Ashe stood beside Deborah, who leaned down and hugged her mother gently, kissing her forehead. "Roarke is bringing Allen by before he takes him to school. I expect they'll be here any minute."

"Such a precious child," Carol said. "So much like you, Deborah."

"Yes, Mother."

"Ashe, thank you for coming back to Sheffield, for keeping watch over us, for bringing Roarke here to help you." Carol closed her eyes, then reopened them, focusing her gaze on Deborah. "I want to talk to you while I still can. I want you to promise me that—"

"Mother, this can wait until you're feeling better." Deborah patted Carol's hand.

"Ashe, would you mind leaving us alone for a few minutes." Carol glanced over her daughter's shoulder at the big man standing guard. "Mother-daughter talk. You understand?"

Ashe squeezed Deborah's shoulder. "I'll be in the waiting room. As soon as Allen arrives, I'll bring him down here."

The moment Ashe closed the door behind him,

Carol Vaughn looked up at Deborah. "I may not live through this surgery, and if I don't—"

"Mother, please, you mustn't talk this way."

Carol held up a hand in restraint. "Hush up. We both know there's a chance that the cancer has spread this time."

"We have to be optimistic, to think only positive thoughts."

"And we shall do just that, but…I want you to promise me you'll tell Ashe the truth about Allen."

"Mother, please…please, don't ask that of me. Not now. Not this way."

Carol gripped Deborah's hand with an amazing amount of strength. "Must I beg you to do this? I begged your father, years ago, not to make us all live a lie. If I had been stronger and stood up to him, none of us would be faced with this dilemma now."

"I'm in love with Ashe. We're lovers. I keep telling myself that he won't leave me this time, that he cares enough to stay. But I'm not sure how he really feels about me, so how can I tell him that I gave birth to his child over ten years ago and have kept that child from him? What if Ashe hates me?"

"Ashe cares deeply for you. He always did." Carol motioned for Deborah to come into her arms.

Deborah cuddled close to her mother's comforting body, careful not to bear her weight on Carol's thin frame. ''What if I tell Ashe the truth and he tells Allen?''

''I don't think Ashe will tell Allen. Not now.'' Carol stroked Deborah's hair, petting her in a loving, motherly fashion. ''But you must tell Ashe. Tell him now. Don't wait. Do this for me. Consider it a last request.''

''Mother!'' Deborah jerked away from Carol, tears filling her eyes. ''Please, don't ask this of me.''

''I am asking,'' Carol said. ''Tell Ashe that he is Allen's father. Tell him today.''

''I can't!'' Deborah turned away from her mother, tears trickling down her cheeks. She swatted them away with the tips of her fingers.

''You must tell him, Deborah. If you don't, Mattie will. She won't continue keeping our secret. And someday, you and Ashe must tell Allen the truth. He has a right to know.''

Deborah swallowed her tears. Her mother was right. The lie had gone on long enough. It was one thing to keep the truth from Ashe when he wasn't a part of their lives, but now that he had come to mean so much to Allen, now that she had fallen in love with him all over again, it was wrong to keep the truth from him.

''I promise I'll tell him,'' Deborah said.

''Today?''

''Yes. Today.''

At that precise moment Ashe knocked twice, opened the door and escorted Allen into Carol's room. Ashe glanced at Miss Carol, then at Deborah's tear-stained face. His eyes questioned her silently. She shook her head, saying ''Not now,'' and went over to stand by Allen at her mother's bedside.

Ashe wasn't a man who prayed often, and most people wouldn't call his supplications to a higher power prayers. He wasn't a religious man, wasn't a churchgoer, but he'd been in enough tight situations to know that even the unbelievers called on God for help when all else failed.

Ashe felt a bit out of place in this small hospital chapel. He could remember the last time he'd been in a house of worship. It was a funeral. Another soldier who hadn't made it back to the U.S. alive. A friend whose body had been shipped home.

He knew Deborah was having a difficult time dealing with her mother's surgery and the threats on her own life. It infuriated him that he could do so little to make things easier for her. At the moment, he felt helpless. He might be able to stand between her and danger, to protect her physically, but he hated being unable to defend her against her own fear and sadness.

Miss Carol's condition was in God's hands; all any of them could do was pray and hope for the best. But the continued threats on Deborah's life were another matter. It shouldn't take Sam long to get the information he needed—who besides Buck Stansell had reason to threaten Deborah? Who had something to gain from her death?

Neil Posey was her partner, owning less than forty percent of the business. But what would he have to gain from Deborah's death? And what about Whitney? Did she stand to inherit anything from Deborah? Deborah had told him that Allen and her mother were her beneficiaries.

Maybe Buck had been lying, covering his tracks, knowing Ashe would have no qualms about coming after him if he thought Buck was responsible for harming Deborah.

Ashe looked at her, sitting several feet away from where he stood. Her shoulders trembled. He knew she was crying. They had come into the chapel nearly fifteen minutes ago, and Deborah didn't seem ready to leave yet. Maybe she found some sort of solace here. He hoped she did. He'd do anything, bear any burden, pay any price, to ease her pain.

When she stood, her head still bowed, Ashe walked up behind her, draping his arms around her. She leaned back onto his chest, bracing her head against him, folding her arms over his where they crossed her body.

She smelled so sweet, so fresh and feminine,

such a contrast to the medicinal odors that mixed with the strong cleaning solutions in the hospital corridors.

"Miss Carol is going to be all right, honey. You've got to hang on to your faith." Ashe kissed her cheek.

"You can't imagine how close Mother and I are. How much we've shared. How we've depended on each other completely since Daddy died." Closing her eyes, Deborah bit down on her lower lip. She could not put off telling Ashe the truth about Allen any longer. She had promised her mother.

"We're all going to come out of this just fine. Miss Carol is a fighter. She's not going to let the cancer win. And I'm going to make sure y'all are safe." Ashe hugged her fiercely, as if holding her securely in his arms could keep the evil away. "I'm going to find out who's behind the threats and end this nightmare you've been living. After that, you and I have some decisions to make."

Deborah's heart skipped a beat. This was the first time Ashe had even hinted at the possibility they might have a future together. Would he feel differently about her, about their future, once she told him Allen was his son?

"Ashe?"

"Hmm-hmm?"

She pulled away from him enough to turn around in his arms and face him. He placed his hands on both sides of her waist. She looked into his warm hazel eyes, seeing plainly the care and concern he felt.

"Let's go to the back of the room and sit. Please. I have something to tell you. Something to explain."

"What is it, honey?" The pleading tone of her voice unnerved him. He sensed her withdrawal from him even though they were still physically connected. The emotional fear he noted on her face scared the hell out of him. "Deborah?"

She took his hand and led him to chairs in the back of the small chapel. They sat side by side. She wanted to continue holding his hand, to keep the physical contact unbroken, but she wasn't sure she could even look at him when she told him the truth.

Her heartbeat grew louder and louder; she was surprised he couldn't hear its wild thumping. Bracing her back against the chair, she took a deep breath.

"Deborah, are you all right?" She had turned pale, her eyes darkening with what he sensed was fear.

"This isn't easy for me, so please bear with me. Let me tell you what I must without your questioning me. Not until I've said it all. All right?"

Ashe reached for her. Shuddering, she cringed, holding both hands before her in a warning not to touch her. "Deborah, what's going on? I'm totally confused."

"Please remember that I didn't know what Daddy did to you eleven years ago." She took another deep breath. "I thought you'd left town on your own, that you washed your hands of me and…"

"We've been over this already," Ashe said. "I don't see any need to rehash it."

Under different circumstances, there would be no need. If she hadn't gotten pregnant the night they'd made love eleven years ago. If she hadn't given birth to his son. If she hadn't kept Allen's identity a secret.

Dear God, did she have the courage to tell him? Could she make him understand? Ashe McLaughlin was a possessive, protective male, one who would proclaim his fatherhood to the world. If she had ever doubted the deep, primeval urges within him, she knew now, only too well, that the man she loved was a man to be reckoned with, a man whose strength was feared and respected by others.

If only she knew how he truly felt about her. If he loved her, if…

"Please, Ashe, listen to me. A couple of months after that night…our one night together…I—I…"

A tight knot of fear twisted in his gut. "You what?"

"I discovered that I was—" she died a little inside "—pregnant."

God, no! No! He did not want to hear this. He couldn't handle the truth. He didn't want to know that Deborah had lied to him. The one woman on earth he'd thought he could trust.

"What did you do when you found out you were pregnant?" he asked, a deadly numb spreading through his body.

Already his voice had grown cold. How distant would he become when he'd heard the complete truth? "I went to Mother. That's the reason she told Daddy. After you left town, Daddy said that I was better off without you, that he and Mother would take care of me and the baby."

"Your father ran me out of town, knowing you were carrying my child?" Nausea rose in Ashe's throat. Hot, boiling anger churned inside him.

"Daddy arranged for Mother to announce that she was pregnant, but due to her age, she was having problems. He told everyone that Mother needed to be under a specialist's care." Twining her fingers together, Deborah alternated rubbing her thumbs up one palm and then the other. "When I was six months pregnant, we went away, then returned to Sheffield several weeks after Allen was born."

Anger, confusion and hurt swirled inside Ashe's mind and body. The truth had been there all along, staring him in the face. Even Roarke had tried to tell him. But he'd been too blind to see, too sure Deborah wouldn't lie to him, too afraid to accept the possibility that Allen could be his son. He hadn't wanted to admit that he was partially responsible for not having been a part of the boy's life for the past ten years.

"Allen." Ashe spoke the one word.

Allen Vaughn was his son. His and Deborah's. Their one passion-filled sexual encounter eleven years ago had created a child. Why had he never considered the possibility? Despite his rather promiscuous teen years, Ashe had been fairly cautious, using a condom most of the time. But he hadn't taken any precautions that night. He'd been so out of his head, needing and wanting Deborah, that he'd been careless—careless with an innocent girl who had deserved far better treatment.

Deborah looked at Ashe then and saw the mixed emotions bombarding him. "Daddy gave me two choices. I could give my child up for adoption or I could allow him to be raised as my brother."

You could have come to me! he wanted to shout. She should have come to him and told him. He would have taken care of her and their child. "You had a third choice," Ashe said.

"No, I didn't. You left town. You never called or wrote. You didn't give a damn what happened to me. You never asked yourself whether or not you might have gotten me pregnant.''

Ashe grabbed her by the shoulders, jerking her up out of her chair as he stood. ''Maybe you didn't feel that you could come to me when you first discovered you were pregnant. I guess I halfway understand your reasoning. But later... Mama Mattie always knew how to get in touch with me. All you had to do was ask her for my phone number, my address. Ten years, Deborah. Ten years!''

''I didn't know how you'd feel about being a father, about our child. You didn't love me. You'd made that perfectly clear.'' She sucked in her cheeks in a effort not to cry, not to fall apart in his arms. Somehow she knew he was in no frame of mind to comfort her. Not now. Not when he was in so much pain himself.

He shook her once, twice, then stopped abruptly and dropped his hands from her shoulders. Glaring at her, he knotted his hands into fists. God, how he wanted to smash his fist against the wall. He wanted to shout his anger, vent his rage.

''Is that why you kept Allen a secret from me?'' He ached with the bitterness building inside him. ''You were trying to punish me because I'd told you I didn't love you?''

''Of course not!'' Seeing the hatred and distrust in his eyes, Deborah knew her worst fears were coming true. "Allen has a good life, surrounded by people who love him."

"Allen's life is a lie," Ashe said, his eyes wild with the hot fury burning inside him. "He thinks Miss Carol is his mother. Hell, he thinks Wallace Vaughn was his father."

"I did what I thought was best." Deborah wanted to touch Ashe, to lay her hand on his chest, to plead for his understanding. But she didn't dare. "I was seventeen years old. My father gave me two choices. Telling you wasn't an option. If I'd thought it was, then I might have—"

"What about later? After your father died? I know Miss Carol wouldn't have tried to prevent you from contacting me."

"After Daddy died, bringing you back into my life was not a consideration. I had to take over my father's business. I had to support Mother and Allen. Besides, you were halfway around the world most of the time."

"Miss Carol wanted me to know, didn't she? Allen was one of the reasons she hired me to protect you."

"Mother has the foolish idea that you once actually cared about me and that if she could get you back into our lives, you wouldn't leave us this time."

Ashe lifted his clenched fists into the air, willing himself to control his rage. He glared at Deborah, at the one woman he thought he could trust. Suddenly, he grabbed her again, barely suppressing the desire to shake her. "I did not *leave* you eleven years ago. Your father ran me out of town. Do you honestly think that anything or anyone could have forced me to leave you if I'd known you were pregnant?"

"Are you saying that you'd have married me for the baby's sake?" Deborah pulled away from him, tears swelling in her eyes. "I didn't want you under those conditions then and I don't want you under those conditions now. I wanted you to love me. Me!" She slapped her hand against her chest. "I wanted you to want me, not marry me because of Allen."

"You've kept my son away from me all his life because of what you wanted? Didn't you ever think about what Allen might want or need? Or even what I wanted or needed?"

Ashe clenched his fists so tightly that his nails bit into the palms of his hands. Pain shot through his head. He couldn't think straight. He needed to escape, to get away from Deborah before he said or did something he would regret. But he couldn't leave her. He was her bodyguard.

"You mustn't tell Allen," she said. "Not now. He's not old enough to understand. That's one of the reasons—the main reason—I haven't told you the truth before now. I was afraid you'd want Allen to know you're his father. I just don't think he could handle the truth as young as he is.''

''I won't do anything to hurt Allen.'' *My son.* Allen Vaughn was his child. He'd looked at the boy and all he'd seen was Deborah. That blond hair, those blue eyes. But Roarke had seen what Ashe had been too blind to see.

''He's a wonderful boy,'' Deborah said. ''The joy of my life.''

''Do you know me so little that you think I'd do anything to jeopardize Allen's happiness, his security? I thought you and I had something special between us years ago. I thought you were my best friend. But you didn't trust me enough to come to me and tell me you were pregnant. And now, when I thought we might have a future together, you still couldn't trust me enough to put Allen's life in my hands.''

''I do trust you, Ashe. I've put all our lives in your hands. I know I should have told you weeks ago, but... I was afraid.''

''How am I going to be able to face Allen and not want to pull him into my arms and tell him I'm his father? God, Deborah do you have any idea how I feel?''

Someone just outside the chapel door cleared their throat. Ashe and Deborah glanced toward the white uniformed young woman.

''Ms. Vaughn, I thought you'd want to know that

your mother is out of surgery and the doctor is ready to speak to you.''

''How is Mother?''

''She's in recovery. She came through the surgery just fine, but I'm afraid that's all I can tell you,'' the nurse said.

The next few hours seemed endless to Deborah. She alternated between the desire to scream and the desire to cry. Silent and brooding, Ashe stayed by her side. The barrier of tension between them grew stronger with each passing minute.

Now, when she needed him most, he was as remote, as far removed from her as if he were a million miles away. He would not leave her unguarded, his sense of honor would never allow him to desert her and put her life at risk. But he could not bring himself to look at her or speak to her.

Ashe was afraid of his feelings, of allowing the bitter anger free rein. More than anything, he needed to get away from Deborah, to go off by himself and think.

The doctor's news had been good. In his opinion, they had been lucky once again. They would have to wait a few days on the final test results, but the preliminary findings were positive, giving them every hope that Carol Vaughn would fully recover.

Neither Deborah nor Ashe had gone for lunch. They had paced around the waiting room, avoiding each other, not speaking, not even looking at each other. Their being together had become an agony for her and she had no doubt it had been as difficult for Ashe. She knew he wanted to get away from her, but he couldn't. He was bound by his honor to protect her.

When Miss Carol was returned to her private room, Ashe went in and said a brief hello. Not wanting to say or do anything that might upset Deborah's mother, he made a quick exit, telling Deborah he would remain outside in the hallway and that she should stay with her mother for as long as she wanted to.

"Did you tell him?" Carol Vaughn asked.

"Yes, Mother, I told him."

"And?"

"And everything is going to be all right," Deborah lied. "He understands."

Carol Vaughn smiled. "I knew he would. He'll take good care of you and Allen."

When her mother fell asleep shortly before five in the afternoon, Deborah kissed her pale cheek and walked out into the hallway.

Ashe stood, leaning against the wall, his hands in his pockets. "Is she all right?" he asked.

"She's sleeping." Deborah glanced at Ashe, but when she saw the coldness in his eyes, she looked away. "I'd like to go home now."

He escorted her downstairs to the parking lot, not

touching her, not saying another word. The drive home was an exercise in torture. For Deborah. And for Ashe.

Suddenly her life seemed void of hope. Where she had felt the joy of being in love, the resurgence of dreams she'd thought long dead, now she felt only loss. Had she lost Ashe again? Or as in the past, had he never truly been hers?

Deborah glanced out the side window of Ashe's rental car, knowing that nothing she could say or do at this point would change the way he felt. When she heard him dialing his cellular phone, she glanced at him.

Quickly he returned his gaze to the road ahead. ''Roarke?''

''How's Miss Carol?'' Roarke asked. ''Ever since Deborah called Allen with the good news, he's been wanting to talk to his mother.''

''Miss Carol is doing real good. We left her sleeping.'' Ashe paused for a second. ''I'm bringing Deborah home, but something's come up and I need to go out. Alone.''

''No problem. Want to tell me what's wrong?''

''You were right about Allen.''

''How'd you find out?'' Roarke asked.

''Deborah told me. Today. While Miss Carol was in surgery.''

''What are you going to do?''

''I don't know.'' Ashe clutched the steering

wheel. "I can't see Allen right now. Keep him inside until I drop Deborah off. Okay?"

"Yeah, sure."

Ashe closed his cellular phone and slipped it back into his coat pocket. "Roarke will take care of you."

"Where are you going?" Deborah wished he'd look at her, but he didn't.

"I need to get away by myself for a few hours and do some serious thinking."

"Ashe, please... You may not believe this now, but...I love you."

Without replying, he drove up Montgomery Avenue, turned into the Vaughn driveway and waited for Deborah to get out. She hesitated for just a moment, hoping he would say something. He didn't. She jumped out of the car, slammed the car door and rushed up on the front porch where Roarke stood waiting. Ashe roared away, leaving Deborah alone, uncertain and miserable.

Ashe McLaughlin was good at that, she thought. Leaving. Maybe she had made a mistake, eleven years ago and more recently, too. But everything wasn't her fault. Surely when his temper cooled and he had time to think reasonably, he would see that he wasn't the only injured party in this situation.

She wasn't sure exactly what she had expected when she told him the truth, but somewhere deep inside her, she had hoped he would understand, that he would forgive her.

"Are you all right?" Roarke asked.

"I've been better," she said.

"Allen's helping Mazie set the table for dinner. He's going to want to know why Ashe isn't with you."

"I gather you suspected that Allen was Ashe's son."

"I saw the similarities. I knew your and Ashe's background. He told me about you, one night when we'd both had a little too much to drink."

"Ashe told you about me?"

"That surprises you?" Roarke opened the front door, placed his hand in the small of Deborah's back and followed her into the entrance hall.

"Why would Ashe tell you about me, about our... Ashe didn't love me. I don't understand."

"Maybe he didn't love you," Roarke said. "But he sure as hell never forgot you. He never got over the way he felt about you."

"I was in love with him then, you know. I'm even more in love with him now."

"Give him time to sort out his feelings." Roarke laid his big hand on Deborah's shoulder. "He has a son he never knew about and he's found out that a woman he'd just learned to trust again has kept a secret from him for eleven years."

Allen ran into the entrance hall, Huckleberry lop-

ing behind him. "How's Mother? When can I go
see her?" Allen glanced around, then stared at the
door. "Where's Ashe? Parking the car?"

Deborah took a deep breath. "Ashe had some
business to take care of immediately. Mother is doing beautifully, and you can see her tomorrow after
school."

"Great. May I call her tonight?"

"Right after dinner," Deborah said.

"Will Ashe be home in time to help me with my
math homework?"

"I'm not sure how long his business will take."
She wanted to wrap Allen in her arms and keep
him safe. For the millionth time in ten years, she
wished she could tell him she was his mother. Dear
God, how Ashe must feel. But he had no idea the
price she had paid pretending to be Allen's sister.
Both of them had lost so much not having the
chance to be Allen's parents. Maybe it really was
all her fault. Maybe Ashe had every right to hate
her. If she'd had the strength to stand up to her
father or the courage to have gone to Ashe with the
truth long ago, things would be different now.

Deborah checked her watch as she followed Allen into the kitchen. Would Ashe return tonight?
Tomorrow? Or would he leave town and never return? Oh, he would return, all right. He might leave
her again, but he would never leave his son.

Chapter 15

Ashe sat in his car, the window down, the crisp night air chilling him. He had to go home, home to Deborah. For the past several hours he had thought of nothing except what she'd told him about Allen. His son. Their son.

He'd stopped by a local lounge for a couple of drinks, then come down here by the river and parked. He hadn't wanted to be around anybody. He'd needed time alone to lick his wounds, to resolve his feelings for Deborah.

The fact that he cared deeply for her complicated his life considerably. If she hadn't come to mean so much to him, he could hate her. But he didn't hate her; and he didn't even blame her for what she'd done. How could he? Eleven years ago he'd taken her innocence and broken her heart. He'd tried to reject her gently, telling himself he was doing what was best for her. If he'd been a man instead of a thoughtless boy, he would have made sure he hadn't gotten her pregnant. That had been his fault. He'd been the one with experience, not her. And she'd loved him. He hadn't appreciated how much the love of a girl like Deborah meant. Now he did.

Why hadn't he, just once, considered the possibility that he'd gotten her pregnant and she'd kept it a secret from him? Hell, he knew the answer only too well. He couldn't have handled the guilt. He didn't blame her for not coming to him, after the way he'd treated her. Back then she hadn't known her father had run him out of town; she'd thought he'd deserted her.

He couldn't justify her keeping Allen's existence a secret after her father died, but he understood her reasoning. He had hurt her badly. She had been afraid to trust her life and Allen's to him.

Things were different now. She did trust him. And she still loved him. That was the greatest miracle of all. Somehow, he'd find a way to make up all the lost years to Allen and to Deborah.

They needed to talk, to come to an agreement on the best way to handle the situation. He wanted Allen in his life, whether or not they ever told the boy he was his father. And he didn't want to lose Deborah, not again. All these years she had stayed alive inside him, her gentle beauty, her unconditional love.

He didn't know exactly how they'd work things, but they would find a way. He'd make Deborah see that no obstacle was too great for them to overcome—together. He wasn't going to lose his son or his son's mother.

Ashe started the car, turned around and headed toward Sheffield, all the while thinking about what he wanted to say to Deborah. When he turned into the driveway, he noticed every downstairs light was on. In the distance he heard sirens. A police siren and an ambulance siren. His heart raced, his nerves rioted. What if something had happened while he'd been off licking his wounds?

He flew to the front door and through the house, calling for Deborah, then he bellowed out Roarke's name. When he entered the kitchen he ran into Allen, who trembled and cried and spoke in incoherent phrases. Huckleberry stood at Allen's side, licking the child's hand.

Ashe grabbed his son by the shoulders. "Allen, what's wrong? What's happened? Where's Deborah? Where's Roarke?"

"Deborah's gone." Allen sobbed, his big blue eyes wide with fear. "I don't know what happened. I heard Deborah scream."

"When did you hear her scream?"

"Just a little while ago. Her scream woke—woke me and—and Huckleberry."

"Where's Roarke?"

"Outside. In the—the backyard. I think he's dead!" Allen threw his arms around Ashe's waist, hugging him fiercely.

Ashe lifted his son in his arms, sat him down on top of the kitchen table and wiped the tears from his face with his fingers. "Are you all right, Allen?"

"Yes. But I can't find Deborah. Where is she? Did they get her?"

"Show me where Roarke is," Ashe said.

"I called 911. Roarke told me to call, then he passed out."

Ashe lifted Allen down from the table. Holding his son's hand, he followed the boy and his dog outside. Roarke's big body rested in a fallen heap on the patio. Huckleberry sniffed Roarke's semi-automatic, which he'd obviously dropped when he'd passed out. The gun now lay in a pool of fresh blood that had formed on the bricks.

Ashe leaned down, turning Roarke slightly. The man groaned, then opened his eyes.

"Hang in there. An ambulance is on its way," Ashe said. "Can you tell me what happened?"

"She was restless." Roarke spoke slowly, his breath ragged. "Worried about you. Thought she…heard your car parking in the back."

"Where is she?"

"He took her." Roarke tried to lift his head. "Told her not to go outside. Couldn't catch her. Couldn't stop her. She thought it was you."

Ashe inspected Roarke's body and discovered he'd been shot several times. Dear God, why didn't that ambulance hurry? If Roarke lost much more blood, he'd be dead before the medics arrived.

"Take it easy," Ashe said.

"I walked out—out the door." Roarke coughed several times. Blood trickled from the corner of his mouth. "The minute I stepped out... Shot me. Kept shooting."

"Did you get a look at him?"

"Big guy. Ugly. Sandy hair. Jeans. Leather jacket." Roarke lifted his hand, but the effort exerted too much of his strength and his hand fell to his side. "Failed. Sorry."

"I'll find her," Ashe said. "You just hang in there until—" Ashe realized Roarke had passed out again.

Four Sheffield policeman stormed the backyard, their guns drawn. Standing, Ashe placed his arm around Allen's shoulders. His son leaned against him.

"Come on, Allen. After we talk to the police and see Roarke off to the hospital, I'm taking you over to Mama Mattie's. I'll get Chief Burton to send one of his officers to stay with you until I find Deborah.''

''You'll find her, won't you, Ashe? You won't let anybody hurt her, will you? You love her, just like I do.''

''Yeah, son, you're right. I'll find her, and I'll never let anybody hurt her because I love her, too.''

Ashe barely contained the rage inside him, and the fear. Dear God, the nauseating fear! If anything happened to Deborah, it would be his fault. If he hadn't left her, deserted her again, then she wouldn't have been in such a tormented state of mind. She never would have rushed outside without thinking, disobeying Roarke's orders. If anything happened to her or if Roarke died, Ashe would have to face the fact that he could have prevented tonight's disastrous events.

Ashe marched into the Sweet Nothings club like a storm trooper. Evie tried to grab his arm, but he threw her off and swept past the bouncer, making his way to Buck Stansell's office. If the man was responsible for Deborah's kidnapping, he'd kill him with his bare hands—after he found out where Deborah's abductor had taken her.

Ashe flung open the office door. Buck jumped up from behind his desk, like a scared rabbit dodging a hunter's bullet.

''Where is she?'' Ashe demanded, as he advanced on Buck, not heeding Buck's bodyguard's warning.

Buck motioned for his bodyguard. Ashe turned on the burly man and, using several expedient thrusts with his hands and feet, brought the big man to his knees.

"Why are you here?" Buck asked.

Evie rushed into the office, bringing two bouncers with her. Ashe pulled his gun from the shoulder holster and aimed it at Buck.

"Call off your goons," Ashe said.

"Take them back inside the club," Buck ordered. "Go with them, sweetie. I can handle things in here."

"Where is Deborah?" Ashe asked again.

"If she's missing, I don't have her," Buck said. "I've been trying to tell you that I'm not behind the recent threats. I thought you were checking into other suspects."

"I'm still checking." With gun in hand, Ashe walked across the room, motioning for the bodyguard to sit. "Someone shot my partner at the Vaughns' home tonight and kidnapped Deborah. What do you know about it?"

Buck eased down in his big velvet chair behind his desk. "I didn't put a contract out on Deborah, but I know who did."

"Keep your hands where I can see them." Ashe

stood in front of Buck's desk. "Tell me what you know."

"I checked into the situation for you, just like I said I would." Buck laid his hands flat atop his desk. "I found out that a prominent Sheffield citizen hired one of my former employees—Randy Perry—to kill Deborah. Randy just got out of the pen a couple of months ago and I didn't see fit to rehire him. He's a bad apple, that one."

"Who hired him?"

"A relative of Deborah Vaughn's, one who had a twofold purpose in wanting her dead."

"Who?"

"The man wanted revenge on his wife's former lover, the one he's cried in his beer about here at Sweet Nothings on more than one occasion. Seems his wife has always compared him to this guy and he's always come up lacking."

"Whitney's husband?" Ashe asked.

"Of course, getting back at you isn't his main reason. The inheritance is. Seems Jamison thinks that old Mrs. Vaughn hasn't got much longer to live, and with Deborah out of the way, his wife would be the logical one to oversee Deborah's estate and take custody of Allen."

"My God! Is Whitney involved in this scheme?"

"Don't know. Wouldn't know what I do if

Randy hadn't stayed buddies with some of my boys and if he wasn't the type to brag to the ladies.''

"Do you have any idea where he's taken Deborah?"

"I didn't even know he'd taken her tonight until you stormed in here. Why don't you pay a visit on Mr. Jamison?"

"That's exactly what I intend to do." Slipping his gun back into the holster, Ashe nodded to the door. "Why don't you walk me out, Buck, old friend?"

Buck chuckled. "Still don't trust me completely? I don't blame you."

Buck walked Ashe all the way outside to his car, then put his hand on Ashe's shoulder. "I'll find out what I can about where Randy's taken your woman. If I learn anything that can help you, I'll send Lee Roy to find you."

Ashe didn't say anything, only nodded, got in his car and headed back to Sheffield, straight to the Jamison house on River Bluff.

The Jamison home sat on the bluff overlooking the Tennessee River. Ashe parked his rental car behind George Jamison's Jaguar. The fury inside him had built to the "kill" stage. His common sense urged him to stay calm, telling him that he must remain in control in order to find Deborah before her kidnapper killed her.

The very thought of Deborah being harmed angered Ashe, and created a pain deep inside him. The hired assassin had been waiting for his chance to get Deborah, and Ashe had given him the perfect opportunity. If anything happened to her, he'd never forgive himself.

He rang the doorbell and waited, checking his gun. After endless minutes of keeping his finger pressed against the buzzer, Whitney Vaughn swung open the double doors and stood in the foyer smiling.

"Why, Ashe McLaughlin, whatever brings you to my house in the middle of the night?"

Ashe noticed she wore nothing but a thin, lavender nightgown, sheer and revealing. "Where's your husband?"

"Not in my bed." She draped her arm around Ashe's neck. He pulled free, walking farther into the foyer. She closed the doors and followed him.

"You want to see George?" she asked. "At this time of night?"

"Where is he?" Ashe went from room to room, turning on lights as he went. "If he's not here, tell me where he is!"

"What the devil's the matter with you, Ashe?" Whitney planted her hand on her slender hip.

"Deborah's been kidnapped," Ashe said. "And I have reason to believe that your husband put out a contract on her life."

"George?" Whitney's large brown eyes widened, giving her an owlish look. "But George would never… What reason would he have?"

"You tell me. For all I know you could be in on it with him."

"I'd never do anything to hurt Deborah. She's my cousin. I care deeply for her."

"Where's your husband?" Grabbing Whitney by the shoulders, Ashe shook her soundly.

"He—he's upstairs in his room."

"Show me." Ashe jerked Whitney around, grasping her wrist. "I don't have any time to lose."

Whitney ran up the stairs, Ashe beside her. Halting, she pointed to a closed door. "That's George's room."

Ashe crashed through the door. George Jamison had one leg in his trousers, the other on the floor. Ashe grabbed him around the neck. When George swayed, Ashe steadied him by slamming him up against the wall. Whitney stepped inside, but stayed by the open door.

"Where did Randy Perry take Deborah?" Ashe tightened his hold on George's neck.

"I—I don't know what you're—you're talking about." George pawed at Ashe's hand, trying unsuccessfully to loosen his hold around his neck.

"Don't play games with me, Jamison. You tell me what I want to know or I'll break your neck. Do you understand me?"

"For pity's sake, Whitney, call the police," George said.

"I'm not doing anything." Whitney glared at her husband. "If you hired someone to kill Deborah, you'd better tell Ashe what he wants to know."

"Please, believe me. I don't know what he's talking about."

With his right hand still pressed against George's windpipe, Ashe reached inside his jacket and retrieved his gun from the shoulder holster. He pointed his 9mm directly at George's temple.

"If you have any doubts that I'd kill you, then you don't know me at all. Deborah Vaughn is the most important thing in this world to me. I'd lay down my life for her. Do you understand what I'm saying, Jamison?"

"Don't kill me," George pleaded.

Ashe despised the weakness in this man. He pressed the 9mm against George's head. "Where has Perry taken Deborah?"

"I don't know!" When Ashe glared at him, fury in his eyes, George cried out. "I paid him $5,000 and promised him $5,000 more to do the job."

"You hired someone to kill Deborah!" Whitney screamed, tears forming in her eyes. "I knew you weren't much of a man, but I never realized what a monster you are. How could you do it? Deborah has taken care of us for years. I don't know what we would have done without her."

"But don't you see, my darling, I did it for us." George tried to turn his head so he could look at his wife, but Ashe kept him trapped against the wall, the 9mm at his temple, Ashe's big hand at his throat.

"With Deborah out of the way and Miss Carol dying soon, then who but to you would the courts award custody of Allen?" George said. "Who but you would be in control of Allen's inheritance?"

"I can't believe this." Whitney slumped against the doorpost, as if her slender weight was more than she could bear. "You're out of your mind!"

"I'd have never thought of killing Deborah. But once the threats started, I thought how lucky for us if Buck Stansell had her killed." George trembled. "Look, Ashe, killing me won't save Deborah. I hired Perry. Yes, I admit it. Once the trial ended and I realized that Buck Stansell wasn't going to continue with his threats, I decided I could hire someone to kill Deborah and everyone would think Stansell and his gang were responsible."

"You sorry son of a bitch," Ashe growled, then returned his gun to its holster. He grabbed George around the neck with both hands, lifting him off the floor.

George gasped for air, his feet dangling, his arms flying about, trying to catch hold of Ashe.

Whitney screamed. "You're killing him, Ashe!"

Not one rational, reasonable thought entered

Ashe's head. He worked on instincts alone. His hands tightened around George's neck. With one swift move, he could break the man's neck. This stupid fool was responsible for whatever might happen to Deborah before Ashe could find her. He didn't deserve to live.

"Ashe, think what you're doing," Whitney cried out, beating against Ashe's back with her tight little fists. "He's not worth it. Do you hear me? George isn't worth it!"

"Put him down, cousin," Lee Roy Brennan said from where he stood in the doorway. "She's right. He's not worth it."

Without loosening his hold on George, Ashe glanced at Lee Roy. "Did Buck send you?"

"We found out where Randy might have taken Deborah."

"A reliable source?" Ashe asked.

"A friend of Evie's," Lee Roy said. "A gal Randy's sleeping with. He shared his plans with her, telling her he'd be coming into another $5,000 after the job was done."

"Where did she say he planned to take Deborah?" Ashe set George down on his feet, but kept his hands around his throat.

"Somewhere close to Deborah's house in downtown Sheffield. Some deserted warehouse."

"What deserted warehouse?"

"My guess is the old streetcar warehouse."

Ashe released George, allowing him to fall to his knees. With expert ease, Ashe snapped the purple top sheet from George's bed and ripped off two long strips. Using his foot, he pressed George over against the bed, jerked his hands behind his back and hogtied the man with the scraps of his own bed sheet.

"Whitney, don't let your husband out of your sight until the police arrive."

"Don't worry," she said. "I'll kill him myself if he even tries to move."

"Come on." Ashe motioned to Lee Roy, who followed him out into the hall and down the stairs.

Lee Roy grabbed Ashe at the front door. "When we find her, she might not be alive."

"She'll be alive! She has to be."

"Even if she is, it could be bad. Randy was in the pen for rape."

"Whatever happens, he's a dead man," Ashe said.

Ashe called the Sheffield police on his cellular phone, telling them where he was going and asking them to send some officers over to George Jamison's home. Lee Roy followed in his truck, the two cousins speeding along Jackson Highway, racing toward downtown Sheffield. Ashe prayed, begging God to keep Deborah safe, offering his own life in place of hers.

* * *

She couldn't bear his touch, rough and clammy. She'd screamed the first time he'd squeezed her breast, but he'd slapped her so hard she'd fallen to her knees in pain.

He was going to rape her before he killed her. He'd told her what to expect.

This was all her fault. Her own stupidity had cost Roarke his life and now would cost her hers. How could she have been so stupid, rushing out to meet Ashe, when in fact she'd run headlong into her kidnapper?

Did Ashe know what had happened? Was he searching for her? *Please, God, please let him find me in time.*

"I ain't never had me no society lady before." Randy Perry snickered as he ripped open Deborah's blouse, exposing her lace-covered breasts.

Deborah tried to back away from him, but he grabbed her, dragged her up against him and thrust his sour tongue into her mouth. Gagging, she fought him, hitting him repeatedly as she kicked at his legs.

He threw her to the floor and came down on top of her, crushing the breath out of her. "You like it rough, huh, society lady? Well, ol' randy Randy can give it to you rough."

He ran his hand up her leg and under her skirt, fondling her hip. When he lowered his head to kiss her again, she spat in his face. He laughed. Then he slapped her.

Deborah closed her eyes against the reality of what was happening to her. She retreated into a silent, constant prayer for Ashe to rescue her before it was too late.

Chapter 16

The old streetcar warehouse stood in darkness, the moonlight casting shadows across the window panes. Ashe could hear nothing except the loud pounding of his heart. He couldn't ever remembering being so scared, not even in battle. But then Deborah's life had not been in jeopardy, only his.

He drove down the street slowly, looking for any sign that someone had broken into the empty building. He circled the block. An older model Pontiac Grand Prix was parked directly across from the warehouse. Ashe eased his Buick up behind it, got out and checked the license plate. A Colbert County tag.

Lee Roy pulled his truck up behind Ashe, getting out and following his cousin across the street.

"It's Randy's car," Lee Roy said. "He got it off

a fellow who brings stolen cars in from Mississippi.''

"That means they're here.'' Ashe removed his gun from the holster before crossing the street. "Look, you may not want to get involved in this. I've phoned for the police. They should be here any time now.''

"All I'm doing is helping my cousin rescue his woman. Right? I don't know nothing about nothing. We made a lucky guess as to who had kidnapped Deborah and about where he'd taken her.''

"Yeah, right.'' Ashe nodded toward the building. "You check that side and I'll check this side. If you find them, don't act on your own. Randy Perry is mine.''

"Got you.'' Lee Roy rounded the side of the warehouse.

Ashe crept along the wall, checking for an unlocked door, looking for any sign of forced entry. Then he saw it. Toward the back of the building, a dim light flickered.

Ashe found a jimmied lock, the door standing partially open. Taking every precaution not to alert Randy Perry to his presence inside the warehouse, Ashe followed the light source, keeping his body pressed close to the wall as he made his way inside, searching for any sign of Deborah.

A lone lantern rested on the floor, spreading a circle of light around it. Deborah lay at Randy

Perry's feet, her blouse in shreds, her skirt bunched up around her hips, half covering the gleaming white of her lace underwear. Ashe garnered all his willpower, resisting the urge to let out a masculine cry of rage. He wanted to kill the big, bearded slob of a man who gazed down at a half-naked Deborah as he unzipped his jeans.

Ashe whirled away from the wall, aiming his gun at Deborah's kidnapper. In a split second, before Ashe could fire his 9mm, Perry fell to the floor, grabbing Deborah into his arms. Lifting her along with himself, he rose to his knees, holding Deborah in front of him, his thick arm around her neck.

"I'll break her neck like a twig," Perry warned Ashe. "And that would be a pity. She's got such a pretty little neck."

"You're a dead man, Perry!"

Randy Perry stood, jerking Deborah to her feet, using her body as a shield. Walking himself and Deborah backward, he kicked the lantern across the floor, extinguishing the flame and sending the room into darkness. The lantern rolled into a corner, crashing into the wall.

Ashe swore aloud. His breathing quickened. It would take a few minutes for his eyes to adjust to the darkness, but then it would take just as long for Perry to be able to maneuver without any light.

Sirens blared like the thunder of an attacking elephant herd. Tires screeched. Doors slammed.

Chief Burton's voice rang out loud and clear, telling Randy Perry that the warehouse was surrounded.

"Don't look like I got nothing to lose by finishing this job, does it?" Perry called out, taunting Ashe.

"Be careful, Ashe." Deborah's voice sounded shaky but strong.

"Deborah!" Ashe couldn't see her now, but he could make out the direction in which Perry was moving from the sound of their voices.

"Don't hurt her," Ashe said. "If you do, I'll kill you before the police come through the door."

"He has a gun, Ashe. Don't—"

Randy Perry held Deborah in front of him as he walked backward, directly past a row of windows. Moonlight created enough illumination for Ashe to see the gun Perry held to the side of Deborah's face, his other meaty hand covering her mouth.

"Let her go." Ashe issued one final warning.

Randy Perry laughed. "No way in hell!"

Ashe aimed and fired. Deborah screamed. Randy Perry slumped, knocking Deborah down as he dropped to the floor. Blood spurted from the lone bullet wound in his head. Deborah looked over at the man's still body, then crawled away from him. Standing hurriedly, she ran toward Ashe.

He grabbed her, pulling her into his arms, encompassing her in his tight embrace. She gulped for air, her body racked with heavy, dry sobs. Ashe rubbed her back, petting her tenderly.

"It's all right, honey. You're safe now. You're safe."

The police stormed into the warehouse after hearing the gunshot. They found Randy Perry lying on the floor in a pool of his own blood and a partially undressed Deborah Vaughn clinging to Ashe McLaughlin.

"Is she all right?" Ed Burton walked over to Ashe. "Did he hurt her?"

"She'll be all right." Ashe slipped his gun into the holster, then removed his jacket and placed it around Deborah's shoulders. "I'm taking her home."

"Maybe you should take her to the hospital. If she's been raped—"

"No!" Deborah cried. "He—he didn't—didn't rape me. He would have, but Ashe—Ashe—"

Ashe lifted her into his arms, carried her past a row of gawking police officers and out onto the sidewalk. She laid her head on his chest. He kissed the top of her head.

Standing by the side of Ashe's car, Lee Roy opened the door. Ashe deposited Deborah inside, got in and looked up at his cousin.

"Thanks," Ashe said. "Pass it along. Okay?"

"Yeah. Sure thing. Glad we made it in time." Lee Roy grinned. "Guess I'll be seeing you from time to time. I figure you'll be staying around these parts to keep an eye on your woman.''

Lee Roy walked over to his truck, got in and drove off. Ashe removed his jacket and draped it around Deborah's shoulders, then pulled her close to his side, started his car and headed southwest.

''Where are we going?'' she asked.

''Allen is with Mama Mattie. Chief Burton has an officer keeping an eye on them.''

''I can't let Allen see me like this, with my clothes—'' She swallowed hard, biting the insides of her cheeks in an effort not to cry.

''He'll be asleep when we get there. I'm sure Annie Laurie can find you something of hers to put on.'' Ashe hugged Deborah, leaning the side of his head against the top of hers. ''It's all over, honey. Go ahead and cry. Let it all out.''

''I can't cry,'' she said. ''I hurt too much to cry.''

''Did you tell Ed Burton the truth? Randy Perry didn't rape you, did he?''

''No, he didn't. He slapped me around. He scared me to death. Oh, Ashe, how can you say it's over? Buck Stansell will just hire someone else to come after me.''

Ashe pulled the car off Shop Pike and into the parking lot of the old converted train depot. Killing the motor, he turned to Deborah. She looked so pale, there in the moonlight, her eyes overly bright and slightly glazed with tears. But she hadn't cried, hadn't gone into hysterics. His strong, brave Deborah. Taking her face in both hands, he lowered his lips to hers and kissed her tenderly.

Still holding her face, he shook his head. "It's over, honey. Believe me. Buck Stansell didn't put out a contract on you. George Jamison did."

Deborah gasped. "George!"

Ashe slipped one arm behind her and crossed the other over her body, bringing her into the comfort of his embrace. "Buck was telling me the truth. Lon Sparks wasn't an important enough cog in their wheel for Buck to make an example out of you. Especially when he found out he'd have to contend with me."

"But George? I can't believe he would… Ashe, are you sure? How did you find out?"

"I got a confession out of George, tonight."

"But—but why would George want to kill me? I don't understand."

"The man has a sick, devious, greedy mind. He thought Miss Carol would die, then if you were out of the way, Whitney would be given custody of Allen and the entire Vaughn estate."

Deborah gripped Ashe's arms. "What about Whitney? Does she know what he did? Oh, dear Lord, is she all right?"

That was his Deborah, kindhearted and loving to the bitter end. "Yeah, she knows. And she's all right. When she found out, she was ready to kill George herself.''

''So, it really is over, isn't it?'' Deborah sighed, her body relaxing in Ashe's embrace. ''Oh, Ashe, I was so afraid. I didn't know if you'd find me in time.''

Ashe kissed the top of her head, the side of her face, his arms tightening around her. ''I had to find you, didn't you know that? I couldn't let anything happen to you. Not now when we've just found each other again. Not when I've realized exactly how much you mean to me.''

The tears she'd been holding at bay rose in her throat, choking her. She swallowed hard. ''I didn't want to die. And I was scared, so scared. I didn't want to leave Allen and Mother and…you.''

''We have a lot to talk about,'' Ashe said. ''But not now. You've been through hell these last few hours. We've both been through hell!''

''I want to see Allen. I want to take him home. Once we're all safe and together, then you and I can talk and work things out.'' She would have to share Allen with his father in the future. Would that mean trips to Atlanta for Allen, or was there a possibility that Ashe would return to Sheffield permanently? ''We can work things out, can't we, Ashe?''

''Yeah, honey, we most certainly can work everything out.''

Keeping one arm around Deborah, Ashe started the car and drove them straight to Mama Mattie's. The moment they pulled into the driveway, Annie Laurie rushed outside. The fading bruises on the side of her face were the only physical reminder of the accident four days ago. After a two-day hospital stay and countless tests, the doctors had sent her home with a caution to take it easy for a while.

Opening the passenger door, Annie Laurie grabbed Deborah when she stepped out of the Buick Regal.

A young police officer followed Annie Laurie. "I see you found Ms. Vaughn."

"You're all right." Annie Laurie glanced at Ashe. "You're both all right." She looked at Deborah's tattered clothing and gasped. "Oh, God, did he—"

"No," Deborah said. "Ashe found us before he really hurt me." She ran a hand down across her torn skirt. "I need something to put on before Allen sees me."

"Allen's asleep. Finally. He's lying on the couch with his head in Mama Mattie's lap. That's the reason she didn't come out here with me. She didn't want to wake him up. Poor baby has been worried sick and we thought he'd never rest."

"Thank you for keeping watch over Allen." Ashe got out of the car and shook hands with the officer. ''The man who kidnapped Ms. Vaughn is dead.''

''Yeah, Chief Burton just called. He said to tell you that George Jamison has been arrested and is in jail.''

''Tell the chief that Ms. Vaughn and I will be glad to answer any questions tomorrow.'' Ashe placed his arm around Deborah's shoulders. ''We'll go around to the back door. Annie Laurie, I hope you find Deborah something to wear before we wake Allen and take him home.''

Deborah and Ashe walked around the house to the back porch, while Annie Laurie went in the front and met them at the kitchen door. Annie Laurie ushered Deborah into her bedroom. Ashe walked through the kitchen and the small dining area adjacent to the living room and stood in the arched opening, looking across the room at his grandmother and his son. His son!

Mattie Trotter placed her index finger over her lips, cautioning Ashe to be quiet. He nodded and smiled. Ashe noticed his grandmother's old photo album in Allen's arms.

More than anything, Ashe wanted to lift Allen in his arms and hold him. His child. His son. Ten years of the boy's life had already passed. Would they ever be able to make up the lost time? Would Allen ever accept him as a father?

When Deborah and Annie Laurie emerged from

the bedroom, Deborah walked over to Ashe and handed him his jacket. He slipped it on, then put his arm around her waist. She took his hand in hers. He thought she looked beautiful in Annie Laurie's little burgundy-checked shirtwaist dress, her long hair disheveled and her face void of any makeup.

"Let's go get our son and take him home," she said.

Mama Mattie's eyes widened, her mouth gaping as she looked at Deborah and Ashe, then down at the sleeping child.

"What?" Annie Laurie said. "Allen is—"

"Allen is Deborah's child," Ashe whispered. "Deborah's and mine."

"But—but… Oh, my goodness."

With Ashe at her side, Deborah walked across the living room, knelt beside the sofa and kissed Allen on the cheek. He stirred, the photo album dropping to the floor. The boy opened his eyes, saw Deborah and jumped up into her open arms.

"You're all right!" He squealed with happiness. "I knew Ashe would find you. I knew he wouldn't let anything bad happen to you."

"And you were so right," Deborah said. "Ashe is my hero." She looked up at him with all the love in her heart showing plainly on her face.

Reaching down on the floor beside the sofa, Allen picked up the photo album. "Mama Mattie's been showing me pictures of Ashe when he was just a kid and then when he was a teenager. He was big for his age, just like I am. How about that?''

''Yeah, how about that?'' Mama Mattie said, glancing at Ashe.

Deborah sat down on the sofa beside Allen. He laid the photo album in her lap. ''Look at the pictures of you and Ashe together. You two must have spent a lot of time together. Mama Mattie has a ton of pictures of you two.''

''They were the best of friends.'' Mattie's eyes glazed with tears.

''Hey, they told me they weren't an item, you know, that they didn't go together, but I think they had a thing for each other.'' Allen looked up at Ashe. ''Come on, Ashe, fess up, you and Deborah were more than friends.''

''Back then we were friends, but we should have been sweethearts,'' Ashe said. ''You know what, pal? I've just realized, very recently, that I've always loved Deborah.''

Deborah raised her eyes, looking at Ashe with disbelief. Had she heard him correctly? Had he just confessed his love? Here, in front of his grandmother and cousin. In front of their son.

''A lot has happened tonight,'' Ashe said. ''Deborah and I haven't had a chance to talk about the future, but I was wondering if I could have your permission to ask Deborah to marry me?''

''Wow-wee!'' Allen jumped up off the sofa,

threw himself against Ashe and hugged him, then turned to Deborah. "Are you going to say yes? It'd be neat to have Ashe for a brother-in-law."

"Don't I have any say in this matter?" Deborah asked, not sure she liked being bulldozed by her two men.

Ashe kept his hand on Allen's shoulder when he spoke to Deborah. "Doesn't look like you get a vote. Allen and I are a two thirds majority."

"Is that right?" The look on Allen's face broke Deborah's heart. She couldn't remember a time when her son had been so happy. He adored Ashe. That was plain to see.

Ashe pulled Deborah up off the sofa and slipped his arm around her waist. Allen grinned from ear to ear.

"Once I was too big a fool to realize what I had," Ashe said. "But now I know, and I'll never let you go, Deborah. Never."

"Isn't this great!" Allen hugged Ashe and Deborah, then spun around to bring Mattie and Annie Laurie into the celebration. "Just think, when Deborah and Ashe get married, they'll sort of be like parents to me. Deborah's always been a second mother to me. Now, I'll have a dad, won't I?"

"Yes, son, you will." Ashe could barely speak, the emotions erupting inside him overwhelming in their intensity.

"I like this just fine," Allen said. "Everything

is working out great. I sure am glad Mother hired Ashe to protect Deborah.''

"So am I," Ashe said.

"Well, it's time we go home, don't you think?'' Deborah patted Allen on the back.

"Could I stay here with Mama Mattie?'' Allen asked. "We've already made plans for tomorrow. She said I didn't have to go to school. We're going to the hospital to see Mother and Roarke.''

"Roarke!'' Ashe and Deborah said simultaneously.

"He's going to be fine,'' Mattie said. "We've called the hospital several times. He came through surgery with flying colors. Looks like he'll be laid up for a spell, but he's going to live.''

"Thank God.'' Deborah leaned against Ashe. "What happened to him was my fault.''

"Can I stay with Mama Mattie?'' Allen repeated his request. "She's going to make biscuits and chocolate sauce for breakfast, then we're going to bake tea cakes and take Mother and Roarke some. Please, Deborah, let me stay.''

"Allen, I don't know. I—''

"Please. Besides, you and Ashe probably want to be alone anyway.''

"He's right,'' Ashe said. "Let him stay. We can pick him up tomorrow.''

Fighting her motherly reluctance, Deborah

agreed. "Oh, all right." She hugged Allen. "I love you, you know."

"Yeah, I know." Allen glanced over at Ashe. "You'd better always love her and be good to her or you'll have to answer to me."

Everyone in the room laughed, Deborah thinking how much like Ashe Allen was.

"You have my word, son," Ashe vowed.

Deborah lay in Ashe's arms as dawn spread its pink glow across the eastern horizon. They'd come home, showered together and fallen into bed, making love like two wild animals. They had fallen asleep without talking. They hadn't discussed the kidnapping or the fact that Ashe had killed Randy Perry, nor had they mentioned Allen and their future."

Ashe stroked her naked hip. "What are you thinking about?"

"About how we need to talk."

"Yeah, I guess we kind of got distracted by other things." He grinned, then kissed her.

"I was too exhausted to think straight and I guess you were, too." She laid her hand on his chest, directly over his heart. "What are you going to do about Allen?"

"I'm going to marry his mother—" Ashe pulled Deborah into his arms "—and be a father to him."

"Are you going to tell him the truth?"

"Someday I think we should. In a few years, when he's a little older and can understand." Ashe nuzzled Deborah's neck with his nose. "We need some time to become a family, for the three of us to bond."

"What about your job? Are you willing to move back to Sheffield? I can't leave Mother, and Allen wouldn't want to live anywhere else. This is his home."

"I can find a job around here. Who knows, ol' Buck might offer me a position as his bodyguard."

Deborah slapped Ashe on the chest. "That isn't a joking matter."

"Let it all go, honey. It's over. Let's don't look back, let's look forward. What's done is done. We've all lived through a pretty rough time, but it *is* over."

Deborah knew she had to face the truth and had to confront Ashe with her fears. She couldn't marry him if he confirmed her doubts.

"I can't marry you." She pulled away from Ashe, but he jerked her up against him.

"What do you mean you can't marry me?"

"I told you that I didn't want you to marry me because of Allen. That was true eleven years ago and it's true now."

"I'm not marrying you because of Allen. Didn't you hear me tell you and Allen and Mama Mattie and Annie Laurie that I'd been a fool to ever let

you go, that I realize I've always loved you?'' Ashe
tilted her chin with one hand while he held her
close with the other.

''There are all kinds of love, Ashe. As much as
I love you, I can't spend the rest of my life married
to a man who doesn't feel the same way about
me.''

''You're confusing me, honey. What the hell are
we talking about here? I've said I love you.''

''Not the way I want to be loved.''

''What does that mean?''

''It means that...'' Pulling out of his arms, she
got out of bed, picked up her robe off the floor and
put it on.

''Deborah?'' Ashe stood, totally naked, and followed her over to the windows.

''I came close to dying tonight,'' she said, her
back to him. ''I realized how very much I want to
live. I've been in love with you for as long as I can
remember, but you didn't feel the same way about
me. You still don't.''

He eased his arms around her, leaning her back
against his chest, enfolding her in his embrace. ''If
a man ever loved a woman, I love you. Nothing
and no one is more important to me.''

She trembled. He soothed her, caressing her
arms, kissing the side of her face.

''You've been a part of me forever,'' he said.
''Maybe I didn't have sense enough to know I

loved you eleven years ago, but you've stayed alive inside me for all these years. I've never been able to forget you. Now I know why.''

She turned in his arms, her eyes filled with tears. ''Why?''

''Because I'm in love with you, Deborah. Deeply, passionately, completely in love with you.''

''Oh, Ashe.''

Lifting her in his arms, he carried her back to bed. Laying her down, he eased off her robe, then braced himself above her. ''Marry me. Let me spend the rest of my life proving to you how much I love you.''

''Yes. Yes.''

He buried himself within the welcoming folds of her body, telling her again and again that he loved her. She accepted him and his proclamations of love. Giving and taking, sharing in equal measure, they reached fulfillment together. Resting in the aftermath, they accepted the beautiful reality of their life, knowing in their hearts that love and happiness was truly theirs.

Epilogue

The whole family gathered around the shiny, new, black Mitsubishi 3000 GT. Mattie Trotter clicked snapshot after snapshot, while Carol Vaughn zoomed in on Allen's beaming face with her camcorder.

"We couldn't wait until after graduation tonight," Deborah said. "We thought you might want to drive it to your class party afterward."

"Wow! I hoped for something like this, but I wasn't sure. Thanks, Mom!" Tall, lanky, handsome eighteen-year-old Allen hugged Deborah. "I'll bet you picked her out for me, didn't you, Dad?"

Ashe grinned. "Yeah. Your mother wanted to get you something a little more practical."

"I helped, too," seven-year-old Martha McLaughlin said, tugging on her big brother's pants leg. "I wanted to get the red one, but Daddy said no, that you'd like the black one better."

"He was right, squirt." Allen lifted his little sister up in his arms. "I think I'll take this baby for a spin around the block. Want to go with me, Martha?"

"You bet I do."

"Don't be gone too long," Deborah said. "You'll want time to go over your valedictory speech one more time. I know you want it to be perfect."

Allen deposited his sister in the car, jumped in and revved the motor. "Listen to her purr."

"Don't drive too fast!" Deborah cautioned.

"Hey, if I get a speeding ticket, my dad will take care of it for me," Allen said jokingly. "He's the sheriff, you know."

Ashe reached out and took two-year-old Jamie McLaughlin off his mother's hip, then turned to watch his older son spin out of the driveway in his high school graduation present.

"Don't worry, honey. They'll be all right. Allen won't take any chances with Martha in the car with him. Besides, he drives like I do."

"I know. That's what worries me."

Everyone laughed. Ashe kissed his wife, saying a silent prayer of thanks to the powers that be for his many blessings.

All the dreams of his youth had come true. He

had married his beautiful society wife and she'd given him three perfect children. Having been elected sheriff of Colbert County when Charlie Blaylock retired, Ashe had acquired the respect and admiration of the community, especially after he'd helped the Feds put Buck Stansell behind bars and break up the local crime ring.

Ashe didn't know whether he deserved his wonderful life, his three great kids and a wife like Deborah, but he spent every day trying to be the best husband and father in the world. And not a day went by without him thanking God for giving him a second chance with the only woman he'd ever truly loved.

*   *   *   *   *